# Malice in Mind

# Malice in Mind

*A.V. Denham*

ROBERT HALE · LONDON

© A.V. Denham 2012
First published in Great Britain 2012

ISBN 978-0-7090-9356-5

Robert Hale Limited
Clerkenwell House
Clerkenwell Green
London EC1R 0HT

www.halebooks.com

2 4 6 8 10 9 7 5 3 1

Typeset in 11/15pt Palatino
Printed in Great Britain by the MPG Books Group,
Bodmin and King's Lynn

# CHAPTER ONE

It was New Year's Eve and they were dressing for a dance at the golf club. Paul emerged from the bathroom where he had been tying his black tie, an art form he had perfected as a teenager, he was often heard to claim. Harriet was standing in front of the cheval mirror examining herself critically, smoothing peacock blue silk over hips that flared with feminine grace and a stomach that was as flat as the design of the dress required.

'Nice colour.' There was an odd edge to his voice.

'That's what I thought when I bought it.' She preened with satisfaction.

'It's far too revealing, though. Perhaps you'd better change. I like you in the black.'

'I don't feel like black tonight, and what on earth do you mean?' Harriet knew that not only did the dress fit like a glove, it made her feel beautiful.

'Are you wearing knickers?'

She blinked. 'No, I'm not. The panty line is visible. But I'm perfectly respectably dressed,' she insisted hotly. 'Don't you dare suggest otherwise. And as for changing, I wouldn't dream of it.'

Paul shrugged. 'Then just be careful tonight.'

Harriet glanced at him but his expression was unreadable. In any case, the babysitter had been late arriving. It was time they left. She picked up her wrap and followed him out of the bedroom.

Harriet Finamore and Paul Marsh were not married. They had been living together for three years, becoming lovers a year after

Harriet's husband, Joe, had been killed in a traffic accident. Paul, a financial adviser, had been Joe's best man.

Were she and Joe's cousin dancing too closely together that New Year's Eve? Afterwards Harriet would have denied it, although there had been a lot of laughter between them. At the end of that dance, Paul claimed her and as he twirled her in a samba, he made a comment lost in the noise of the band.

'What did you say?' she laughed, as they came together.

He did not reply but grasped her little finger as he spun her out again, twisting it. The pain was excruciating.

'What's the matter?' he asked, as she stopped in the middle of the dance floor, holding her hand against her breast.

'My finger. I think it's dislocated.'

'My God, Hari. How did that happen?'

'As you spun me out. Ouch,' she exclaimed, as he took hold of her hand to examine it. 'That really hurts.'

Paul instantly became solicitous. 'What a stupid thing to have done. Ice. You need ice.' His hand on her shoulder, he propelled her over to the bar where he demanded ice, insisting that it was put in a polythene bag. Then the ice and her hand were wrapped in a towel. 'But you'll be all right until midnight, won't you? Come and sit down over here.' He led her to an unoccupied table well away from the band. 'We'll get you home immediately after they've played *Auld Lang Syne*. Don't move and I'll be back in a bit. Promised this dance to Eva.' He bent down and kissed the top of her head.

She sat there unaccompanied, unnoticed, sober and, while the bonhomie grew ever more frenzied, the evening was ruined for her. Later she allowed him to put her to bed as though she were an invalid. But her little finger throbbed for weeks afterwards, as if in sympathy, whenever she thought about that night.

She never told a soul about what had happened. It was just a stupid accident, she decided.

*

'If you must play boys' games, stay in the Territorial Army,' Felicity Ormston declared to her husband. The year was 2003. 'But if you do have to serve abroad for six months, I shall take the children and leave you.' There was steel in her voice and her body language was defiant.

'You knew there was the possibility that I'd have to go abroad when you married me,' her husband, James, countered. He had fallen in love with Felicity the first time they met and in the beginning their marriage was blissful. The advent of children had changed all that. They were her absolute priority and, while he could not fault her for that, increasingly he felt sidelined.

'I knew about the annual twenty-seven training days. Not that you'd be sent to fight abroad.'

'Fel, no one knew there was going to be a war,' he protested. 'No one knew we'd be deployed to Iraq, to yet another Gulf War.'

Like many another, he supposed, James had gambled on there being no conflicts that would involve him directly when he first joined the Territorial Army. By profession he was a structural engineer, not a regular soldier, but the chance for new experiences, the friendships which still endured, had given him such confidence in himself and his abilities that he was by then a major.

A sociable woman, Felicity thoroughly enjoyed the life that went with being a young officer's wife in those early years, but when James went abroad to serve in Iraq as a sapper, she did leave him, taking the children. She bought a house in Cennen Bridge, in Glamorgan, to be near her parents. Then, after the Iraq war and promotion to lieutenant-colonel, James went to Afghanistan.

There were too many fatalities. This time there were many soldiers who were wounded, James among them. It was no big deal, losing a kidney, they assured him. His body would adjust. After all, he had been a supremely fit man when he arrived in Helmand Province.

James Ormston had never really believed that his wife would carry out her threat to leave him. Losing the children, Jessica and Matthew – particularly his son – was what hurt the most and, desperate to have access, he agreed to all the terms she dictated. Now James began looking *around for a base for himself that was still within easy distance of work and his children.*

*Just before he was deployed to Afghanistan he had found a cottage on the very edge of Cennen Bridge, one of a pair of former labourers' semi-detached cottages. His neighbour was an elderly widow in poor health but with a family who visited frequently and who agreed to keep an eye on his place. It was isolated, which suited him on his return. He was no company for anyone any more.*

*Two men had died under his command.*

Paul never mentioned that incident with her finger again. For a time Harriet even believed that it had been an accident.

A year or so later they left Ashley, Harriet's eleven-year-old daughter, with a babysitter while they went to have dinner with friends. The evening was convivial, a delicious meal with rather too much wine flowing. Harriet was driving home – Paul always drove to wherever they were going, but there was an unspoken agreement that she would drive back. So Harriet only ever drank one glass of wine. Brad, who had been sitting next to her at dinner, was an extrovert with a reputation for flirting with anything in skirts. That should have exonerated her, if nothing else. A woman with whom Brad did not flirt outrageously was entitled to consider herself slighted, his wife maintained to her female friends.

It had been the usual: a hand on her thigh, which she returned to him, several leers, a suggestive remark. Harriet did not rise to any of these, dismissing them with gentle banter. On the way home, however, Paul took exception to one remark in particular. What had Brad said? Harriet couldn't remember it accurately. Something crass, like preferring women with a nicely rounded bottom like hers. 'You must remember then that I thanked him for the compliment and dropped my fork.' In the ensuing confusion Brad had turned away from her.

'I do remember. All of it. I remember exactly what was said, by

Brad, by you.' Paul had not said anything more while she was driving. Maybe that should have alerted her? But the moment the babysitter had been paid and had gone home he rounded on her.

'Why did you laugh when Brad became smutty? Why did you encourage him?'

'I never encouraged him.'

'Why didn't you object when he touched you?'

'It was only Brad. You know what he's like. He behaves in exactly the same way every time you meet him. He's incapable of taking no for an answer. He's really a very boring man.'

'So you liked what he did. Slut!'

'How dare you call me that!'

'I dare, because it's true. And this is what happens to sluts!' He slapped her face. Once open-handed, a second time with the back of his hand, his signet ring drawing blood at the corner of her mouth as the contact came.

Her head ringing, the pain exploding behind her eyes, Harriet fell awkwardly on to the couch, the short skirt of her black dress riding up to expose her thighs and the lace of her black knickers.

His hands were already unzipping his trousers, readying himself as he gazed down at her for one moment. And then he fell on her. It was over very quickly and it was not until several days had passed that Harriet acknowledged to herself that he had raped her. She had not agreed – had not been in a state of mind to agree – that he should penetrate her then and there, where they might have been interrupted by Ash. The more she thought about it, the more certain she was that no one could have called what Paul did to her that night an act of love.

The following day Paul told her outright that she looked a bit rough. 'I guess I was a bit rough, too, last night.' He even grinned sheepishly. 'It was probably that last glass of brandy. Got something to put on that cut on your lip? Just as well we aren't going out tonight. Wouldn't want anyone to think I knocked you about, would we?'

For Harriet that episode marked a watershed in their relationship. Afterwards, the sex between them was never the same. The trust that had always existed between them had been eroded, and where it would all end she did not know. If she left him, where would she go?

Harriet's own parents had retired to Malta soon after her wedding to Joe. When he died they immediately suggested that she should sell everything and come with Ashley to be near them, since she was their only child. But Harriet had a supportive group of friends; Ash was settled at school. Her parents had always been a self-contained unit from which she had often felt excluded as a child and she could not believe that this would ever change.

Now there were weekly telephone calls – although not always at convenient times. But their visits to their daughter, who lived near Guildford, became less frequent, and not only because of their increasing age. Money was tight, they explained. Somehow it was rarely convenient for her to take Ashley to visit them. Life was like that sometimes, she tried explaining to her daughter.

Months later – months during which Paul's acts of violence had become more and more frequent – Harriet thought again about that brutal sexual assault, and knew that she should have left him then. Or, at the very least, she should have made it clear that she would not stand for such treatment ever again. It was entirely her own fault that she had become his victim, Paul's punch bag.

# CHAPTER TWO

In the kitchen of the house that she shared with Paul, Harriet raised her head dazedly from the pine table against which she had slumped. She hurt. Badly. His last blow had landed on already bruised ribs. She moved carefully, her breathing shallow. Nothing seemed to be broken. Shakily she poured herself a cup of strong coffee. This could not go on.

Paul Marsh closed the front door behind him only five minutes later than usual, although he was unconcerned about the time. He always allowed for the build up of traffic. He flexed his right hand, adjusted his tie and smoothed his unruffled hair. He unlocked the car, got in, put on his seat belt, started the engine and drove smoothly out of the wrought-iron gates of his mock Tudor house.

Harriet grimaced. The coffee was not making anything better. *This could not go on.* How many times had she said that to herself? Too often, and the beatings were happening ever more frequently. Yet the look on Paul's face that morning as he told Ashley to get out and go to school had freaked her out. It was cold, calculating. She had always thought that he loved Ash as if she were his own daughter. Now? Now she did not know what to think.

Still in a daze, Harriet cleared the kitchen and made the beds. Then she sat in the kitchen once more, her hands clasped round another mug of coffee. As she had bent over the double bed, smoothing the sheets, all she had wanted to do was to lie down, pull the duvet over her head and seek oblivion. She had even taken off her shoes. But something, some vestige of pride forbade her to give in.

She finished her coffee. Then she went upstairs and packed methodically for herself and Ashley, filling her small car with all the essentials that occurred to her. She wished that she was brave enough to say to Paul's face, 'You have hit me for the very last time. I'm leaving you.' It was all she could do just to write the words she needed to say to him and leave the note for him to find.

She was shivering with apprehension as she left, and not only because she was afraid that he would come home and find her before she had made her escape. Slinking out of the house while he was at work made her feel as if she were a thief in the night rather than a woman leaving an abusive relationship.

She went to the bank, then she saw her solicitor. She met Ashley outside the school gates. Then she drove westwards, fleeing to the safety she craved, towards Wales, to the home of her old schooldfriend, Florence.

'I can't tell you how difficult it was, even writing him that note.' Harriet had seen Ash settled for the night and now she sat in Florence Harding's sitting room, looking as exhausted as she felt. 'In the end I couldn't bring myself to set down on paper even a portion of how I really feel.'

There was no need for an explanation. Florence knew very well that Paul had represented security, for, since the death of her husband, security was the one thing that Harriet prized, even above emotional fulfilment, which everyone who knew her thought that she had found with Paul. 'Some security you've had, wondering the whole time when you'll have the next quarrel,' was the only acid comment she permitted herself.

'It wasn't always like that, Flo.' Harriet defended the man with whom she had been living. 'Not at first, and never the whole time.'

'So he was unpredictable? Scary.'

'When Joe died Paul was great and I relied on him totally. I never imagined someone could change so much.' Perversely it seemed essential that she should defend Paul to Florence, who was her oldest friend. 'I suppose I confused love with gratitude.'

She saw the raised eyebrows and sceptical look on Florence's face and smiled defensively when Florence commented drily, 'The poor boy threw his toys out of the pram because what he thought he wanted was out of reach? How very mature.'

'It was as much my fault as his. I should never have agreed to live with him. It was asking for trouble.'

Florence Harding had never married. A watercolourist and illustrator of children's books, she lived alone. She had known Harriet Finamore since they had fought over who had the right to play with the set of brightly coloured building blocks at nursery school thirty-eight years before. She had been going to say that she'd never really cared for Paul. Then she thought better of it. 'At least you never married the man.'

'I always expected us to marry. I wanted Ashley to get used to Paul before we did the formal stuff.' Harriet lowered her head as she sighed deeply. At forty-one her figure was trim and her thick fair hair which was trimmed to just below her ears and worn with a fringe, screened the expression in her violet eyes and concealed the tremble on her mobile mouth. 'I seem to have made so many bad calls, don't I?'

'If you're referring to your marriage with Joe, well, he wasn't the world's easiest. We all know that, but he did give you Ash.'

'Yes, he did, didn't he?' Harriet's voice brightened. Arrogant and opinionated, Joe had nonetheless been a lovely man, her mother had always said.

The only comment Ashley had made that afternoon, when she had been confronted at the school gate with a car full of luggage and the news that they were going away for half-term, had been an anxious, 'You haven't forgotten Mick, have you?' The brown-haired bear had been her father's gift to her when she was three and, although she would not admit it to anyone, she hated going to sleep without him beside her. Now she was tucked up in the double bed in Florence's guest room with her battered teddy bear in her arms and a satisfying pile of books on the bedside table.

Florence reached over and poured Harriet another glass of wine. 'The one thing that bothers me is, won't this be the first place Paul comes looking for you? What happens when he arrives on my doorstep?'

Harriet shook her head as she picked up her glass. 'I thought of that. This morning I went onto a site for women's refuges on the house computer. He would have discovered that easily enough. Then, in my note I told Paul that he was not to try to find us and that I'd be in touch with him about the rest of our stuff through my solicitor. I'd already cleared that with William Crosse, of course. I put a London postcode into the satnav Paul gave me for Christmas, then I left the satnav in its box on the bookcase.'

'Is Paul really that gullible?'

Harriet shrugged. 'Probably not, but by the time he realizes what I've done and where I have most likely gone, I won't be here. I have brought my laptop with me and as I have always preferred not to use the house computer that is all he will discover. You do understand that, don't you, Flo?' she asked, anxiety in her voice. 'I haven't come here to disrupt your life. Ash and I just want a refuge for a few days while I find us somewhere to rent.'

'How about money?' Florence asked bluntly. 'Decent rental properties don't come cheap around here.'

'Even now, I have a good income with the interest from the insurance money from when Joe was killed and from renting out our house. I've never felt beholden to Paul, although the interest rates have fallen so much.' Was that one of the things that had gone wrong between them, Harriet wondered for possibly the first time? 'I suppose in the back of my mind I always thought that I'd be able to return to the house, if things went wrong with Paul, but the Letts seem so settled that I agreed to an extension of their tenancy only a month ago. Besides, Box House is too close to Paul.'

'Did he know you regarded Box House as your bolthole?'

'Probably not. He would know that you can't get rid of tenants without due process. He also knows how much I like them.'

'So what are you going to do now?'

'I need a job,' Harriet declared the following evening. She had thought about nothing but her future all day. 'But I haven't worked since I married Joe. I have no skills....'

'I wouldn't say that,' Florence protested mildly.

'I would. But what on earth can I do to earn a living? What do you suggest I could do? Cleaning? Checkout counter? I can't even add up unless I see the figures written down.'

'You don't need to add up. There are machines to do the job for you nowadays,' Florence commented. 'You could work for a supermarket, of course. I'm sure management would look upon you as a steadying influence.'

'Even though I'm on the run from my violent lover?'

'If that's how you see your situation. But I can't see you sitting behind a till for hours at a time. You have far too much energy. What do you like doing most?'

'Gardening,' replied Harriet immediately. Her face clouded. 'I quite forgot to leave Paul instructions for watering the hanging baskets. They'll be ready to put out at the weekend. If he neglects them the plants will die.' She smiled at Florence's expression. 'Worrying about my hanging baskets is the least of my problems.'

'But knowing about plants and gardens could provide you with an income, couldn't it?'

'I suppose so,' Harriet agreed doubtfully. 'But I have no paper qualifications, neither could I provide references.'

'I could describe your garden. People are always on the lookout for a good gardener. I'm sure there would be no problem in finding the first job. Then you'd have a local reference for the next. What about working in a garden centre? There are two in this area, although the nearest one isn't very modern. At least there you'd have company while you work.'

'I'd like to keep a low profile, particularly in the beginning. Still, I might try a gardening job. But first I need to find us accommodation. And then there's Ashley's schooling.'

'The local primary has a good reputation.'

'How could I have forgotten about schools? I should never have left Paul just now. This is such an important year for Ash.'

'Calm down, Hari! Do you have the money to go private?'

'No. If Ash wants to go to university, I'd like her not to be saddled with enormous student loans, so I'd be prepared to finance her then. I'll need to look for somewhere to rent in a good secondary school catchment area,' Harriet went on. 'Do you have a local paper?'

They scanned the agency columns, Harriet ruling out flats and anything on a large estate.

'How long do you think you've got?' Florence asked.

'Until Paul comes looking for us, do you mean?' Harriet made a face. 'Do you know, the way he's been behaving over the last few months I'm not sure. Maybe he's even relieved that we've gone. He might phone you, but I begin to think that he might not be so very keen to instigate a countrywide search. I wonder if he has come to hate me as much as I loathe him for what he has made of me – tried to make of me,' she amended, a look of determination on her face, 'a victim.'

For a moment Florence looked shocked. 'Do you see yourself as his victim?'

'Yes, no. No longer. But I hate him. I will not be his victim ever again,' Harriet declared. 'I hope I never even see him again.'

# CHAPTER THREE

Cennen Bridge was a pretty, bustling market town, the area wooded and green, eminently safe. Helmand Province could not have been more different, James thought, although Camp Bastion, the hastily erected base camp, was a haven of Western normality with its enclaves of allied troops. He missed the strange juxtaposition of Western cuisine and the Afghan way of life with little market stalls that sold Eastern carpets and brassware as if to passing tourists. Just as the military hoped it might be again sometime, in a more settled future in the villages they were trying to protect, where the dwellings were behind high walls connected by narrow alleys.

Eventually there would come a kinder time, they hoped fervently, when boys and young men would be free to fly their kites, aiming to sever the strings of an opponent's prized possession and bring it down, but in battles where only paper and string were trashed instead of bringing about the ruination of lives and livelihoods, as was happening now.

At Camp Bastion was also the base hospital, another haven after the dust and noise of battle, where pain was alleviated by efficient nursing staff using powerful drugs, where failure was explained away as part of the psychology of war. He'd spent time at the base hospital after being wounded.

Harriet handed the estate agent a sheet of paper. 'Just in case you have something for rent that isn't on an estate, here is the name and also the contact details of my solicitor. These are my bank details. I imagine you will want to check. As I mentioned, currently I am staying with an old friend. She is happy to vouch for me.'

'I'm sorry there isn't much else to offer you. Ah ... you know Florence Harding? Hang on a moment. I've just remembered....' Matthew John, the estate agent, went to a filing cabinet and pulled out a folder. 'There is one property on my list which might be suitable. I hadn't mentioned it before because it's not the most modern of cottages and nowadays clients seem to prefer all the latest mod cons. The previous owner died after a long illness and her heirs have only just got probate. They have talked about selling but in the present climate....' He shrugged. 'It has two bedrooms, a sitting room, a back kitchen and scullery that hardly merits the term utility room, as you will see, if you would like to view it. There is a bathroom and it is furnished....' His voice tailed off as he recalled the double bed in which Mrs Jones had breathed her last. 'I would need to do a check on the appliances, of course.'

'And make sure it has been thoroughly cleaned?'

'Er – quite. Why don't I take you out there to have a look at it?'

'And the rent?' Harriet prompted gently. He told her. 'If I like what I see, I'll take it.'

She switched on her mobile phone when she left the small cottage and as she reached her car the ringtone sounded. She dug in her bag for it but there was no reply when she said, 'Hello?'

The caller had not yet rung off. The silence was palpable. She repeated herself. 'Hello?'

Again there was no answer. Bother, she thought. I wonder who that could have been?

'It's fantastic, Flo,' Harriet told her friend over supper. 'Ash, you'll love your room. Mr John agreed that if I paid the rent Mrs Jones's son and daughter are asking, he would see that the rooms are all given a coat of paint and the carpets – which are only rugs anyway – are cleaned. Oh, and he suggested a new bed in my room.'

'Because Mrs Jones died in it? Yuck, Mum! That is so gross.'

'Everyone has to die somewhere,' Harriet commented.

'Yeah, but then, I suppose you don't have a new bed in hospital every time someone dies there. Or a new stretcher for an ambulance,' Ashley said quietly.

Florence froze. She was unused to such frank discussions of events she would have preferred were left under the carpet.

'No, dear. Think of the expense,' Harriet answered, as if it had not occurred to her that Ash was remembering how her father had died. Ash had been very young when the accident happened, but she had worshipped her father and she had always been happiest when she was in his arms. It was something of a miracle, Harriet often thought, that Ash had developed as normally as she had.

'What about bed linen and so on?' asked Florence. 'China, cutlery, a decent easy chair?'

'The family have already gone in and taken away everything they think is of value. I'm to have my pick of what's left so that they can call the place furnished. What I don't want, they'll pay to have removed.' She grimaced. 'I think Ash and I will have a job to find much that we want to use, but that'll be fun, won't it, love? Then, once I've sorted out our finances, we'll do some shopping.'

'And what about your good things that you left at Paul's?'

'Paul's a pig,' said Ashley firmly.

'Ash!'

'Well, he is, so. Otherwise we'd still be living with him and we'd have all our own things. It stands to reason.'

'Dear, sometimes people just don't get on with each other. That doesn't make them bad.' Harriet saw the look on Florence's face and sent her a silent message pleading with her friend not to interfere.

'Then why did he punch you in the ribs the morning we left, before he sent me off to school? I had to wait ages for the bus. Did you do something really bad? Because if you say you did I just don't believe you!' the girl ended passionately.

'You saw…?'

'It wasn't the first time, was it, Mum?'

Florence got up clumsily. 'There's ice cream in the fridge,' she said thickly. 'I'll go and fetch it. No, leave the plates, Ash. I'll deal with them later.'

'Why did you never say anything before?' Harriet asked her daughter, once Florence had gone into the kitchen. Her face was pale, her throat tight. 'He never … did he?'

''Course not,' replied Ashley scornfully. 'He knew I'd kick him in the balls if he so much as touched me.'

'Touched you?' Harriet's voice was strangulated, the sexual implication assuming more importance than the language.

'Well, you know, if he ever hit me. But he didn't.'

'He loved you. You were like his own daughter.' That, at least, she had always believed. 'I think that Paul would have liked nothing better than to have had children of his own.'

'Why didn't you have his baby, Mum?'

This was the strangest conversation, Harriet was thinking, her daughter asking her why she hadn't had a baby with the man to whom she wasn't married. 'Because we weren't married.' The answer was an honest one, even though it was evasive.

'People do have babies when they're not married. There's Annie in my class. Her sister's pregnant and she's in Year 11.'

'I know they do. I wouldn't because I think that a child needs a father as well as a mother. I suppose I stayed with Paul for so long partly because I thought of him as your substitute father.'

'Some father.' There was a world of scorn in the child's voice. 'And you were, like, his own wife. He still hit you.'

'Ash, I never thought it would end in this way. I never thought I'd need to leave Paul, but it's not good to stay with someone you no longer trust. Yes, he did hit me, but that was because we weren't getting on.'

'Sometimes I don't get on with Poppy. I'd never hit my best friend.'

'I should hope not. But feelings between a man and a woman

are different. They can hurt each other badly, and quite unintentionally.'

'Paul hit you deliberately.'

'I know, dear. It was a really bad quarrel.'

Florence, maybe judging that the conversation was becoming too heavy, returned to the room in time to hear her friend's remark. She snorted audibly as she set down a tray on which were three bowls of pink ice cream and a plate of wafer biscuits.

'I'm going to miss my friends,' Ash sighed. 'Do I have to go to school on Monday?'

'I've arranged to see the head teacher first thing on Monday morning. If she can take you, I expect you'll be starting immediately.'

'Will I need to learn Welsh and wear a uniform?'

'There's a grey skirt and a red jumper, for when it's cold,' Florence said. 'Welsh won't be a problem for you, Ash. I'm sure you'll find it fun to learn. Help yourselves to the ice cream.'

'Strawberry ice cream. Goody. It isn't raspberry, is it, Aunt Flo?' Ash paused, her spoon in the air.

'It is strawberry. Your mum said that's your favourite. So, you're off to see the school on Monday? I must introduce you to Fiona who lives down the road. She's about your age and will also go to the comprehensive in September.'

'So I won't be going to St Crispin's, after all?' asked Ashley, her voice neutral. 'That's where all my friends are going.'

'That's right, pet. I'm sorry about your friends but it looks as though we shall be living here from now on, so I suppose you will need to transfer to the local comprehensive,' said her mother.

'It's a new school, purpose built a year ago. State of the art science labs, I'm told, with a splendid sports hall.'

'Do they play hockey?' asked Ash more eagerly.

'Not a clue,' replied Florence, for whom all forms of sport had always been anathema. 'You'll have to ask your head teacher. Come on, eat up or your ice cream'll get cold.'

Ashley giggled. Soon afterwards she went to bed without a murmur, her plea bargain on how many chapters she could read settled to her satisfaction.

*At first James had taken the injury philosophically – did you take anything that hurt so much quite so phlegmatically as that word made it sound? he wondered. They were efficient at the hospital in Camp Bastion and apparently there were no complications. As luck would have it – luck? – he had been injured only a short time before he was due to go home at the end of his six months' deployment. It must have been luck that he'd not been one of the fatalities, like the others. He didn't permit himself to dwell on his men who had been killed. It still didn't seem right that he had survived while they had died. Stupid, they'd called him, the mind doctors. Well, maybe their language had been a little more diplomatic.*

*He'd spent a couple of months in hospital on his arrival back in the UK, too ill to attend either the reception for his men at Wootton Basset or their individual funerals. Then he'd gone home to his parents to convalesce with only a scar to show outwardly for all the pain he had endured. Or so he'd thought several weeks later as he returned home to Cennen Bridge.*

*There was a man called Harry coming to live next door, he'd been told. He didn't think he could cope yet with a neighbour, sane, capable and healthy....*

# CHAPTER FOUR

They were washing up after Ash had gone to bed when once again Harriet's phone trilled. 'Excuse me,' she said, putting down the tea towel and going into the hallway. 'I suppose I'd better take this.' Her mother sometimes phoned at this time. 'Hello?' There was no reply. Harriet returned to the kitchen. 'No answer.'

'The reception is better on a landline around here.'

'If it was important, I expect whoever it was will phone again.'

'You don't think it was Paul, do you?'

'Paul? I don't suppose so.' Then Harriet remembered the call she'd had that morning. She went cold. 'Paul? I wonder if ... No. It couldn't have been Paul. He'd have said something. Texted me, at least, if—'

'If what?' Florence asked, mystified.

Harriet explained the call she'd had that morning. 'I thought nothing of it, then.'

'So that might have been Paul, too?'

They looked at each other silently.

'I think you need another glass of wine,' said Florence gently. 'Paul doesn't know where you are, and he won't find out by making silent calls to you. I think you should dismiss the calls and forget all about him, don't you?'

Sycamore Cottage was one of a pair of semi-detached early twentieth-century labourers' cottages which had been sold separately some twenty years previously when the estate to which they belonged had fallen on hard times. The paintwork of Oak Cottage was fresh and the front lawn had been recently mown. Sycamore Cottage was shabby; its paint peeling. At least the grass had been cut, but the back garden, which must have been used for vegetables in the past, resembled nothing more than a wilderness of nettles, couch grass and bindweed. Yet instead of her heart sinking, Harriet discovered an intense desire to return the garden to its former productivity.

Inside, the walls were now magnolia and the exposed beams had all been treated for woodworm, but neither varnished nor painted, which she had feared. On the floors were three richly hued rugs, which Harriet, who had learned a thing or two from Joe about oriental rugs, suspected were worth a lot more than the family had realized or they would have removed them.

'The fridge-freezer, washing-machine and cooker are all new but I'm afraid I decided we couldn't run to either a dishwasher or a microwave,' said Matthew John, who had come to show Harriet and Ashley round. 'Upstairs there's one new bed. The family decided to let you have all of Mrs Jones's linen. They suggest that what you don't want could go to a charity shop.'

The bathroom was basic. There was a new piece of vinolay on the floor, a new immersion heater and also, to Harriet's relief, a new lavatory seat. 'It's cleaned up well,' she said. 'Lawnmower?' she asked, looking out of the window.

'An old-fashioned push mower in the garden shed, along with some useful tools which you are welcome to use.'

'I like it here, Mum. When are we going to move in?'

'The lease starts on Friday,' Harriet told Florence, while they were having supper. 'But I can go in tomorrow to do some sorting out and Ash has promised to wash the china and glass.'

They were still discussing the various things that had to be done before the move when Florence's phone rang.

'Excuse me,' said Florence. 'Won't be a minute. Hello?' There was a pause. Harriet and Ashley heard her say cheerfully, 'Why, Paul, I've not spoken to you for ages. How are you all?' Then quietly she closed the door between the kitchen and the hall where her landline was.

Ashley looked at her mother, her whole face a question. Harriet put a finger to her lips. Neither of them said a word.

After a minute the door opened and Florence returned. 'That was Paul,' she said.

'We gathered,' answered Harriet. 'I'm so sorry to have involved you in all this,' she added contritely. 'It's not right that you have to lie on our behalf. I should never have presumed so on your friendship.'

'Don't be a fool.'

'I didn't think he'd call you quite so soon.'

'Well,' said Florence, casting a meaningful glance in Ashley's direction. 'No harm done. Now, Ash, let's take the plates into the kitchen. Then while your mum and I clear up I guess you're entitled to an hour or so of television before bed. How does that sound?'

Ash mentioned her favourite DVD and won a surprisingly easy agreement, Harriet's only condition being that her daughter read for a shorter time than usual once she was in bed.

'OK, Mum.' She sounded subdued. Harriet gave her a quick hug. 'Everything is going to be fine, love. Please don't worry.'

'I think I might open a bottle of wine,' said Florence comfortably. 'We'll sit in the conservatory and watch the sun setting.'

'Sounds good to me.'

It was not until they were relaxing in Florence's small but comfortable conservatory that Harriet broached the subject of the phone call again. 'How did Paul sound?'

'Hurt, puzzled, a bit anxious. Not angry. It seemed a little mean not telling him that you were both safe.'

'I had a feeling it would be something like that. He has this habit of brushing aside what he's done, as if it wasn't his fault at all, as if I'm the one who's being totally unreasonable. When something goes bad between us he sounds so plausible I sometimes wonder if he's right and I am wholly in the wrong. Then the bruises remind me that even if I have done something stupid he has no right to hurt me.'

'Bruises?' Florence said sharply.

In answer Harriet lifted up the loosely fitting cotton sweater she was wearing. There was a large blue-black mark across her ribs under her left breast overlying a mark that spread further and which was fading into a dirty yellow. 'The worst of the pain usually only lasts for a few days. Then it's just spectacular colour, until the bruising fades.'

'How long has this been going on for?'

'Three years, I think.'

'Three years!' Florence absorbed the information. 'Why on earth haven't you mentioned any of this before? I just supposed this was a particularly bad row that had ended with him slapping you hard, and so you'd left to give him time to apologize for what he'd done.'

'I've left for good. They say most women don't leave the man who abuses them until he has hit them thirty times.'

'Thirty times! That's unbelievable. And who's they?'

'Women's groups. Medics, I suppose. In the worst cases the women land in hospital with broken bones and still return to their abuser. The nursing staff come to recognize them.'

'How come you know so much about all this?'

'I did a bit of researching. Mainly because I wanted to stop it and didn't know how. I don't think you can,' Harriet said sadly, 'stop it, I mean. Stop the behaviour, once a pattern has been established.'

'Has Paul ever broken one of your bones?'

'He hurt one of my fingers badly. It could have been a break. I never had it X-rayed. After the second time, when Ash asked what had happened to my face, Paul never hit me where it showed. That time he told her that I had been clumsy and had fallen.' She did not tell Florence that Paul had stroked her cheek and then he had smiled at Ash and said, 'I've tried kissing it better but not with much success. Perhaps this will do the trick.' She had thought of Judas, but she had not dared to say anything out loud.

'So he punched you and you let him get away with his violence? Why did you stay with him for so long?'

'I stayed for all the usual reasons women remain in abusive relationships. Inertia, for one. There's always the hope that this will be the last time. I'd think that if I was more careful he wouldn't need to hit me again.'

'Unbelievable. I misunderstood … I never imagined…. Hari!'

'And where would I go? Should I involve anyone else? Money. All the usual issues. But for me, there was Ash.'

'You said that Paul always regarded Ashley as his daughter.'

'It hurt him that she would never call him Dad. I was afraid that one day he would make an issue out of it.'

'Was that why you never had a child with him, the fact that he abused you?'

'I'm not sure. Yes, I suppose it was there, in the back of my mind, that I couldn't quite trust him as I had in the beginning. In the beginning I trusted him implicitly.'

'Why did you keep it all to yourself? Couldn't you have confided in me?'

'Maybe because I knew exactly what you would say.'

'That you should leave him immediately.' Florence shook her head in perplexity. Then she reached out for Harriet's hand that lay on the arm of the chair and squeezed it. 'You have one funny way of expressing your faith in a man.'

'This man, maybe. And he didn't hit me often. Months would go by and it was as if there was, or ever had been, no violence at all. Then, this time he hit me twice in as many weeks. I had promised myself that I wouldn't be a victim. Well, I can see now that I had been one of those, a victim, ever since the beginning. And I knew it had to stop, although I would not involve the police. Nor would I be one of those women in hospital who was lying there, black and blue all over and with broken bones. But the time had come when I knew that I just had to leave or that is what would have happened to me.' She sat back as if suddenly she was exhausted.

Hari must be exhausted, Florence was thinking. To have gone through all that without anyone to confide in would have been shattering. 'If you couldn't even tell me, perhaps you should have involved the police,' was all she said.

'And have everyone know exactly what was happening?' Harriet shuddered. 'That was the one aspect I couldn't bear. In the end, of course, we left in something of a hurry. I brought my jewellery, our passports and a few other documents. I picked up some photos, not the albums but the ones in frames on the book-case, but I had to leave behind pictures and books and all our winter clothes which I'd just put away for the summer.'

'You make it sound as though they won't be there for you when you send for them.'

Harriet shook her head sadly. That was exactly what she had thought as she drove away from Paul's house, yet what else could she have done? 'My guess is that Paul will wait until he is sure that we aren't coming back and then he'll get rid of absolutely everything.'

# CHAPTER FIVE

Florence took in the revelation that Paul was not the suave, caring man that she had always believed him to be. 'How wrong can you be about a person? But he can't do that, get rid of your possessions, just throw them out.'

'Who's to stop him?'

'What about a restraining order?'

'My guess is that he'd insist that it was too late, that he'd already disposed of our things. He'd be very apologetic, but there would be nothing left.'

'Hari, you still have keys, why not go and collect some of your things one day when he's at work? I'd come with you. There would be no bother, if the two of us were together.'

Harriet smiled cynically. 'You've never heard of changing locks? It's his house. He has every right to do that.'

'Aren't you a common law wife, or something? You have rights, too.'

'That's a myth. Under the present law, there's no such thing as a common law wife. I have no "rights" as you call them. The house is his and almost all the contents, come to think of it, because I got rid of most of my stuff when I let my house.'

'Why did you do that?'

'The tenants wanted to rent unfurnished. I only kept a few pictures and my books and a favourite chair. Paul has excellent taste and his house was fully furnished. At the time it seemed the sensible thing to do.'

Ash appeared in the doorway. 'I've switched off the telly, Aunt Florence.'

'Thank you, dear. Good film, was it?'

'The best.'

'I'll come and kiss you goodnight in a bit,' said her mother. She watched Ash wander back through the kitchen. 'Work,' she said abruptly. 'I need to find a job. Not just for the money. I think it's important that Ash sees me trying to build a new life for us.'

'The first thing to do is to see if anyone is advertising for a gardener in the local paper. Then there are always adverts in the local newsagent's window. It's worth a try. And if Paul hasn't already destroyed your things, maybe one day soon you'll get them all back.'

Harriet grinned. 'A new winter wardrobe mightn't be a bad idea, at that. I'm sure that Ash would agree.'

It was all very well joking with Florence about the destruction of their property. At the back of Harriet's mind there lurked the nagging suspicion that she had no idea what Paul was capable of doing next.

By the weekend, when they were ready to move into the cottage, Harriet had met the head teacher of the primary school who declared herself delighted to offer Ash a place, particularly once she discovered that the girl played the oboe.

Florence was as good as her word and before the move she had invited Fiona to tea. Fiona was the same age as Ash and her family had lived in Cennen Bridge for generations. Fiona was quick-witted and shrewd. If the friendship lasted, Harriet thought that her daughter would be accepted by the other children all the sooner.

The girls circled round each other suspiciously for a while until Florence served tea on her best china, when they looked at each other across the chocolate biscuits put out by Harriet as an aid to friendship, and they both giggled and became instant best friends.

The day before the move she had been interested to find a Welcome card on the doorstep. It was addressed to Harry and Ash and it was from their elusive next door neighbour who signed himself James.

When Ash saw it she remarked, 'I suppose someone's told him our names and he's jumped to the usual conclusion. Won't he get a shock when he discovers he's got two women living next door.'

Harriet, who by now was philosophical about the contraction of her name, smiled inwardly at Ash's description. 'We'll just have to hope he's no misogynist.'

'What's that, Mum?'

'Someone who doesn't like women.'

'Like Paul, you mean?'

'Not at all,' Harriet said decidedly. 'Paul doesn't dislike women, he's just not very fond of me any more.'

'He was Dad's best man, wasn't he? I wish we had our photo albums with us. I like to look at the pictures of your wedding.'

'I know you do, love, and I wish we had brought everything with us, too. At the time, when I was packing the car in a hurry, it did occur to me but it seemed such an effort. I mean, where do you begin?'

'Does Paul hate us now? Does he hate us for leaving him?'

'Hate is a strong word.' Harriet paused. Was Paul learning to hate them? One thing she had learned about Paul over the years was that he had strong feelings towards people. Of those he liked, he would hear nothing wrong. By contrast, those for whom he had taken a dislike, he could think of nothing good to say about them.

'I never truly believed that Paul loved me,' Ash declared. 'That's why I could never call him Dad. It didn't seem right.'

'Didn't it, sweetheart? I did wonder. I always knew that he would have liked you to think of him as your dad. I think he looked on you as the daughter he didn't have and I'm sure that he believed I would come to love him, in time.'

'Why didn't – don't you love him, Mum?' she asked, in a small voice that betrayed all the uncertainties of a life that had never seemed certain since her father had died.

'I don't know, darling. Love is a strange thing, at least, the love that is between a man and a woman. It's different, indescribable really. You can't call it to order. It's either there or it isn't.'

'Poppy says it's chemistry.'

Harriet laughed. 'Wherever did Poppy get that from?'

'One of her teen magazines,' Ash answered uncomfortably.

'Ah. One of those magazines I said were too old for you?'

Ash shrugged. 'Anyway, I suppose it was a bit hard on Paul that we lived with him and you didn't love him.'

'I didn't exactly not love him,' said Harriet quickly. It made her sound calculating and she did not want her daughter to think ill of her. In any case, she had believed that love would come with time. 'I just didn't love him in quite the way he would have liked.'

'Unconditionally.'

'That's a grown-up word,' said her mother, and immediately apologized. 'I didn't mean to sound patronizing. Although you are quite right. Paul did want me to love him unconditionally and something prevented me from doing that. Still, it's nice to know we have a welcoming neighbour and let's hope we manage to meet him soon.'

*After a while James almost forgot the wound. The scar was there, when he showered, neat but fading, but after six months or so the pain had left him. Instead there were nightmares when he woke with a jerk, covered with cold sweat.*

*Then it got worse. Only you couldn't call these nightmares because they happened at any time, any place. The only times he could be sure they would not plague him was while he was playing the piano at home, or listening to a CD, or in the church playing the organ, practising for the Sunday service for which he played occasionally when the local organist was unavailable, having one of his attacks of gout. But they still happened, and without warning.*

*It was as if he entered a tunnel and at the end of it, beside it, there was the noise, the explosion that wrecked so many men's lives. There was the vision of men falling, the dreadful sight of men screaming for, despite the noise that sometimes came with his nightmares, there was no real sound coming from the men, his men. Their mouths were open, gaping, but the sound of their screaming did not come from them. It was all in his head, blood-chillingly real.*

*Then would come the flash of the explosion, the inevitable pain in his own body that followed....*

*That was when he woke up, to shiver with the coldness of the sweat that bathed his body. If he was in bed, he would curl into the foetal position until he stopped shaking enough to be able to drag himself up, strip off his sodden clothing and change his sheets. If he were in the open it would be different. He would have to stand stock still until he felt the stares of the passers-by boring into him. Only then would he, or could he, move.*

After she had left Ash at school on the Monday morning, Harriet walked purposefully towards the newsagents where she scrutinized the postcards in the window. They pleaded for information for lost pets, advertised availability to clean, offered for sale various household items and finally stated that gardening was required one day a week, offering what Harriet thought was an astronomical fee for the service. She went to consult Florence.

'The Ormstons? Joanne and Gareth. I only know them by sight. The garden used to be beautiful.'

'They're offering fifteen pounds an hour. That's a fortune.'

Florence looked at her quizzically. 'It's obvious you've not had to employ a gardener recently. There is the problem of garden rubbish and tools. Most of the town isn't permitted to have bonfires and it's usual for jobbing gardeners to provide their own tools.'

'I never thought about tools, although there are ancient tools in my shed. There should be something I can find. I'd have to use a client's mower, though, since I really don't want to go to the expense of buying a machine until I'm properly set up and I can't see myself with much credibility if I take round an antique machine that I probably have to push.'

'I suggest you ring them and fix an appointment.'

'I'll do just that and afterwards I'll go through the shed and sort out what tools I can use and what I have to borrow.'

Later that morning when Harriet, dressed in an old pair of jeans and a shirt, was in the shed happily going through Mrs Jones's old gardening tools, her mobile phone rang. She frowned and began to search for it under a pile of old gardening magazines which were destined for the tip.

'Hello?'

There was silence the other end.

'Hello?' she repeated. She went out of the shed into the garden. It was probably just bad reception, she decided as she repeated her greeting for the third time. 'This is Harriet Finamore,' she added. There was still no reply.

Paul, she thought, going cold. Was she right? Was he hounding her out of revenge because she had left him? What could she do about it, if she was right?

*Stop this,* she told herself. *Stop this right now.* If it was Paul, he was out to demoralize her, and at the moment he was succeeding. But she had vowed she would no longer be a victim. She would not be Paul's victim, ever again.

# CHAPTER SIX

Gareth and Joanne Ormston lived in a stylish modern bunga-low on the edge of the town. There was a small front garden with a lawn that needed mowing and flower beds full of rose bushes (and weeds) bordering the path to the front door. Plenty of work there, Harriet thought, as she rang the bell.

There was a pause before Joanne Ormston opened the door. She was younger than Harriet had expected, probably in her late thirties. Of medium height, she was slim, very attractive with expensively tinted hair and an expertly made-up face. She was wearing jeans and a white shirt but where Harriet's jeans had come from a chain store, Joanne's were obviously designer.

'Do come in,' Joanne said expansively, holding the door open wide. 'It is so good of you to come to see me. You can't imagine how I've longed for someone to offer to take over the garden.'

'How do you do, Mrs Ormston.'

'Joanne, please.' She pronounced it, Jo-anne. 'And you are?'

'I'm Harriet Finamore, though people usually call me Hari.'

Joanne took Harriet into the sitting room, a light, airy room with minimalist modern furniture and a cream carpet. 'Old Mrs Harris was an inveterate gardener and when her arthritis got too bad she employed a marvellous man called Benjamin. But he retired, so, as you see, Hari, we're in a mess and neither of us gardens.' Involuntarily Harriet glanced at Joanne's hands which were soft and white with extremely long, painted nails. Joanne grinned, knowing what Harriet was thinking and, after a moment, Harriet grinned back, already liking her immensely.

'Gareth runs a haulage business and I lease a gallery in Cennen Bridge. We're renting for the moment as we're doing up an old property on the edge of the town. When I say we're doing it up, I really mean we have the builders in.'

'I've moved into Sycamore Cottage, on the other side of town. I much prefer older houses but I guess they all have their problems.'

'Are you now! Well, come and have a look at my garden and tell me what you can do for me.'

Joanne opened French windows into the back garden which was laid out to beds full of herbaceous plants. A fountain set in stone played in the centre of a stone patio. It was all very quiet, very tranquil, if badly neglected.

'You have the makings of a delightful garden,' said Harriet. 'I should be very happy to take it over for you.'

'Shall we go back inside and talk about the details over a cup of coffee?'

Harriet declined the coffee saying that she had to collect her daughter from primary school after her first day there, but within a short time it had been decided that she would spend four hours a week in the garden. She would even start the following day. 'With the front, I think, to give a good impression.'

'Exactly. I think you and I are going to get along excellently.'

Harriet was standing outside the school gates when her mobile phone rang again. Bad timing, she thought. One or two of the other mothers had nodded to her and it would have been the perfect opportunity to get to meet them. 'Hello,' she said, her back turned to the cluster of women.

As before, there was silence.

'Hello?' she said, more sharply this time. This was no cold call, she concluded. This was deliberate. It had to be Paul. Did he know where she, they, were? Was he deliberately trying to rile her, or did he have a worse scenario in mind?

The silence continued. Then it seemed to change. Distinctly she heard the sound of heavy breathing.

'Is that you, Paul?' she asked sharply. 'Are you trying to upset me, because if you are, it won't work, you know.'

She had the sense that the call had been concluded before she finished speaking.

'Mum. Mum, what are you doing here?' Ash asked, coming up behind her. 'My mum doesn't usually come to meet me,' she said to the girl beside her, whom Harriet saw was Fiona. 'I'm perfectly capable of getting myself home,' the girl ended indignantly.

'Of course you are, dear. I just thought I'd come and meet you as this is your first day. Hello, Fiona. Did you both have a good day?'

'It was all right,' Ash told her.

'Great.' All right in Ash's terms was actually high praise. 'Let's go home and have some tea.' And forget about Paul, she thought. After all, he couldn't possibly know where she was. Could he?

*James was leading a patrol from Camp Bastion, three armoured patrol vehicles making for a village where they'd been told there was Taleban activity. The road – if you could call the unmade track they were on a road – ran between low, scrubby hills and crossed streams that at this time of the year ran virtually dry. They had to be especially cautious when they were using the crossings, because it was there that the Taleban left IEDs, their improvised explosive devices. A man would need to go ahead at these crossings, probing until he was satisfied that it was safe. So it was a slow, nerve-racking business.*

*This time it had gone so smoothly. That is, until they were almost at the village. It happened without warning. Stupid! It always happened without warning. There was an explosion and the second vehicle was hit. The other two stopped. In spite of the danger the men scrambled out. You had to. You had to get to your own, do what you could do, although anyone with sense could see that two men were lying on the roadside badly injured. Immobile.*

*He and his men ran back. He was out front when the second explosion happened.*

*He spun round. It was the third patrol vehicle. The driver had inched out into the road to pass the second, his own triggering another IED. James saw a mutilated body fly through the air. It landed feet away from him. He knew at once who it was. Darren Warren-Brown. Corp was already radioing for the medics but God knew in this ruckus when they'd arrive. Not that it mattered. Darren had been married only weeks before they were flown in. His wife had given birth to a baby girl a month ago. He'd been so proud, showing off the photos. He'd never see either of them now. There was yet another soldier, nineteen the previous week, whose face was shattered so that the only way to identify him would be by his tags and there was a gaping hole where his stomach had been.*

*In his dream, in which he was not sure whether he was in his bed or – or where? James moved restlessly.*

*He wondered just how many people would truly miss him if he didn't return. Jess and Matt, at least for a time. His wife? Considering she had kicked him out, he doubted if she would give his death more than a single thought.*

Over tea – fish fingers and frozen peas, by no means gourmet cookery but aimed to please Ash – Harriet told her about the gardening job. 'Mrs Ormston, who runs The Gallery in town, seems nice and her garden could be a picture. But no one else seems to be advertising. I'm not sure how I can find more work.'

'What about the other people this – did you say his name was Benjamin? – worked for?'

'Ashley Finamore, you're not just a pretty face, are you, my pet?'

'As in, that's a good idea?'

'Exactly so. When I go to Joanne Ormston tomorrow morning I'll see if she has a contact number for Benjamin.'

'Forty pounds for a morning's work is fab.'

'Mm, it's a start,' said her mother. 'Unfortunately forty pounds isn't going to pay our bills by a long way.'

'Are we very poor, now that we've left Paul?'

'Paul didn't keep us,' answered Harriet, smothering indignation. 'It's true that I didn't pay him rent, but I did the cooking and the cleaning and the gardening, as you know. Then, out of my money, I paid for half of the bills, gas, electricity, council tax and so on. He seemed satisfied that we were paying our way, although he insisted on providing for all the food. I think our outgoings in Cennen Bridge will be a lot less than they were, if we're careful, so we shouldn't be worse off.'

'Mum, is that our neighbour's car?' The sound of a car leaving next door was a timely interruption. Ash was now peering out of the window. 'He's gone. Have you seen him yet?'

'No, and I don't even know his surname. I expect we'll meet him soon enough, though. I suppose one of us could go round when we know he's there.' Then she thought that she wasn't yet prepared to open herself, or Ash, to the scrutiny of new neighbours. 'I think we'll just have to wait until he's ready to visit us. But that reminds me, I noticed from the bathroom window that what looks like a new plum tree has fallen over. I think his lawn is due for mowing. If I see the man who cuts his lawn I'll mention it.' She had a better idea. 'I'll pin a note to the door of his garden shed if our neighbour isn't there.'

The following morning, after receiving no reply when she rang the doorbell, Harriet went into the back garden of Oak Cottage with the note and some sticky tape. There were windows at the side of the shed and one of them was broken. It would not have been visible from the house. She wondered if a branch of the plum tree had fallen on it. It was just possible, she decided, looking at the angle of the tree as it lay on its side, although a little unlikely. Perhaps it had been broken accidentally some time before. Then she looked more closely at the tree. It had not fallen. It had been savagely uprooted, so damaged that she doubted if it would even survive careful re-planting. Who would have done a thing like that? Best left, she decided, shaken all the same. She removed her note and went home to her own garden.

When she went to work for the Ormstons later that morning, Harriet said to Joanne, 'If you have a contact number for your Benjamin, I could try and persuade him to give me a list of his clients. It's a bit presumptuous since I've yet to pull a weed for you, but I thought I ought to speak to him before he leaves Cennen Bridge for good.'

'I thought of that, also, but I'm afraid it's already too late. Benjamin left a month ago and I don't know where he's gone.' She saw Harriet's face fall. 'However, I do know that he worked for John and Mary Smithson who live in The Old Vicarage. That's the large stone house opposite the church. You could try them.'

Harriet thanked her profusely and went home via The Old Vicarage, which had probably ceased to be a vicarage sometime during the previous century. It had a small front garden behind a stone wall, but from the general layout of the surrounding dwellings she judged that its back garden was extensive, probably going behind some of the smaller cottages and extending down to the small stream that ran through the market town.

While she was pondering the best way of introducing herself, Harriet's phone rang. She took it out of her bag. Then she set it on the seat beside her and regarded it warily. How ridiculous! she thought. As if it were going to bite her.

'Hello,' she said brightly. There was silence.

'Go to hell, Paul!' she ended the call abruptly. Then she giggled. It could have been anyone. She hoped she hadn't offended a prospective employer.

Then, making up her mind to call on the Smithsons immediately, Harriet resolutely switched off her phone.

# CHAPTER SEVEN

'Begin at the beginning,' Mrs Smithson said encouragingly, as they sat down in the dining room. 'Who are you and why do you think I might employ you in my garden? As it happens, I do need someone because our daughter is getting married this summer and I need the garden looking immaculate.'

Valiantly Harriet marshalled her thoughts and made a pitch for a job.

An hour, a cup of instant coffee and a tour of the garden later, it was agreed that she would give the Smithsons a morning a week until after the wedding, working under Mary Smithson.

Harriet left the house reeling. Not only was she promised another forty pounds, she had in her bag the name and address of one more of Benjamin's clients; judging by the name, Beechwood Grove, the owners of a large property on the outskirts of the town.

'Well done,' Florence exclaimed, when Harriet had finished telling her friend about the two jobs she had landed. 'You have done well.'

'And there is still Beechwood Grove I could try.'

'Beechwood Grove used to belong to one of the old local families but there were only daughters and they've married and left home. The mother, old Mrs Tench, is in a nursing home. The new people are young and likely to be a bit impoverished.'

'I'll go and see them, all the same.'

'Think I'll make myself a cheese sandwich. Join me?'

'I shouldn't. I must start getting my own garden to rights. I need to get some vegetables in. It's too late for a lot of things, but I'm going to buy seedlings and there are always tomatoes and salad stuffs. I thought I'd go to the local garden centre next.'

'I expect they're all right for vegetable seedlings. It's the more exotic stuff they don't do.'

Harriet's phone rang, interrupting them. 'Hello? Harriet Finamore here.' She spoke without a thought of who might be there. The silence was palpable. 'Stop this, Paul! You are becoming a pest. Leave me alone.'

'Is that Paul?' Florence's voice was bell-like in the background.

This time he spoke. 'I thought you might be with Florence. Come home, Hari.' It was a command, not a plea.

'After what you did to me? I'm never coming back.'

'We'll see about that. I don't believe you can live without me.'

'I shall prove you wrong, if it's the last thing I do.'

He laughed. Cynically. 'Be careful what you wish for, my dear.' Then he put the phone down.

Harriet switched hers off. 'Yes. That was Paul,' she said stonily, 'and he has now discovered my whereabouts, if he wasn't sure about it before.'

'Of course, he recognized my voice. I'm so sorry, Hari.'

'Not your fault.'

'You told him to leave you alone. Has he been pestering you? How long has this been going on for?'

She told her what had been happening. 'I suppose he wasn't sure until now where I was.'

'At the very least you must change your sim card.'

'I don't use half its facilities. I'll put it away for Ash and get something cheaper this afternoon.'

'Good. Then at least you'll know he can't contact you again.'

'But what if he comes looking for me?'

Florence looked at her helplessly. 'Can't you get injunctions – or things like that – to prevent someone from pestering you?'

'I suppose so. But I'm sure it takes time and a solicitor.'

'Are you afraid of Paul?'

'I'm not sure,' Harriet confessed slowly. 'I became wary of him because I was never sure when his next assault would happen. In the beginning I'd have trusted him with my life.'

'I can see that. How awful that he changed.'

'How awful that I made him change.'

'Harriet Finamore! This is not your fault.' Florence looked at her sternly. 'Say it after me! This is not my fault.'

Harriet regarded her friend for a moment. Then she said meekly, 'This is not my fault.' She repeated it, a little more firmly, 'This is not my fault.'

'I'm not sure I'm convinced. When he comes looking for you, you'll have to sound even more positive than that.'

'So you do think that he will come for me?' Harriet shivered with apprehension.

'Possibly. Probably. Now that he realizes he can't spook you by heavy breathing down the phone, he's bound to try to intimidate you some other way. You'll just have to tell him to his face that it's over. Finished. Unless he's completely insane, which doesn't sound like Paul, he'll listen and accept your decision.' Resolutely Florence went back to the breadboard where she had been working when Harriet arrived. 'I'm making enough sandwiches for the two of us,' she added gruffly. 'Yours are in clingfilm. You can eat them whenever you feel hungry. Now, go away. I've got work to do.'

Later, as she walked to the garden gate after her sandwich lunch, a man drove into the driveway of the other cottage. He saw her and stopped the car, winding down his window.

'Hello,' he called. 'Are you looking for Harry?'

'Um,' said Harriet. 'Not really.' He was good-looking, dark, with chiselled features. She guessed he was probably in his forties. It was as they had thought; James, whatever his name was, obviously believed there was a man living next door.

Suddenly she remembered the uprooted tree and how she was convinced it had been done deliberately. Uncertain about his reaction if he knew that she knew about it, she allowed the misapprehension to continue.

'I don't think he can be in. Perhaps you'd better come back?'

'I'm just leaving,' said Harriet, even more awkward now. 'I have to go to the garden centre. I need some seedlings.'

'Brownlows, I hope?'

'It is the nearest garden centre.'

'You'll find it a bit of a mess today. Don't let it put you off because the prices are good and you've got your work cut out here, haven't you? I've not seen you before. Are you going to work for them regularly?' He was looking at her oddly as she nodded, but it was obvious that she was leaving the premises, so he just grunted, engaged gear and drove to the side of his own cottage.

Harriet got into her car. Not a suspicious man, and he seemed nice enough. She supposed that it wouldn't be too long before she would have to apologize for not introducing herself properly before.

She had already ordered a new mobile phone online. Now Harriet went to Brownlows, the nearby garden centre, which was just down the road from Sycamore Cottage. The place was in turmoil, as she'd been warned, with a skip full of shattered glass and old, broken window frames. A builder pushing a large wheelbarrow towards the skip nodded as he passed her.

'Looks as though you've got quite a job on,' Harriet said.

'Storm damage from a couple of nights ago,' he replied.

The glasshouse must already have been in a fragile state, she thought, and it was probably too old to have had toughened glass. 'I didn't think the wind was that strong. Still, it's a good opportunity to make a really good job of re-building it now.'

'If you ask me, it wasn't,' the man said. He nodded significantly and touched the side of his nose. 'Ill wind, and all that.'

Harriet turned away. Vandalism or a dodgy insurance claim? Still, it was really none of her business and anything that made Brownlows look a little more up to date had to be a good thing for the owners. She found a pair of secateurs. They weren't the best but she thought they would do. She also found some strong gardening gloves. The whole garden centre was not particularly impressive and on closer inspection the stock looked tired. There were very few people around and no sign of any employees other than a girl at the till. She chose a bag of potting compost and a packet of cut-and-come-again lettuce seeds. She bought some tomato plants, a courgette plant that was limp but which she was sure would recover with a good watering and a dozen healthier-looking runner bean plants. Next year, she promised herself, she'd have her own seedlings.

The young, harassed woman balancing a baby on her hip who answered the door at Beechwood Grove, appeared nonplussed when Harriet offered to do some gardening work for her.

'Gardening?' she repeated vaguely.

'I've just come to live in Cennen Bridge,' she said. 'Mrs Smithson, at The Old Vicarage, suggested I should come to see you as I'm new here and looking for work.'

'Why don't you come in and we'll talk about it. You'll have to excuse the mess. The baby's teething and I've not had time to clear up after the twins.'

While Vicky Heard made the coffee – proper coffee – she plied Harriet with questions: Where was she living? 'Next door to James Ormston? Nice man.'

That was Harriet's first impression. She remembered his eyes. Nice eyes, with a hint of sadness in their depths, she'd thought.

'I could do with a gardener but with small children it would have to be organic gardening,' Vicky added, in the sort of tone that brooked no argument.

'If I worked for you, it would be your decision entirely. You might just have to expect the results to be different from other gardens.' Harriet thought it was expedient not to mention that she had already discovered that the Smithsons had murderous intent towards slugs and regarded chemical fertilizers as miracles of modern science.

'Come and have a look at the garden. Robin has a ride-on mower to keep a swath of grass roughly cut for the twins to play on.'

There were untidy borders, some stately trees, a large beech, three silver birches and two conifers. There was an empty pond.

'The pond can't be filled until the children are much older.'

'Of course not,' Harriet agreed. 'You could make it into a sandpit perhaps.'

There was a kitchen garden behind a brick wall that was totally overgrown. 'We hardly ever come in here,' admitted Vicky.

'I'm afraid it would need an army of gardeners to set this to rights. You should get some raspberries from these canes, at least, and over there is a blackberry, which will probably be productive as it's in full sun.'

'Blackberry jam,' said Vicky. 'I could do that.'

By the time the twins returned home it had been settled that Harriet would give the Heards four hours a week and that Robin would continue to use his ride-on mower for rough-cutting the grass.

The twins, at nearly four, were like pent-up puppies when they erupted from the people-carrier, which drew up in front of the house as Harriet was preparing to leave. As she said her good-byes she nodded towards the boys who were already fighting over a football.

'You might get them to sow their own seeds,' she suggested. 'Probably veggies rather than flowers. Perhaps they could have a competition to grow the biggest pumpkin for Hallowe'en. Children who are encouraged to grow their own plants in the garden are less likely to uproot your precious things.'

Vicky laughed. 'I'm not sure that I haven't just got myself a guardian angel, Harriet Finamore, but Beechwood Grove is certainly not going to be the same place as before.'

# CHAPTER EIGHT

He was between the two burning vehicles, bodies on all sides. Some were groaning, beginning to move. Two lay horribly still.

*Unbelievably there was a third explosion. For a moment, when the noise abated, there was no sound other than heavy breathing. His? Once again James was not sure where he was. There, or at home?*

*Then the explosion came again; it was coming increasingly often. But that was ridiculous. There had only been three explosions. Often? That surely meant that with a conscious effort he could stop this pain-filled nightmare. The noise hurt his eardrums – for this time there was sound and his sight was affected, too. No, it was the swirl of smoky dust that covered the track, covered the bodies, that was making it difficult to breathe.*

*Yelling like maniacs, those of the men under his command who were still on their feet scattered, to re-group with him where it was safest before they engaged the enemy. They'd need to pick up their wounded and their dead before they left the scene of battle. You didn't ever leave any of your men exposed to the tender mercies of the enemy.*

*There was a burst of gunfire, another explosion. The noise was deafening. In the midst of it James suddenly felt as though he had been punched in the kidneys by a tank. He gasped and the pain shot through him. Slowly he slumped to the ground.*

Life began to settle into a routine. Ash went to school and, as Harriet had suspected, by becoming friendly with Fiona, settled in quickly. Of their elusive neighbour nothing more had been seen. A man who did grass cutting in the village came fortnightly to deal with his lawn but, apart from the postman, no one else ever called. On a visit to Matthew John to check on the payment of a bill for a faulty drain that had required a plumber, Harriet thought to question the agent to see if he were any the wiser.

'James Ormston is in the Territorial Army. He spends several weeks a year training. Someone told me he's been in Afghanistan where he was wounded. He's some sort of an engineer, they say, but I don't know who he works for.'

Ormston. Could he be a relative of Joanne and Gareth?

One afternoon Harriet had just finished unloading her car and was letting herself into the cottage through the back door which led to the kitchen when she sensed that there was someone behind her. She whirled round and her heart began to pound.

Within arm's length was a man. No stranger. This was Paul.

'Hello, Hari,' Paul said evenly. 'So this is where you've been hiding yourself? You know, I expected you home long before this.'

'W-what are you doing here?'

'I've come to take you home, of course. Ash as well. I suppose she is at school?' When there was no reply he went on, 'You'll just have time to pack for the two of you before she returns. I'd like you to get a move on, though. I've wasted enough time already today and we don't want to be too late back, do we?'

'How did you find me?' she managed at last.

'Running to Florence was your natural choice. Hearing her voice in the background when I called you was all I needed. Once I was here, I asked at the post office. Simple.'

He sounded so reasonable, so like the ordinary Paul of the past that it confused her. 'So why didn't you come and find me sooner, if you really want me back? I am never coming back to you, Paul.' She swallowed the fear that threatened to engulf her.

'My dear, that sounds a little dramatic. How can you say that when we haven't even discussed why you left me so abruptly?'

'I'm sure it can't really have come as such a surprise.'

'We lived together happily for a number of years. Why leave me now? Why do it the coward's way, without any explanation.'

'Be-because I don't want to be with you any more. I'm – we're – happier on our own.'

'You deserted me on a whim?' His left eyebrow was raised in the quirky way she had once found so beguiling.

'No whim, Paul,' she protested. 'I left you because I decided that I won't allow you to hit me any more.'

He lifted his hand, and she flinched visibly. He smiled gently as he moved nearer. He reached out and stroked her cheek and she forced herself to stand very still. 'Silly girl, you know that I love you very much.' He spoke with a sincerity it was hard not to believe.

She said shakily, 'You have a very strange way of showing it. I'm not going to change my mind, Paul. Ash and I have left you and I –we're – not coming back.'

'I think you might have to. Consider this, my dear, how will you manage? You're not a very capable woman, after all. We both know that you need looking after by someone who takes care of all the little difficulties in life. Someone like me.'

'A control freak? Someone who gets his kicks out of being violent, of hitting a woman with no provocation? Go away, Paul.' Her voice rose. 'I'm not going anywhere with you, ever again.'

But the back door was wide open. Paul turned to see if they were being observed. Apparently they were not. 'Yes, my dear, I think you are.' She shuddered as again she heard the dulcet note in his voice that had often preceded violence. Then he put his hand on her shoulder and, pushing her none too gently inside the cottage, he shut the door firmly behind them.

Even in the throes of a panic that threatened to overwhelm, Harriet noticed that Paul had not thought to lock the door. She was shaking. She took several shuddering breaths in an attempt to calm herself, knowing that it was essential that she should not break down. Ash was due home and she sensed in the depths of her being that she must not do anything to provoke Paul into hurting her so much that she could not protect her daughter. She had always believed that Paul sincerely loved Ash and would never do anything to harm her, but could she trust him?

'Why should you want me to come back to you, now that you know I don't want to live with you any more?'

'I don't think you've thought this through. Quite simply, I don't believe that you refuse to be with me.' He leant negligently against the kitchen sink as though he belonged there of right. He was the same man she remembered. No casual look for Paul; certainly no jeans or a sweatshirt. He was wearing his cavalry twill trousers, a sports jacket under which was a checked shirt and a tie.

The arrogance of the man was incredible. Unusually for her, it made Harriet begin to feel angry. She moved her shoulders to relieve the tension in her muscles and challenged him directly. 'What will it take to convince you that I mean what I am saying?'

Paul examined his nails as though the state of them was the most important thing on his mind. 'But that's obvious. You left in such a hurry. You left most of your things behind. What am I to believe, that you have dumped your winter clothes, all your books and most of your other possessions, merely in order to leave me? I don't think so. You have never been anything other than careful with your belongings. That was – is – one of the facets of your character that has always endeared you to me. You see, it showed me that basically we are very much alike.'

Her intake of breath was a hiss of denial. Then she said, as calmly as she was able, 'Of course we'd like our winter clothes, our books, my father's pictures.' She shrugged. 'But despite what you say, they are only things. Once I can afford it, we can replace what we actually need.'

'And how would you do that?' he asked, disbelief apparent in his voice as he straightened, moving away from the sink to examine the fridge which he opened, adjusting the placement of three yoghurt pots before closing the door again. 'You haven't got that much actual cash available, have you? And I should know. Haven't I managed your finances all these years? You've had no cause for complaint, living with me, have you?'

'I'm willing to believe that you managed my affairs scrupulously. You wouldn't have wanted us to lose by mismanagement because that would have reflected badly on you.' She sensed rather than saw his rage that she might ever have questioned his motives and again her courage almost failed her. She went on unsteadily, 'It stops here. I am perfectly capable of managing my own affairs. I don't want to live with you any more. Go away! I don't ever want to see you again.' As though he was merely amused by Harriet's impassioned declaration, Paul made no move to go. 'I want nothing more to do with you,' she cried. 'Don't you understand?'

He sighed gently. 'I repeat: How will you manage?'

'I have a job.'

'You? Do you mean to tell me you are working? Doing what?' Once again there was disbelief overlaid by mockery in his tone. 'Don't tell me that you have had to become a cleaner?'

'No, and there's nothing wrong with domestic work. I've done it ever since I was married, but—'

'And we both know you couldn't serve in a shop to save your life.'

Harriet bit back the angry retort that there were plenty of jobs a woman could do if she had to put food on her child's plate. 'I don't work in a shop,' she said, as calmly as she could.

'Of course you don't.' He said it soothingly as though he quite understood her difficulties. 'You might as well admit it, Hari, you need me.'

'Neither Ash nor I need a man who is violent. You have hurt me for the last time.'

Once again he smiled and took a step closer. 'Not only incapable, almost hysterical, I would say. I suppose you are a fit person to take care of a child?'

The insinuation stung her into her response. 'Don't you dare even try it, Paul. There are already people in this town who think that I am perfectly sane and capable. What is more, my solicitor knows why I left you.'

'You told William Crosse why you left me?'

She heard the timbre of his voice change from gentle solicitude to something that sounded nearer to anger. 'I told him exactly why I left you. I asked him not to tell you where I was proposing to live, although from the beginning he knew that he could contact me through Florence.'

'I see. Such a pity that you chose to involve a third person,' he sighed. 'So unnecessary. I don't count Florence, of course,' he added dismissively. 'She would say anything to support you. Now I really don't think I can let such treachery pass.' Before Harriet could react, Paul's left fist slammed into her stomach, winding her so that she bent over double, coughing and retching. When she eventually straightened, he slapped her face with his open right hand, and followed this with a swingeing blow with the back of his hand which knocked her off her feet.

Harriet lurched heavily against the corner of the substantial wooden kitchen table, the shock of that and the blows he had already inflicted threatening to spiral her into unconsciousness. As she collapsed onto the floor at Paul's feet, he kicked her viciously in the ribs.

'Leave my mother alone! Get away from her, you pig!'

Through a haze of pain, Harriet heard her daughter screeching at Paul at the top of her voice. Ash....

# CHAPTER NINE

Dazed as she was, Harriet realized that Ash had returned from school. Ash. There was no way she could possibly permit Paul to do to Ash what he had already done to her. She opened her mouth, but only a croak emerged.

'Hello, Ash. Come to join our little party, have you?'

Ash took no notice of the man, but dropped to her knees by her mother's side. 'Mum! What's he done to you?'

'It's all right, Ash,' Hari mumbled weakly. 'I tripped. I—'

'That's right,' said Paul, over their heads, his voice sounding solicitous again so that even through the haze of pain Harriet was amazed by his talent of being able to switch off emotions. 'It was a stupid accident.'

'N-no accident,' Harriet muttered, trying her best to get to her knees at least, but Ash, although she tried her best to support her mother, was not strong enough to bear her weight and Harriet slumped to the ground again.

'I saw you kick her. I hate you! Leave us alone!'

Shaking her head in an attempt to clear it, Harriet was aware only of her daughter by her side, first yelling at Paul at the top of her voice as she got to her feet, then launching herself towards him, fists flying. Afterwards Ash told her proudly that she had managed to hit him twice.

How it would have ended Harriet did not know, but in the moment that Ash was forced to take a breath another voice, a man's deep bass voice, interrupted the ugly scene as he caught

Ash by the arm. He held her away from Paul as Ash, realizing that she could no longer reach the man whom she loathed, fought to release herself.

Through the haze of pain, Harriet recognized James, her neighbour. He was not alone. Behind him, her face registering horror, was a woman she also recognized: Joanne Ormston.

'What's going on? Good lord! Harry, are these women pestering you? Stop it, you little termagant. Just stand still.'

'James, I don't think it's quite what you think ...' Joanne started to say, but her words were drowned by Ash's shriek.

'Leave me alone. Let me go!' But eventually Ash's struggles abated and she stood as tense as a wild creature waiting for the moment to escape, for the moment, quiet.

Joanne moved past James to go to Harriet, sinking to her knees beside her.

All the same, the man's hand still grasped Ash's wrist. 'But—' his voice tailed away, as though its owner had only then become aware that the notion of female harassment did not quite marry with the sight of one of those females – the woman he had taken for the gardener – lying curled up defensively on the kitchen floor. She remained motionless, still incapable of moving, his own companion bent over her solicitously.

'Who the devil are you?' Paul demanded.

'James Ormston. You know, I'm your neighbour.' He remembered then that he was not alone. 'This is Joanne Ormston, my sister-in-law.' Joanne was now helping Harriet onto a kitchen stool. 'I'd shake hands but,' James shrugged, 'I'm a little occupied at present. I'm sorry it's taken me such a long time to get acquainted but I've been ...' he hesitated, 'away. There must be something I can do to help?'

He spoke quietly but there was something in the timbre of his voice, arresting, compelling, that was sufficient for the repugnant, heated atmosphere of the scene to abate just enough for the participants to take a breath.

It was Ash who spoke first. 'He's been hitting my mum. He's hurt her badly. Can't you see!'

Paul said tightly, 'It's none of your damn business.'

'No, it isn't,' answered James equably. 'Although it certainly sounded as though someone required a little assistance. I saw the child arrive. I wondered what she was doing here.'

'I live here,' replied Ash indignantly.

'Do you now?' His eyes narrowed as he scrutinized her carefully, but his hold on her wrist slackened.

'I'm Ashley Finamore. I've lived here for ages.'

'So you are Harry Finamore,' James said distastefully, eyeing the other man up and down. His voice suggested that the delay in seeking his acquaintance had been of no consequence after all.

'James, you've got it wrong,' said Joanne, shaking her head.

'I'm Hari Finamore, Harriet Finamore.' Harriet spoke for the first time. She caught her breath as pain in her ribs shot through her again and she clutched her side. Ash wrenched her wrist from James's loosened hold and she pushed both Paul and Joanne out of the way to go to her mother, standing by her protectively.

'It's all right, love,' Harriet said tightly, fighting to control her breathing, for her sore ribs hurt abominably. 'I'll be better in a moment. All I need to do is to catch my breath.'

'A wet flannel might be a good idea, Ashley,' said James easily, although his eyes had hardened as he saw the blood at the side of the woman's mouth. 'Run it under the cold tap and squeeze it dry before you bring it back. Joanne?' He nodded towards the other woman.

'Perhaps you could show me where the bathroom is?' Joanne said to Ash, her voice reassuring. 'We'll bring a couple of flannels for your mother. I'm sure she'll be better soon.'

Now,' James said to Harriet, once the two had left the room, his own voice gentling, 'do you want me to call the police?' It was plain that he was not of the same opinion as Joanne.

'No,' said Harriet, shaking her head. 'I just want him to go and never to come near me again.'

'I think that might be arranged.' He turned to Paul and, while he spoke quietly, the steely edge to his voice was more menacing than if he had shouted. 'Do you understand? I don't think a squad car would take all that long to arrive and I'm very happy to call one, if necessary. Unless, that is, you leave at once. So, whatever-your-name-is, get out.'

'But Hari and Ash are coming home with me. I'm not leaving without them. That's why I am here. I came to fetch them.' Paul sounded so unutterably reasonable that Harriet blinked.

Even James seemed taken aback. He looked questioningly at Harriet and she shook her head vehemently. Then he turned back to the man. 'Get out!' he repeated softly.

'I will send for our things,' Harriet said, looking directly at Paul for the first time since he had assaulted her. 'But we shall not go back to you. Ever.'

'I've always known you are a fool, Hari. And disloyal. Haven't I looked after you well, you and the child, all these years?'

'It's over, Paul. I don't love you and I will not go back.'

'You heard the lady. Out.'

Even then Paul stood his ground. 'You know, one day you'll be sorry you said that.'

James moved. He moved so fast his actions were blurred, but in a moment Paul's right arm was pressed into the small of his back and he was being propelled out of the kitchen door. 'I'd like to leave you as marked as you've left her, but you aren't worth it,' he snarled.

To the amazement of both Harriet and James, Paul stood his ground just outside the kitchen door, although he was massaging his wrist as he made one last appeal. 'Hari. Is this what you truly want?'

'Please just go, Paul. It's over.'

He shook his head as though he couldn't understand her. Then he turned away, saying over his shoulder, 'I really do hope you don't ever regret this decision.'

'Amazing,' said James, gazing after him as Paul got into his car, grinding his gears as he drove off. 'I am so sorry you had to go through that,' he turned back to Harriet. 'I had no idea.'

'Of course you didn't.' The grinding of his gears actually betrayed just how agitated Paul was. She hoped there would be no further trouble. 'No one in Cennen Bridge knows the truth about my dire past, other than that I have recently ended a relationship. Except for Florence Harding, that is. She's my oldest friend.'

'I know Florence.'

'We stayed with her while I was finding somewhere to rent.'

Ash and Joanne returned to the kitchen, both carrying flannels. 'Here's your flannel, Mum. And I found a clean one for Joanne. They're both nice and cold and we've squeezed them really dry. Shall I mop up the blood for you?'

The adults were relieved to hear relish rather than repugnance in her childish voice. Yet Harriet was grateful that at least the true extent of the violence had not been perpetrated in Ash's presence.

'I think I'd better do it,' she said. 'Let me just hold one against my mouth to stop the bleeding. I'll use the other in a moment.'

'Did he kick you?' asked James abruptly, as he noticed how Harriet was favouring her side.

'Only the once. Ash interrupted him.'

'But this has happened before?'

'Yes,' she admitted sadly, 'but never quite so prolonged or quite so violently.'

'Ghastly man. You're well out of that, Harriet.' Joanne turned to James. 'I've already met Harriet. She works for me.'

'Does she? Shall I send for a doctor?' he asked Harriet then, narrowing his eyes as he assessed the damage to her face.

'Oh, heavens, no. I shall be all right.'

'You don't think he's broken a rib?' asked Joanne. She had told

Ash who she was and the girl had not hesitated to pour out her hatred of the man who once more had hurt her mother.

Harriet tried a laugh by way of denial, and winced perceptibly.

'That's it. Get your mother's things, Ashley. We are taking her to the hospital to get her X-rayed.'

'Really? That is well cool.'

'But of a coolness that should most definitely not be happening. Do you think you could manage to walk, Hari, if I support you with my arm? Otherwise I might have to carry you.'

'Probably not a good idea,' said Harriet with a smile, and winced again. 'It's all right. I may not be able to run, but I'm perfectly able to walk. If you insist we go, that is.'

'I'm sure it would be for the best,' said Joanne. 'Look, James, this obviously isn't the best of times for you to show me those papers. In any case, I have to get back to the gallery as I'm meeting a client in half an hour. So I'll be in touch in a day or so. But Gareth and I really do need to sort this out, you know. He says it's so....' She shrugged and turned back to Harriet. 'You obviously won't be in a fit state to work for a bit. I'll expect you when I see you. OK? Do hope you feel better soon. 'Bye, Ash. Take care, both of you. See you, James.' With that, she was gone.

# CHAPTER TEN

Harriet had a cracked rib. She was told that there was no point in having it strapped but that she should be careful for a day or so.

'Thank goodness it's Friday and I don't have to go to work until Tuesday,' she sighed, as they all got back into the car.

'But Joanne has already told you that she doesn't expect to see you until you're better.'

'I don't think my other ladies would take kindly to it if I have time off so soon after starting to work for them.'

'Other ladies? What do you do for them?'

'Mum's a gardener.'

'Are you? I thought you worked in the gallery. That's interesting.'

'Mum, I'm st-ar-ving. Absolutely starving,' Ash interrupted dramatically. 'I haven't had anything to eat for positively yonks.'

'Oh, goodness. Of course you're hungry. What are we going to do about it?'

'Feed her, of course,' James replied. 'What would you like, Ash?'

'Fish 'n' chips.'

'Absolutely,' said James. 'I couldn't have chosen better myself. There's a shop on the corner here, I seem to remember. With a bit of luck I can park. There,' he said, pulling into a side street. 'Come and help me fetch the food, Ash,' he said, undoing his seat belt. 'Fish and chips all round, I take it?'

'Are we going to eat it in the car?' asked Ash. Paul had never so much as permitted a toffee to be consumed in his car.

'I thought we'd have a picnic.'

Harriet said anxiously, 'Are you sure? Wouldn't you rather see Joanne this evening? She seemed a little agitated.'

'It's not that important,' he said easily. 'I expect Gareth is just fussing. We'll have a picnic and then I shall see both of you safely back home. Right?'

The picnic area James knew of was delightful. High on a hill overlooking the town, its backdrop was mysteriously shady at that time of the evening with oaks and ash and sycamores and underlying feathery ferns. There were two unoccupied wooden bench tables in the shade of the trees and two more on a grassy area in the evening sun. James parked the car near one of these and there he settled Harriet with a rug on the seat.

Harriet sat down carefully. So long as she moved cautiously the ache in her ribs was not too unbearable. She accepted the parcel of fish and chips and sat toying with the food which they ate with plastic forks from a plastic container he took from under the front seat of the car.

'There's nothing like being prepared,' she commented, with a hint of amusement in her voice, noting with relief that Ash was clearly enjoying her unexpected supper. 'You must have been a boy scout.'

'In the dim and distant past,' he agreed, with an answering grin.

'What do you do for a living?' she asked him, after she had chewed carefully on a succulent chip, having prudently eschewed both salt and vinegar because of her cut lip. 'I heard that you are in the Territorial Army. Is that right?'

'I'm an engineer, but I have had amazing experiences with the Territorials.'

'Maybe it's been a little more than a hobby, then?'

'Mm. I've seen active service in both Iraq and Afghanistan.'

'That must have been difficult,' Harriet commented diplomatically.

James chose to take her literally. 'Oh, you know, firms are under an obligation to let their people go when necessary. At least it means that we have a job to come back to when our stint is over.'

'And of course that's essential,' she said.

'Mum, are you going to finish your chips?' Ash broke in impatiently, 'I'm still hungry.'

Harriet sighed. 'They are very nice, love, but I haven't much appetite tonight.' She pushed her bundle of food towards her daughter. 'You eat what you want.'

'I should have thought of giving you something more bland,' said James apologetically. 'Stupid of me.'

'Not at all. Besides, it's Ash we're feeding, isn't it.'

'Mum doesn't ever buy fish and chips.'

'But I do cook oven chips occasionally. You must be glad to be home again, James.' She remembered that she'd been told that he had been wounded. Not a subject to bring up tonight.

'Do you go to the local school, Ash?' James asked.

'I've started at the primary school.'

'Ash is going to the comprehensive in September.'

'It's funny, we've hardly seen you since we came here. Where were you when you were away?' Ashley had no compunction at all about exercising her curiosity. 'Were you sick?'

'Ash, it's not very polite to ask personal questions.'

'I've been in and out of hospital,' James answered diffidently. 'You see, I got a bit of a wound in Afghanistan.'

'Have you been fighting?' asked Ash, open-mouthed.

'Yes. Anyway, now I'm home and it's back to the day job.'

'You must be very brave,' said Ash admiringly.

It was no wonder that Paul recognized a man he dared not openly challenge, Harriet was thinking. 'Will you have to go back?'

'I have an ongoing commitment to the TA, but I won't be called up for active service again because of the hospital bit. Afghanistan was something else. Unforgettable. The job was grim at times, though my men were fantastic. In many ways it's a shame, but I think it means my days with the TA are about over.'

'If you have men, I guess you must be an officer?' Ash looked at him consideringly.

He nodded and licked his fingers before he replied, 'That's right.'

'Are you a captain, or something?' asked Ash, visibly impressed.

'Lieutenant-Colonel. Rank comes with age,' he replied easily. 'Inevitably you get to the age when senior vacancies are few and far between. It's about the right time for me to go.'

Rank came with qualities of leadership, Harriet thought shrewdly.

'Do you like fighting? Was it bad, being wounded?'

'Ash! I said no more questions.'

But he answered, 'I don't particularly care for the fighting bit, Ash. Not many of us do, you know, although we know it has to be done. It's the life, the camaraderie, and yes, the action bit that I enjoy. There's nothing like it, really. As for being wounded?' he shrugged. 'It happened. I should have known better and kept my head down. Fortunately the medics in Camp Bastion did a good job on me.'

'I expect your family was relieved when you came home.'

'I was one of the lucky ones.'

Why did Harriet wonder if he really believed that? There was something in the timbre of his voice that suggested otherwise. 'They all probably worried, anyway.' Was he unmarried? It was an easy assumption. She hadn't yet seen a woman next door.

He grimaced as if in anticipation of her unspoken question. 'I'm divorced. My wife wanted me to leave the TA. When I refused, she left me. My children are more glad I'm back than my former wife is.'

'So you do have children,' said Ash.

'I have a boy and a girl. Matt, short for Matthew, is eleven, and Jessica is fourteen.'

'I'm just eleven. Where do they go to school?'

'They both go to Windcote College.'

'So I won't see them, ever,' said Ash.

'I don't know about that. They live nearby with their mother, but they'll be coming to visit me every other weekend and, of course, they will stay during the school holidays now that I'm home. Felicity manages a hat shop and her parents live about five miles away. She's very good at her job.'

Harriet could detect a degree of pride in the expertise of his former wife, which was touching. 'It sounds as though you've both managed to stay on good terms with each other. That's good, especially for the children.'

'I never wanted the divorce in the first place,' said James. 'When it became inevitable, there was no need for either of us to make life more difficult than it was for the other and neither of us wanted to upset the children any more than was absolutely necessary.'

It sounded to Harriet as though, given the opportunity, James would go back to his wife. She wondered if this Felicity felt the same way about him. She sighed inwardly. His experiences with his wife seemed as sad as her own, first with Joe and then with Paul.

'Eat up, Ash. I think your mother is getting tired. She should probably be lying down.'

James could not possibly have heard that sigh. It must have been intuition, a sensitiveness you did not often find in a man. Attractive and sensitive. And still in love with his wife. Then she realized that a man used to living in close proximity to an enemy would develop acute senses. 'I'm fine, really I am,' she told her daughter. 'You don't have to gulp your food. We don't want you getting indigestion.'

Nevertheless, James insisted that they should not linger. When Ash had finally finished and, without prompting, had packed away the debris of their meal, he put Harriet into the car again with infinite gentleness and drove home carefully. Once there, he urged her to go to bed with one of her painkillers.

'I think you should have a hot bath first. Tell you what, I'll bring round a casserole tomorrow which we can eat here and you can lie on your sofa in comfort while I do all the work. Is that a good idea?'

Harriet agreed that it was and she thanked James gravely. In truth, she was hurting more than she wanted to admit, and the thought of lying flat in bed and falling asleep for the first time in many weeks, safe in the knowledge that she would not wake up to find Paul on her doorstep, was persuasive.

Ash was also looking sleepy but, again without any prompting, she thanked James enthusiastically for her supper and informed him that they both preferred chicken casseroles to anything else and that her mum wasn't too keen on peppers unless they had been skinned. 'They give her wind,' she said candidly.

'Oh, they are known for that,' agreed James, without the faintest flicker of amusement, which endeared him to her mother. 'Sleep well, both of you.'

Ash waited until the garden gate had clicked shut. 'He's nice, isn't he? Just think, we could have had anybody for a neighbour.'

'He certainly is,' agreed Harriet. 'I think we are very lucky.' Then she thought that it would be as well if she were careful not to become too friendly. That was how all the dreadfulness had begun with Paul, allowing him to take over her problems.

'D'you want the bath first?' By the sound of her, Ash seemed to have no doubts about the niceness of James.

'You have your bath first, love, then I can have a nice, long soak. I'll come and kiss you goodnight when you're in bed.'

Later, as she eased herself into the hot water, Harriet reflected that, bruises and a cracked rib notwithstanding, her much dreaded encounter with Paul had had a positive result. He had walked away, worsted for the very first time, and for the first time in a long while she felt safe.

# CHAPTER ELEVEN

The following evening, after a casserole that Ash pronounced "wicked", Harriet agreed that she might watch a DVD until bedtime since it was a Saturday. It was warm enough that evening to sit outside, and she and James made themselves comfortable on the sheltered terrace that Harriet had already made weed-free and colourful with bedding plants, petunias and ageratum, neither of which needed too much watering.

James had noticed her occasional wince. 'You'll have to cancel work this coming week,' he observed.

'I can't possibly do that,' Harriet objected. 'I've not worked for my clients for very long and I really can't let them down, especially the Smithsons with their wedding looming. I'll be well enough to do something that isn't too strenuous.'

'If you don't tell them about your accident, I shall,' he said, and Harriet believed him. 'Besides, that cut on your lip needs explaining.'

'I definitely don't want them to know about Paul. It's so humiliating to have to admit to being beaten up.'

'I'm glad to hear that you can already find something amusing in what happened to you. At least it proves that the wretched man hasn't totally demoralized you.'

'No, I suppose he hasn't.' She reflected on that for a moment. Perhaps the truth of it was that, having made her escape from him, she no longer feared Paul's reactions in the way she had for so long.

'All you have to say is that you had a fall. That's not a crime.'

'I suppose that's better than sounding wimpish and admitting that I was beaten up by my ex. Besides, I've decided that I don't want to be thought of as a victim. Not here, in Cennen Bridge, so I shall definitely go to work. There are plenty of jobs I can do that will not stretch me too much.'

'There's very little in the garden that doesn't take bending and stretching, or have you perfected techniques that the rest of us could copy? And are you working full time?' He speculated about the circumstances that could make a victim of a woman whose character came over as totally resilient.

'A little exercise will do me good,' she was maintaining stubbornly. 'I have three jobs, but that leaves me with time to spare. Why?'

'It's just … well, you see, I've had to give up my engineering job but by coincidence I've been left a garden centre. It's called Brownlows. It was a family business.'

'That one? What's happened to the former owners?'

'Bill Brownlow was my mother's brother. He was unmarried and died recently. He left the garden centre to me and a sum of money to my elder brother, Gareth, who inherited the family haulage business. But, of course, you probably know what his business is. Grateful as I am to Bill, my problem is, I don't know too much about the finer points of gardening.'

'I suppose that accounts for its general state.'

'Excuse me?'

'Oops. Sorry, but on the couple of occasions I've been there, I've not been too impressed. Then there was all that work being done on repairing the glasshouse. I hope it was the one in the worst state.'

He looked at her appraisingly. 'Did you hear that it was storm damage?' When she nodded he added, 'Someone took a sledgehammer to it.'

'Good heavens. How dreadful! What have the police done?'

'I didn't involve them. As you said, it was the one needing the most repair. And it could have been caused by the storm.'

She digested this information. It really wasn't her business. 'I am impressed by your low prices,' she added, with a mollifying smile.

'I see.' Frowning, he digested that. 'When you're feeling better, perhaps you'd like to come and have a proper look at it?'

'Are you offering me a job?'

'I'm not sure. Would you be interested?'

'I'm not sure,' she countered. 'But I'd love to have a really good look over the place.'

'That's a date.'

'That reminds me. Did you get your fallen plum re-planted?'

'Gordon did it immediately you mentioned the problem.'

'More storm damage?' she asked.

'Probably.' He changed the subject abruptly. 'What about your belongings that are still in Paul's house?' She'd mentioned that problem earlier. 'Have you decided what to do about them?'

'Not really. I can't ask a removal firm to go and fetch the stuff. It would be far too difficult to explain where everything is.'

'And Paul might have moved them, anyway.'

She had thought about that, too. 'There really isn't much. A chair that belonged to my mother, silver and a few pictures that my father inherited from his father, books and an old cabin trunk of our winter clothes. I wouldn't want to bother with anything else.'

'Then I suggest that you arrange a date with Paul and we hire a small van and drive over together.'

'You'd do that for me?'

'Why not?' he said equably. 'I'll sort out a van and you can settle up with me once we're home. I think the sooner the better, don't you? It would be best to do it next Saturday as I've promised Matt and Jess to take them out on Sunday.'

'It doesn't have to be next weekend,' Harriet protested, 'and I wouldn't want to disrupt your time with your children.'

'One day at a time is all that Felicity allows me at present.

Besides, I think it would be as well to get the job over as soon as possible, don't you? Phone Paul tomorrow and leave him a message. That way, if he has moved any of it, he'll have time to collect it all together without loss of face. Best all round, that.'

Indeed, it would be. Harriet was lost in admiration. There was no way she could have brought herself to drive over to Paul's on her own in a month of Sundays, she told him.

'I think you are a lot more positive than you give yourself credit for,' he declared. 'But drink up, Ash's film finished ten minutes ago and it's time you were both in bed.'

*Through the darkness he heard noise. Someone had once told him that you only worried when there was no noise. That was when you were dead. He tried to smile because at least the noise meant that he was still alive. Or perhaps it was the wine. They'd told him that wine and some of the drugs they used didn't always help with post traumatic stress disorder.*

*The men on either side of him let him fall as they themselves came under fire, falling into a ditch. Involuntarily he screamed as he hit the ground. Then they were dragging him, their hands hard under his armpits, his feet trailing in the dust, catching on stones. He was hurting so much that he tried to tell them to let him go, leave him be. But somehow the words wouldn't emerge through his clenched teeth. There was dust in his mouth, too. His tongue felt swollen with it. Improvised explosive devices! He should have been more wary. He should have known better than to have led his men into a trap. Could it have been prevented? Probably not, given the Snatch vehicles that were inadequate for the job they were supposed to be doing. Damn war. Damn all wars!*

The following morning Harriet was in her own small front garden tying up some tall delphiniums which she had rescued from a tangled heap of groundsel and goose grass. She was delighted to find that her ribs only ached when she bent right over. A 4X4 drove up just before midday and a woman and two children got out and went into James's garden. The woman let them into the cottage, coming out a few minutes later looking decidedly irate. This must be Felicity with James's children, Harriet decided, trying not to appear too curious an observer.

'I say,' the woman called across the space of the two gardens, 'I suppose you must be the gardener.'

'Um ...' began Harriet, taken aback by the woman's aggressive tone.

'Mr Ormston is supposed to be looking after the children today and he isn't at home.'

It was scarcely her concern, Harriet thought with a degree of indignation. 'I expect he isn't back from the church yet,' she said, her own voice conciliatory. She had seen him leave the cottage at around 9.30, smartly dressed, and she had wondered if that was where he was going.

'Damn. I suppose he's had to fill in for the organist. Again.'

It was news to Harriet that James played the organ, although she knew that he liked music because almost every evening now she heard classical music coming from an open window.

'He knew very well that I have to be at the Richards' by noon and it's a quarter to already. I've told the children to watch TV until he gets back and that if they want anything they're to ask you.'

'Um ...' repeated Harriet. Then she rallied. 'I can't just go in to James's house and sort out his children,' she protested. 'Anyway, I'm not his gardener, I'm his new neighbour and I've never even been inside his place.'

James's former wife eyed Harriet up and down dismissively. Then she consulted her watch, frowned, waved her car keys and said over her shoulder, 'I imagine the place is much the same as yours. Mirror image and all that. As you must be a practical sort of person, I'm sure you'll cope.'

Harriet watched the car move off, the woman inside taking no further notice of her than if she really had been the jobbing gardener. On a Sunday? That most people were considerate of their jobbing gardener's feelings, good gardeners being hard to come by, was a fact of life that Harriet was already coming to appreciate. This employer undoubtedly lost her gardeners soon after she found them, she thought cattily.

So what was she going to do now? she wondered. She could remain within sight of the cottage windows and hope that the children were content to wait for their father in front of the TV – or she could go and introduce herself and hope that James did not think that she was being intrusive.

The decision did not have to be made. Ash came outside to ask what was going on. 'Was that kids arriving next door?'

Harriet explained it appeared that James's children had come to spend the day with their father but that he must still be at church. She told Ash that his wife had mentioned that James played the organ. 'I expect organists are almost the last to leave a church.'

'It would be fun to hear James play.'

'I think I must have done a couple of times, through the wall. He plays very well. At first I thought it must be a recording.' Mood music you might call it.

'Do you think we could go to church one Sunday when he is playing? Fiona's friend sings in the choir.'

'Would you like to do that?'

'I think I might like to try. Can I go next door and see James's children now? Can I Mum?'

'Yes, love. Why not? I think that's an excellent idea. Why don't you invite them here for a glass of lemonade while they are waiting for their father? You can all have it in the garden so that they'll see him as soon as he gets home.'

# CHAPTER TWELVE

Harriet watched while Ash ran next door and rang the doorbell. After a moment it was answered by the boy. She could see her daughter issuing the invitation quite unselfconsciously. Oh, to be that young and innocent again, she thought. Then she thought that nothing on earth would induce her to repeat all the agonies of the teen years which Ash and she, naturally in the guise of the Wicked Witch of the West, still had to endure. She gave a wave and went inside to prepare a jug of lemon barley, adding a plate of ginger biscuits. Then she went out into the front garden again.

Ash had already brought the two children with her. Youngsters rather than children, she amended. The three were standing around looking awkward.

'Hello, I'm Hari,' she said, using the diminutive. 'You must be Matthew and Jessica. Would you like some lemon barley water while you are waiting for your father to come home?'

'I don't drink squash. I'd much rather have a Coke,' said Jessica.

'Mum doesn't allow Coke,' Ash told her solemnly. 'She says it makes me hyperactive.'

'Does it?' asked Matthew interestedly. He turned his large, expressive eyes on Harriet. 'Have you done a proper scientific study of what it does to Ash?'

'It doesn't do me any harm,' commented Jessica. She was very slender, wearing jeans that did not disguise prominent hip bones and a crop top that emphasized an already developed figure and showed two inches of firm, bare flesh above the jeans. She twiddled with her fringe which hung fashionably long over her eyes.

Privately Harriet thought that drinking caffeine probably accounted for the girl's manners. She answered, 'I don't have to do a scientific study of what it does to Ash. All I've had to do is read the evidence that other people have found. So, no Coke in this household until Ash is old enough to choose what to do with her life. Lemon barley water, anybody?' she asked cheerfully.

'Me, please,' said Ash.

'OK,' Matthew agreed, pleasantly enough. 'Er – thanks,' he said as Harriet passed him a glass.

'What about you, Jessica, will you change your mind?'

'I suppose so. If you've not got anything else.'

'I could fetch you a glass of water.' The look the girl gave her was withering. Much the same as that of her mother, Harriet recognized. 'Or you could go without.'

Jessica sighed heavily. 'Lemon barley water.' Her 'please' came grudgingly late.

'Biscuit, anyone?'

'Thanks,' said Matthew, taking two and glaring at his sister.

'I don't like ginger biscuits,' announced Jessica.

Harriet said sympathetically, 'Oh, dear. I guess you'll just have to wait until your father returns, then. You see, we haven't been here long, and I only have things in the pantry that both Ash and I like.'

'I like chocolate biscuits.'

'So do I. For a treat,' said Harriet. 'Unfortunately, besides being more expensive than the plain ones, they are fattening. That's why I don't buy them very often.'

'Mum never eats chocolate biscuits,' offered Jessica.

'There you are, then,' said Harriet. 'How sensible of her.'

Jessica regarded her with narrowed eyes. She must have concluded that Harriet was not being ironic because, eventually, she gave her a tentative smile. 'You may call me Jess,' she said graciously. 'Have you come to live here for good?'

Harriet explained that they had wanted to find somewhere new to live and that she had needed to find work. 'I'm a gardener, you see.'

'Mum says that gardeners today are rubbish,' said Jessica. Her brother must have given her another of his looks because she added defensively, 'They need telling everything, Mum says.'

Why was she not surprised by the attitude? Harriet thought before she answered carefully, 'I think a lot of people believe that professional gardening is an easy job that anyone can do. If it's your own garden it doesn't matter if you have the odd failure – and a lot of that is inevitable – but it takes stamina to work in someone else's garden because it is labour intensive and you do need to know what you are doing. I mean, it wouldn't be a good idea to dig up all someone's best plants and leave the weeds.'

'Do you know what you are doing?' asked Jess.

'My scientific know-how is a little rusty,' Harriet admitted cheerfully, 'but I did go to college to study gardening, so I reckon I can tell a weed from a flower.' Not for a moment was she going to confess to this ill-mannered teenager that she hadn't finished her course because she had left to marry Joe.

'Do you have to know science to do gardening?' asked Matthew, sounding interested.

'Of course you do. Even if you want to garden organically. You know, pest control, compost and all that. Then you need to understand crop rotation for growing the best vegetables.'

'Mum doesn't grow vegetables. She buys them from the supermarket. She says they're cheapest there.'

Harriet was about to declare that she liked to support a shop that sourced its vegetables from local suppliers when, fortunately, James arrived home. She watched as the two children went to greet their father, Jessica embracing him exuberantly, tall as she was, leaping up into his arms and giving him smacking kisses on his face. It was as if she needed to make absolutely clear to bystanders the affection that existed between them. Matthew was less demonstrative, accepting the hug his father gave him without showing any resistance but from the manner in which he stayed close to James it was apparent that he, too, was pleased that they were together again.

One of the children must have explained that Harriet had given them some refreshments because James came over to thank her.

'Think nothing of it,' said Harriet. 'I hope you all have a lovely day together,' forestalling any polite invitation that she and Ash should join them. Then, giving them a wave, she gave Ash a little push in the direction of the front door.

'Mum,' protested Ash, once they were inside. 'I think James was going to ask us to go next door with them.'

'Yes, dear, I think that he was, being a polite man. But it wouldn't have done, you know. He's not seen his children for ages, not for any length of time on their own, I mean. It's hard for a father and his children to be separated, and don't forget, he was in Afghanistan. That must have been a strain for his family.'

'I suppose he might have been killed, not just wounded,' said Ash. 'That would have been pretty awful.'

'It would, indeed. So now they need time together, and without strangers around.'

Ash considered this for a while. 'My dad's dead,' she said in a small voice. 'And now I don't even have Paul.'

Harriet's heart smote her. She sat down on a kitchen chair and pulled Ash towards her. 'Come and have a cuddle,' she said, ignoring the twinge in her ribs. 'As long as you don't think you're too big for cuddles. I know you haven't got your dad, and now you've lost Paul. It's awful about your dad. But we're better off without Paul,' she added defiantly.

'Well, naturally I'm sorry about Dad,' Ash said stoutly, giving Harriet a kiss on her cheek, 'but I'm not really sorry about Paul. He was perfectly horrid to you the other day and I don't think he was always very nice when we lived in his house.'

Harriet shifted Ash's weight until the bones of her thin hips were pressing on her own good side. 'Paul and I were not always happy together,' she admitted.

'I knew that.'

'Did you? We were, at first. But you told me he was always nice to you,' Harriet said, her heart thumping with dread as she prepared to be confronted with evidence of child molestation. 'Were there times when he wasn't nice to you?'

'Only when he shouted at me.'

Harriet's heart lifted fractionally. 'I shout at you at times.'

'I don't much like you when you shout at me.'

'No. I don't suppose you do. But Paul didn't upset you in any other way, did he?' she persisted.

'Do you mean did he act inappropriately?' the child asked.

'What's that?'

'You know,' said Ash candidly. 'They told us about it at school. You are supposed to tell an adult you trust if some man or other does things to you that you don't like.'

'Oh. I'd forgotten.' She was torn between thankfulness that she did not have to go into the sordid details of what constituted inappropriate behaviour and rage that it should be necessary for a child to be aware of it.

'Paul wasn't like that. Except for the times when he got cross, he was all right. It's a pity about Dad, though,' she ended wistfully.

'Yes, it is,' Harriet agreed softly. 'So, love, you see why I thought that it was important for Matthew and Jess to be with James on their own today.'

'Matt's OK. Jess is a pain, but James is all right.'

'He is, isn't he? It's so kind of him to offer to arrange for a van to go and fetch our things from Paul's next weekend. And, although Jess may come over as a pain, I think she was probably just a bit defensive with new people. I expect you'll get on with her better next time you see her.'

'If all the girls at Windcote are like her, I'm glad I'm not going there next year.'

Harriet decided not to comment on that remark. 'What would you like to do when James and I go over to Paul's house?'

'I'd like to stay with Aunt Flo.'

'Then we'll see what can be arranged.'

Harriet decided to telephone her clients on the Monday to tell them that she had had an accident. 'I shall come to work,' she promised, 'but I thought I'd better warn you that I'm not quite as mobile as usual.' She was going to spin them the story about a fall but apparently Joanne had already told both Mary Smithson and Vicky Heard in lurid detail about Paul's vicious attack on her. 'As I'm slowed down, I suggest that you pay me seventy-five percent of my usual wage for the next couple of weeks,' she offered gallantly.

Vicky Heard was entirely sympathetic and only John Smithson, who had answered that call, took her up on her suggestion. Mary Smithson was horrified about what Harriet had endured and she was so outraged at the possibility that she might lose an efficient gardener through what she called sheer stinginess that, when Harriet examined her cheques, which were paid at the end of the month, she discovered that nothing had been docked by anyone.

Certainly, due to James's intervention, her injuries were far less than they might have been. But the bruises that faded through blue-black, then a garish greeny-black to yellow persisted for over three weeks, reminding her, if she needed it, of what male violence could do to a woman.

# CHAPTER THIRTEEN

The hospital at Camp Bastion was quiet, eerily quiet compared with the noise of the battlefield. Could you call the compounds of Helmund Province a battlefield? No more and no less than the miles of scrubby land that divided the sparse settlements. Yet they were equally dangerous, which was sometimes easy to forget. There was a grandeur about the scenery that was unexpected. It was harsh, totally unforgiving, yet there was a nobility about it that belied the poverty of its people.

In the unmade-up streets of the villages there was often a menacing quiet – when you were totally absorbed in your surroundings, waiting for an attack that sometimes never came at all, or if it did, was quite out of the blue. Then occasionally the unexpected happened – an approach from a friendly face, the offer of tea. You accepted, of course you did, although for the man in charge it was always with his eyes watchful for enemy action.

The children were friendly enough, even though the friendliness sometimes came with the outstretched hand hoping for sweets or a biro. James thought that the women were beginning to regard them as something other than implacable enemies. This was apparent particularly when you were escorting a medical team to conduct a surgery in a village. Then it was always the men first, afterwards the children and finally the women – provided that their husbands agreed that they might be examined. Fortunately they were always able to take with them a female medic to enable this to happen. It also gave the Afghan men pause for thought, that the soldier with medical know-how was a woman.

They were training the Afghan men now in the hope that one day

*soon they would be capable of taking on the Taleban themselves, allow-
ing the Western soldiers to go home.*

*At Camp Bastion there was bustle but it was purposeful. There were
nurses, soft hands. There was pain, too. Pain....*

*It got better, of course. As pain does. But the nightmares did not.*

*PTSD, they said it was, once he was back in the UK and he had
decided to tell them what had been happening to him. Post traumatic
stress disorder. A form of flashback. It was a common enough occurrence,
they assured him. It was what must have felled so many men from the
trenches in the First World War. Although they called it cowardice, in
those days.*

*It could easily be treated, they assured him. Some sufferers responded
to counselling, others needed a few weeks on drugs, although a few even
had difficulty responding to a mixture of the two. He was coming out of
it. Slowly.*

*For some reason or other, it was a help having neighbours. Analysing
it, he assumed it was because he did not feel quite so alone as he had
when the cottage next door had been empty. He liked Hari, he decided.
She was independent but with a fragility about her that he appreciated
in a woman. When he thought about the man she had been with for the
past few years he wanted to do him serious damage. The way she had lain
on the kitchen floor, slapped, punched and kicked, made his blood boil.
You didn't do that to your worst enemy.*

*He couldn't see Harriet Finamore as anyone's worst enemy.*

As Florence agreed, with alacrity, to have Ash for the day, James
and Harriet were able to leave in the van after an early breakfast
the following Saturday, although Florence did suggest prudently
that Ash should arrive with her overnight things. 'If you don't
think you'll be back by her bedtime, ring and she can stay the
night with me.'

There was little heavy traffic on the road so early and they
made good time but arrived to find no sign of Paul at his house.

'That's a relief. I was even afraid that Paul might have changed the locks out of sheer spite,' Harriet commented, as she opened the front door. James raised an eyebrow and she added, 'You must be wondering why I lived with him for so long.'

'I expect he had his good points,' he commented. She flashed him a grateful smile. Paul had been good to her, at first.

Yet once inside the house, there was no sign that she and Ash had ever lived in the place. None of her pictures were on the wall – the living room had even been re-decorated in her absence. It was as if he had thoroughly expunged her from his life.

'A re-decorating job would explain why your paintings aren't on the wall, too,' said James reasonably, as he looked around. 'Where do you suppose Paul has put them?'

The whole house was devoid of her belongings, neither attic nor garage yielding a thing. 'I don't understand it,' Harriet said in bewilderment. 'Where has it all gone? Make a pot of tea, preferably good and strong and I'll have to think.' She produced a tin of biscuits. 'These are Paul's chocolate biscuits. Have one,' and she thrust the tin towards James. 'I think we need some comfort food.'

'Isn't there even a garden shed here?' James asked, helping himself to two biscuits.

It was all there, stacked in cardboard boxes, along with the old cabin trunk into which Harriet had packed clothing. Ash's toys and games were in a large box. There was even the battered easy chair that Harriet said had belonged to her mother, a canteen of silver cutlery and a small, cracked leather case with faded initials that had belonged to Harriet's father containing a few packets of old family photographs. She exclaimed over that with delight.

'I feel stupid, not having thought about the garden shed,' Harriet confessed.

'I don't see that you should. A garden shed is far more vulnerable than a garage and Paul might have left you a note.'

It still took them some time to carry everything round the side of the house to the van and pack it so that nothing would shift on their homeward journey. So it should not have been too much of a surprise when Paul drove up and parked his car behind the van.

'You left the gate open. I expected you to have been long gone,' he said. 'What kept you, Hari?'

'It took time to find everything,' answered Harriet tightly. 'Nothing was left where I expected to find it.'

'Do you suppose I needed reminding of you at every turn?' he asked sarcastically. 'If I find you've made a mess, you'll be sorry.'

James moved a little closer to Harriet's side. 'We have almost finished and then we'll leave. It is all tidy inside.'

Harriet remembered their foray into his chocolate biscuits and felt a twinge of guilt, which she suppressed.

'So I should hope. There was no need for you to go inside the house at all. Don't forget to leave your keys,' he added pointedly.

'Except for using the loo, we wouldn't have needed to go inside at all if I had known that you'd put everything in the shed,' said Harriet.

'I left you a note sellotaped to the back door. Now, get on with the job and just go, will you? I hoped I'd never see you again.'

Harriet opened her mouth to respond angrily but then she shut it. They had used the back door from the kitchen and so they had missed the note. Besides, dignified silence best suited the situation and there was James next to her to add substance to her right to be there, doing what she was doing.

'Goodbye, Paul,' she said clearly, as he went back to his car, carefully manoeuvring it round the van then putting it away in the garage, which he made a show of locking. The set of his back as he went towards the front door suggested that he would not demean himself by adding anything to what he had already said.

'Dreadful man!' she exclaimed as she got into the car and snapped her seat belt on, furious with herself for being so upset by him and with Paul for riling her so easily.

'You don't have to see him, ever again.'

'No, you are quite right, I don't. But if you had not been with me I think I might very well have gone to pieces over all this,' she admitted shamefacedly. Then with a sudden lift of her spirits she lent across and gave him a peck of a kiss on his cheek. 'Thank you so much, James, and thank God it's all over.'

She sat back, quite oblivious to the flick of movement as a curtain in a downstairs room fell back into place.

It had taken them far longer over the whole business of collecting her belongings than Harriet had anticipated. She rang Florence, then told Ash she'd see her the following day. 'Goodnight, love.'

They had only had a sandwich lunch. Once Harriet had finished her phone call, James insisted that they should find somewhere to eat. 'No need to hurry back, after all, and personally I'm famished.'

They found a pub that served meals and as they ate they talked about their families, Harriet explaining that her parents were in Malta, James telling her that his parents were dead and his sister blamed him for his split with Felicity. 'The man is always in the wrong.'

She thought he sounded bitter. 'Do you think you might get back together with her now that you are home from Afghanistan?'

'That is never going to happen,' he declared. 'Do you think it will take you long to get over Paul?'

'He means nothing to me. I used to hate him. Now? Now I feel only contempt. Paul and I are finished, thank heavens, and now I have a fresh start. Really, I'm very lucky.'

'Plucky,' said James, and covering her hand which lay on the table with his warm one, he squeezed it gently. 'You are a plucky woman, Harriet Finamore. I shall call you Harriet from now on, it's a beautiful name and it suits you.'

His comment gave her a warm glow but her answering smile was constrained and she extricated her hand gently. She liked this man. Too much? There had been a frisson when he touched her but that he had rescued her from a particularly nasty situation meant nothing more than the kind act of a friend. She did so hope that they would become good friends. But the complication that came with emotions was something she just knew she could well do without.

'Do you think you could spare the time to come and have a look at the garden centre with me? I could certainly do with some advice.' His query broke into her reverie.

'Of course, James. Not too sure about the advice bit, but I'd very much like to see over Brownlows properly. Early next week?'

This might be just the opportunity she needed, she was thinking – extra hours without the business of finding more private clients, if James was prepared to offer her work, although that was not what he was offering her, yet, she reminded herself cautiously.

What with the two journeys, the delay in finding her belongings and the break for dinner, it was nearly eleven o'clock before they arrived back at the cottages.

'We'll unpack immediately after breakfast,' said James. 'I have to collect the children at ten, so I'll return the van with them.'

'I could take the van back on my way to Florence's. It would be no problem. And I'm sure Ash won't mind walking home.'

'Are you sure, Harriet? I'm taking the children out for the day.'

'It's a deal, and no more than you deserve for all the help you've been. Thanks, James. Thank you so very much. I don't know what I would have done without you.'

'You'd have managed very well, but I'm glad I was there for you.' With that, he came close and dropped a kiss on the top of her head. 'See you soon,' he said, then turned, and strode to his own front door.

She watched him go with a thumping heart. *Now what did he have to go and do that for?* she pondered crossly, quite forgetting the grateful peck she had already given him.

## CHAPTER FOURTEEN

Harriet arrived early at Brownlows on the appointed day, partly because she had promised to find a crab apple for the Heards. Although they would need to plant between November and January, she thought that she would take a photo to recommend a tree while it was in full fruit. She was looking for a *John Downie* which had large red and orange fruit but all she could find was a *Red Sentinel*.

As she moved round the outside area she thought that it was looking even more run down than on her previous visit. It was end of season, but did there have to be quite so many chipped ornamental pots for sale? The stands where bedding plants were on display all looked as though they needed a coat of preservative while the gravel paths between the stands were weedy. As for the plants themselves, she thought that she would not be tempted to buy many of them for they were all full of weeds and some were obviously pot-bound while others showed signs of infestation.

'Not a very edifying sight.' James's voice came from behind her left shoulder.

'Not terribly,' Harriet agreed candidly. She turned round and registered shock. James had a large bruise on his forehead and his left hand was heavily bandaged. 'What on earth has happened to you!' she exclaimed.

'A bit of an accident,' he shrugged.

'It looks like it. What sort of an accident?'

'I was going home last evening, didn't notice a slow puncture, had to take evasive action because of a lorry on that first bend and slewed into the hedge. I bumped my head on the steering wheel and sprained my wrist.'

'How awful. Poor you.'

'My own fault, I suppose. I should have noticed there was something wrong with the car. Fortunately I was driving very slowly, following a tractor from the farm next door.'

'But you are all right otherwise?'

'A bit sore. But I'll heal,' he said cheerfully, 'and the car only had a small dent in the nearside door. Anyway, it's good to see you.'

'If you're sure you want me here today. What did you want to show me, James?'

'Everything. I know about engineering and running a business but I've no experience in horticulture. Here I don't know what to do. I don't even know where to start. What do you think I should do?'

'I'm not quite sure I'm the person you should be asking,' Harriet replied, taken aback. 'I know about gardening, but I've absolutely no experience in running a business.'

'Then between us we ought to be able to sort something out, don't you think?' James said cheerfully.

Surely he didn't mean that he was intending to take her advice just like that? Too much responsibility! 'What I'd most like is a cup of coffee,' Harriet said firmly. 'But I forgot,' she shook her head. 'There isn't a coffee shop here.'

'That's one of the ideas I've been contemplating. Come into the office. Christie's on the till and Gordon is in the garden turning the compost heap. You know, I've always thought it was a pity my uncle didn't concentrate a little more on the commercial side. Apart from a coffee shop, and the inevitable loos, everywhere you go nowadays you can buy garden furniture, ornaments for the house as well as the garden and books by the dozen. Even Christmas decorations.'

'Oh, please,' Harriet shuddered. 'A very nasty modern abomination, if you ask me. No one should put up Christmas decorations until well into December.'

'I bet the garden centres make a mint, though,' said James shrewdly. 'And think of all those Christmas trees and wreaths they sell. Aesthetically you may be right and I know my uncle thought like you. All he would sell is local Christmas trees.'

'Norway Spruce which shed their needles even before you've got them home, and a bit of mistletoe? I'd sell Nordmann Fir or a Blue Spruce.'

'There you are. I thought you'd understand.' They went into the wooden shed that housed the office and various pieces of equipment. It looked as though a bomb had hit it. 'Don't tell me. This is another of the jobs I have to do. I may look as though I like working in chaos but this is what I inherited and I'm in the process of trying to make sense out of it all.'

'You'd better let me make the coffee,' Harriet said, seeing his clumsy movements. At least the mugs were clean, she noted thankfully as she took her coffee, and they both sat down at the table which was littered with opened envelopes, trade journals and what appeared to be account books.

'I'll be fine in a day or so. But as for here, where do I start, Harriet? What should I be doing?'

'Look,' she said soberly, after a pause that had the effect of making him look even more anxious. 'I think we ought to get one thing straight. You've recently rescued me from a nasty situation. I must have come over as pathetic. You don't know anything about my capabilities, except what you've seen and that wasn't too edifying.' He began to object, but she forestalled him. 'I suppose you believe me to be honest, which may be flattering but is hardly wise, on your part. You have no idea whether I can give you good advice or not.' Too much responsibility. What if it went wrong?

'Of course I don't expect any such thing,' said James, with a touch of irritation. 'There's so much to do. I just don't know where to start.'

'OK. I'll just throw some ideas at you. What you do with them is entirely up to you. First things first. You claim to understand business – which is more than I do. But do you know what your overheads are? Do you know what your cash flow is? Is there any surplus? I mean, do you know what capital you have to play with?'

'Not too much capital. I'm working on the overheads and the cash flow. My uncle had let things slip in the last few months.'

Years, more like, she thought, but did not say. 'Your staff. You need to make sure you are paying them on time. Otherwise, if they are good they'll go elsewhere. Even if they aren't worth keeping, they'll leave you. Do I have to mention insurance?' Thankfully he shook his head. Then he smiled at her boyishly. 'You are great, Harriet. You've got both foresight and energy. More coffee?'

'I've not done anything except give you a few tips.'

'You know, when I asked you what I should do first, what I really meant was what I should do in the garden to make it look a place that someone might want to buy from.'

After a moment, Harriet threw back her head and laughed. 'You must think I am the world's worst.'

'I was thinking of appearances. Of course I know that what happens to the business side is more important if I'm not to bankrupt the place, though I would so like to make some changes.'

'If you really want my advice, tell Gordon to forget the compost and clean up the gravel. You'd better throw out the plants that can't be rescued and spray the ones that can. Later on you should do something about those awful stands. It's a wonder some of them haven't collapsed already. And your insurance company would really like that, especially if a dreaded third party was involved. Now, I must go. Um, James, will you let me know how things go?'

Harriet got up to leave and James went with her to where she had parked her car. As she drove off, she wound down her window and leant out. 'One more thing, get rid of all those broken pots. You could sell a few at a big discount, but most of them aren't worth the space they occupy. See you.'

She drove off, her mind in something of a turmoil. She had known that the local garden centre was not one of the best. On the other hand, its prices had always seemed reasonable and for that alone she had patronized it, saving her employers, and herself, a tidy sum of money. It would be a pity to see the place go under, but with inexperienced management she very much doubted if it had anything of a future.

James did not call her and a few days later she realized that he seemed to be away. His absence from the garden centre wasn't going to help its recovery, she thought. Where was he? She hoped there was nothing wrong.

A week later Harriet was working in Florence's front garden, cutting the edges of her tiny lawn, when she was accosted across the low stone wall from the pavement outside.

'I say, will you come to me for a couple of hours a week? And what do they pay gardeners in this area nowadays?'

'Excuse me?' Harriet came back from trying to decide which was the more fragrant rose, the *Mary Rose* or the *Scepter'd Isle*. She had thought she would suggest to Florence that she should plant a pink tree rose on either side of the garden gate. The *Mary Rose* was honey-scented; the *Scepter'd Isle* had a strong perfume of myrrh with a hint of musk.

She straightened, laid her edging shears on the grass and went towards the gate. 'Ah, hello, Mrs Ormston,' she said, recognizing the woman who had called out to her.

'I'm looking for a gardener. Would you add me to your list? Please,' Felicity added belatedly, when Harriet did not reply.

Working for Felicity Ormston would be sheer hell, Harriet was thinking. 'I'm so sorry,' she said eventually. 'I'm afraid that won't be possible.'

'But you only have three jobs and after the wedding it is doubtful if Mary Smithson will need you any more.'

Mary Smithson had told Harriet only that week that she would need to give her notice in the autumn. 'A bind, but John says we have to retrench.'

'I'm sorry,' Harriet repeated. 'I don't want any more work.'

'What do they pay you, ten pounds an hour?'

'Fifteen pounds,' said Harriet, and could have bitten her tongue. That made it sound as though she was in the market for more work.

'Do they really?' By the note in Felicity's voice she seemed to be re-considering the matter. 'I could pay a little more.'

'I'm so sorry,' Harriet said insincerely. 'It's not a matter of out-bidding the opposition, I just don't have the time.'

'But you have managed to take on Florence Harding.'

'I do a few hours for Florence in exchange for child minding,' Harriet said furiously. 'Not that it is—' her voice tailed off. There was no reason to make herself as unpleasant as this woman. 'I'm sorry,' she said, yet again. 'Thank you for inquiring,' she added, as graciously as she could. Then she turned away and picked up her edging shears again.

'Well, really,' Felicity said crossly, as Harriet moved away. 'I thought the offer of work would be mutually beneficial. It appears I was wrong.'

Much better to allow her the last word, Harriet thought. Who was she kidding? It was perfectly obvious that all the woman was doing was attempting to establish a relationship – of sorts – with her ex-husband's new neighbour. Yet on reflection much later she thought that the encounter reflected better on herself than on James's former wife.

# CHAPTER FIFTEEN

Harriet went round to Joanne Ormston the following morning intending to make sure that the borders were pristine, the dahlias and the Michaelmas daisies were properly staked and that the dead heading was up to date. She was not expecting the news she heard.

'I'm so sorry, Hari, but we're going to have to give you up.'

'Have I done anything wrong?' Harriet blurted out, wondering if she had inadvertently killed a precious plant.

'Don't be an idiot. Anyway, do you really think I'd know if you'd pulled up a plant instead of a weed? Come inside and have a cup of coffee and I'll explain what all this is about.'

Harriet followed Joanne into the house which was looking a lot less pristine than it had done on her first visit. There were packing cases everywhere. 'You're moving,' she exclaimed.

'At long last.' They went into the kitchen and Joanne produced a cafetière already prepared with cups and saucers on a tray. 'Milk, sugar?'

'Just milk, thanks.'

'As you know, we're only renting this place. Gareth and I've lived in Cennen Bridge since we were married, to be near the business, but Gareth has always wanted a country place and about nine months ago we bought a run down property about three miles away. Well, it's as ready as it's going to be with our present finances so we're moving in and the other improvements will have to be done around us. If only that wretched uncle of his hadn't willed the garden centre to James we'd be doing all right. But you don't want to hear about family matters do you?' Harriet made sympathetic, if uncomfortable, noises. 'Oh, I suppose Gareth does as well as he can considering he's not much of a business man.' Joanne sounded disparaging. 'The gallery does reasonably well in the summer when there are tourists around, but during the winter months – except for Christmas when people are looking for presents – things are not so good. What I need to find is the new Hockney or Clarice Cliff. Someone, anyone who will make my fortune. Chance would be a fine thing. If the gallery had done a little better maybe we'd have had the cash to do a proper decoration job on the house instead of just getting the essentials done, like the roof and window frames.'

'But you wouldn't think of closing The Gallery, would you?'

'Certainly not. I love my work and I'd be bored stiff without it. Besides, it does make just enough money to keep it in the black. Then, we have friends here. Gareth's family is here. It's just the present times. You know, difficult cash flows. I had such plans when I opened it. Oh, well.'

Harriet thought of her own problems and how she had been forced to make the decision to leave the place that had become familiar to begin again. And with a daughter. Did that make it easier or more difficult? She was not sure.

'Is there living accommodation at The Gallery? I mean, nothing you could rent out?'

'It has a tiny kitchen and bathroom on the first floor. Sometimes I do a retrospective up there which means I'm not losing space downstairs. I have a very small stockroom. The property has attic rooms but none of them have windows. I suspect servants slept there in earlier times and how they managed I've no idea. If I had the money I'd convert it to a self-contained unit. Money again. Or the lack of it. There is another good sized room on the first floor that I rent out for classes. That helps. Damn finances,' Joanne said disgustedly. 'You are always short of money when you most need it, aren't you? Anyway, the agent our landlord uses agrees that it would be fairer on you to give you notice. He seems to think that any new tenant will make his or her own arrangements.'

'Oh, well. Never mind,' said Harriet. 'Shall I just do a tidying up job today?'

'That would be great. I'll miss seeing you around, you know.' She smiled at Harriet and put her hand on her arm briefly.

Harriet was touched. She had not had the time to make many friends so far in Cennen Bridge. 'Then I'll just have to make sure I call in to see you at the gallery every so often. Not necessarily to purchase, but to keep in touch.'

'You must come round and have a kitchen supper, soon.'

'I'll look forward to that.'

It was a beautiful, late summer Sunday with a tinge of crisp freshness in the air that hinted at autumn. Ash was having a sleepover at Fiona's house but instead of having a leisurely breakfast Harriet got up, deciding to walk through the wood that bordered the town, up and on to the hill where James had taken them for a picnic the evening Paul assaulted her. The panoramic view was breathtaking with mountains in the background.

The berries on the rowan trees were turning orange and a few leaves were already browning at the edges. It was at times like these that she almost wished that they had a dog. A dog would be a good companion when she was on her own. But you couldn't take an animal to someone else's garden and Harriet had always thought that it was unkind to keep a dog and leave it for hours without the companionship that the animals craved. Maybe they'd get a kitten instead.

She was due to go to the Heards the following day but she remembered that she had forgotten to buy twine to use there, so she decided to go to Brownlows before going home. It occurred to her that she could see what, if anything, had been done since her last visit. She was also curious to discover if James was there. She thought that he must still be away as she had not heard any sound, or seen any sign of him since their meeting. It seemed strange, not to say unwise, that he should leave his new venture in the hands of a surly, unco-operative man and an inexperienced girl.

What met her after she had parked her car was an even greater mess in the yard than she had found before. The old pots that she had suggested should be thrown out were strewn on the ground below the shelving on which they usually stood. Those that were not chipped or broken before now lay in large pieces.

Christie, the girl who worked there, was contemplating the destruction, her hands on her hips, a wheelbarrow and shovel by her side, her dejected stance indicating that she didn't know where to start the clearing up.

'Anyone would think a hurricane had hit this,' Harriet said, approaching her. 'Did the stands collapse, or something?'

'I don't know,' replied Christie. 'The stands are all right. Perfectly solid.' She kicked one which did not budge an inch. 'It was like this when I came to work. James said he'd do paperwork by the till if I started to clear up. It's just deciding where to begin.'

'Is his hand still hampering him?'

'No, the bandages are off. But there has to be someone near the till at all times.'

'Of course. Silly of me. When did this happen? Last night? Was it vandalism?' Harriet asked, shocked that anyone could do such a wanton act. Yet, vandalism again? She remembered what the builder had said when she saw him clearing up the broken glass from the collapsed greenhouse. He hadn't believed that it was storm damage, nor had James himself, she remembered.

'We suppose it was last night. Everything was fine when James left, at any rate. As for who did it, I don't know. Stupid boys who like to fool around, I guess.'

'Isn't the garden centre locked at night?'

'There is a padlock on the gate but no one has used it for years.'

That had better be rectified, Harriet thought to herself. 'Well, good luck. I hope it doesn't take you too long to clear up the mess.'

Christie shrugged. 'I'm probably better off doing the job myself than listening to Gordon's moans about his back.'

'I'm sure he isn't that bad,' Harriet countered cajolingly. By the look on the girl's face she hadn't succeeded. 'I guess it can't always be easy, working with a much older man.'

'You can say that again. Sometimes Gordon's a right pain. Still,' she conceded, after a pause. 'I suppose that when you get to be as old as him you can't help being a sour old devil.'

'Perhaps his back really does give him pain,' said Harriet gently.

Christie had the grace to look a little ashamed of her outburst. 'You could be right,' she admitted. 'But he still isn't going to help me clear all this mess up, is he?' She turned back to what she was supposed to be doing and Harriet left her to it.

Not exactly a happy ship, Harriet thought, as she found the twine she required and went to the till with it. There was no one else around but James was there, surrounded by paperwork.

'James, I'm so sorry about that mess outside. You must have reported it to the police this time?'

'Harriet. It's good to see you again.' He put down his pen and smiled at her. She noticed that the lines on his face appeared even more pronounced than she remembered. 'I was hoping to call in this evening to tell you I am back. No,' he sighed. 'I haven't reported it. There didn't seem much point. Besides, I'm not convinced that it was done by local youths.'

'If it wasn't human vandalism, how do you imagine it happened?'

'It could have been a fox.'

'Those stands seem solid enough to me. If a fox had jumped up and knocked a few pots down, it'd have frightened itself to death by the noise and tried to get away, not run amok among the whole lot.'

He shrugged. 'It could have been more than one animal.'

She doubted that very much. 'The insurance won't pay out unless you do report it,' she mentioned cautiously.

'I'm not going to bother to claim. As you yourself told me, those pots weren't worth the space they occupied. I'd rather bear the cost of replacements myself and keep a no claims bonus.'

'But if whoever caused the damage thinks he, or they, have got away with this again, won't it happen for a third time?'

'Third time?' He regarded her keenly. 'Ah. I gather someone's been talking.'

'Oh, you know,' she answered uncomfortably.

'It's all right. I shan't ask who. Still, you are cheerful. That's a possibility, I suppose. I prefer to regard this as a one off. However, I am investing in a stouter chain and a good padlock for the gate. It was my fault we'd got slack about locking up at night. And I'm going to make a habit of doing a late evening inspection visit.'

'I'd offer to stay and help clear up but I'm due for a Skype call from my parents,' she said. 'It's good to see you again.'

'You, too. I hope I won't have to be away any more for a while. And, if it was vandalism, I imagine that the message'll get round that it's not going to be so easy another time.'

'It's rotten luck, anyway. Come and have supper this evening. I'm going to do a fish pie. Ash prefers fish that's either coated in breadcrumbs or comes in small pieces.'

'Thanks.' His face cleared and Harriet felt warmly pleased that she had thought to invite him.

'A fish pie sounds good. I'll see you both later.'

# CHAPTER SIXTEEN

Harriet drove to the Heards, thinking that James had taken the mishap very well considering that he had only recently taken over the garden centre.

'I've not found you a *John Downie* crab apple locally,' she told Vicky, who came out to see her as soon as she got out of the car. 'But I did look it up in my book and this is what I think you should plant.' She reached into the car for her tried and tested gardening manual, opening it where she had left a bookmark. 'Good, large fruit, for a crab apple, with plenty of colour. When I was a child my friend and I used to push crab apples on to the end of a stick and see who could flick them the furthest.'

'Thanks for that,' said Vicky drily. 'Remind me not to allow you to tell my children of your exploits.'

'Sorry. Do you have anything special in mind for me today or shall I just carry on with the borders?'

'Actually, I wanted to talk to you about that,' said Vicky guardedly.

This time Harriet, whose heart had given one hard thump, did not immediately conclude that she had done something wrong but she managed to maintain an interested demeanour. 'Oh, yes?'

'Actually, Robin and I were talking about our finances over the weekend and we came to the conclusion that … that—'

'You can't afford me any more.'

'Yes. No, I mean, we're awfully sorry and you've actually taught me so much. It's just that—'

'I've done myself out of a job.'

'I suppose so. Do you think a month's notice would be fair?'

Harriet sighed inwardly. But there was nothing else for it. 'In four weeks I could leave everything tidy. There are jobs that should wait until later to put the garden to bed for the winter but so long as I tell you what has to be done you can do those for yourself.'

'I hate this,' said Vicky passionately. 'I've loved having you come here and I was so looking forward to next spring.'

'These things happen,' said Harriet philosophically. She had never been the sort of woman who believed that things were meant, but losing two jobs in almost as many days and having being consulted by a man who, by his own admission, knew very little about the finer points of gardening surely had to mean something.

Ash seemed delighted that James was coming to supper and volunteered not only to set the table but wash the salad herself. As she bathed and changed, Harriet wondered if she was wise to invite James round. It probably wouldn't do to make a habit of it. On the other hand, he must have had a difficult few days and could do with a little home comfort. There was a lot to be said for a sympathetic ear in times of trouble.

She was aware that because they lived next door in a small town, gossip – particularly anything to her detriment – could make for an awkward time for both herself and for Ash. So she sensed that she had to be doubly careful. But outwardly at least the atmosphere between them was nothing more than might have been expected between close neighbours who were still getting to know each other. That was what she told herself.

Yet Harriet was finding that James was beginning to occupy far too much of the space in her head – his former life, what he was doing at that precise moment, heaven help her, when would she see him next? Be sensible, she admonished herself. Nothing is going to come of this. Get over him, woman!

James declared the fish pie one of the best he had ever eaten.

'Flatterer,' said Harriet, pleased all the same.

They ate fresh peaches after the fish pie. 'I like fresh ones better than tinned peaches,' said Ash.

'So do I,' agreed James.

It was too chilly to drink their coffee outside so Ash went upstairs and they sat down alone to drink their coffee.

'I know,' said Harriet. 'I don't really approve of schoolchildren having a TV in their bedrooms, but with only the one living room there didn't seem much choice. I do try to regulate what she sees and for how long.'

'And Ash is a very sensible girl.'

Harriet held up crossed fingers. 'She's not yet a teenager.'

'Jess is going through a difficult phase,' commented James cautiously.

'Poor Felicity.' For the first time Harriet felt a twinge of sympathy for James's former wife. 'At least Matthew hasn't entered his Gothic period yet.'

'Nor the one where his jeans are permanently at half mast.'

'I often wonder what happens when young men like that really have to run for anything, like a bus.'

Harriet was invited for the promised kitchen supper at Gareth and Joanne's new house a few days later. Kitchen supper meant something informal but to add to the occasion, the Ormstons had also invited a pleasant couple, Tom and Marlene Evans, whom she did not know.

It was a convivial evening, the only awkward moment occurring when Gareth made a snide remark concerning his brother's ill-health, making it sound as though post traumatic stress disorder was something to be ashamed of. 'It's no wonder Brownlows isn't doing too well. That yard always looks a mess. Young James hasn't a clue when it comes to the nitty gritty of running a business.'

'I'm sure that eventually James will make a success of it. He's got tenacity, that man.'

'Another of your ex's, Marlene?'

'Certainly not, Gareth. I just think that a man who has the guts to go and fight won't let a little thing like a health problem get in the way of making a good living.'

'I think you're absolutely right,' said Harriet quietly. James's ill-health was news to her. She decided that it explained a lot, particularly his absences. She liked Joanne but her husband was very different. Bitter, as though he believed the entire world was against him. How very different he was from his brother.

'There you are then, Gareth,' said Joanne, in the tone of voice that insisted the subject was changed. 'More potatoes, anyone?'

It appeared that Felicity was not the sort to let anything drop until she had succeeded in getting her own way. A few days before the Smithson wedding Harriet was in a border not far from the house when she was aware that Felicity and Mary Smithson were heading in her direction. Not wanting to have to engage in conversation with them, she ducked behind a large clump of phormium. She had looked in her gardening book and was almost sure that this was *Tenex* by the way its tall, dramatic form stood out in the border and, for her immediate purpose, made a good screen. She loved all the grasses; the way they swayed in a gentle breeze was pleasing in a mixed border, giving substance to the planting.

'Your little gardener is very much a law unto herself, isn't she?' Felicity was saying as the two women drew nearer, 'although I must say your garden is looking a picture this year. Then, you always did have green fingers.'

'Harriet is extremely co-operative and knowledgeable and very hard-working,' answered Mary warmly.

'I'm sure she understands that you know far more than she ever will. I suppose you don't have any difficulty with her?'

'Of course not and as to my gardening knowledge being better than hers, apparently Harriet did a course when she was young. She knows far more of the Latin names than I can ever remember.'

'Oh, Latin names.' Felicity made them sound almost obscene. 'I gather her circumstances are a little straightened, so to speak. I thought I'd try to get her to come to me. She said she hasn't got time.'

'Then she probably hasn't, don't you think?' Mary said gently. 'There are only a certain number of hours in each day and she does have her daughter to take care of.'

'That's as maybe. What James sees in her I can't imagine.'

This was too much. Harriet decided that she had no option but to make a noise behind the grasses and reveal herself. It was all her own fault. She should have braved Felicity the moment she realized they were walking towards her. Drat, she was thinking as she emerged from behind the phormium but they had already walked on.

She paused to re-adjust the string she had used to keep a clump of miscanthus from collapsing in the middle, its large orange/bronze plumes still sufficient to screen her. It would need dividing next year, she thought. She knelt on the grass in front of a clump of blue fescue that the rain in the night had flattened and with gentle fingers she teased it upright.

'I thought you were working in this border this morning,' Mary Smithson said behind her. 'It's all right, Felicity has gone. If it's any consolation, I'm sure you were right not to agree to work for her.'

'I really didn't think I had the time.'

'Not with your daughter to consider. And besides, it would put you in an impossible situation, living as you are next to James.'

'Precisely.' Harriet decided that it would be best to admit that she had overheard their conversation. 'I'm afraid that I was behind the phormium just now.'

'I thought so. I caught sight of your green T-shirt. Never mind Felicity. We all know she can be a bit of a bore. She'll get over her failed rescue bid. Eventually.'

Would she? Harriet had her doubts about that. Yet, wherever she worked and whatever her prospects were, Harriet knew that she would much prefer to stay well away from Felicity Ormston. This was not proving easy as both of them were invited to the Smithson wedding, Harriet sure that her invitation was a thank you for her help with the flowers.

On the day of the wedding, they were not seated together but after the meal James danced with Harriet no less than three times, holding her close and making it plain that he wanted to be with her, which, with the champagne, was making Harriet feel positively light-headed.

Inevitably Felicity accosted Harriet afterwards. 'I like your dress,' she commented, eyeing her up and down, 'but the hat was a bit of a disaster. You should have come to me.'

Harriet had taken her hat off some time before. 'I wear hats so infrequently,' she explained weakly, for want of anything less revealing – like that she probably couldn't afford Felicity's prices.

'I daresay I could have given you a discount,' said Felicity, making it very clear she understood exactly why Harriet had not come to her.

'But if you'll forgive me, Felicity' (as they were at a social event she was brave enough to use the woman's first name) 'I think the bridal pair are going and I promised Mary that I would look after her confetti for her.'

'I thought John and Mary frowned on confetti.'

'They do, if it's commercially produced from paper. I made this out of rose petals, lavender and rosemary, all from the garden.' There really was no point in making an enemy out of James's ex-wife, she thought. 'Here, take a handful. I have a whole bag here and a little goes a long way.' Laughingly tipping some of the confetti into Felicity's hand, Harriet edged her way through the throng towards the mother of the bride.

# CHAPTER SEVENTEEN

It was the following Monday and the weather had broken. Harriet, on her way to the shops, met James at the garden gate heaving boxes into his car. Seeing that he was about to drop one of the smaller ones that he had balanced precariously on top of others, she stopped to help him. They stood talking together afterwards while the fine drizzle turned to a more steady downpour.

'You'd better get on with what you were doing,' he laughed at her as she adjusted her weather proof hat, an Australian Akubra that had seen better days but which she refused to replace.

'I've plenty of time. Weren't the Smithsons lucky with their weather?'

'And did I tell you that everyone commented on how beautiful the garden looked and Mary insisted that it was all your doing?'

'No one would believe that, not of Mary, but it was good of her,' said Harriet. 'I shall be losing my job there, soon, also.'

'Losing your job there, also?' He picked her up sharply.

Harriet reminded him that his sister-in-law was moving and that the Heards had decided they couldn't afford her any longer.

'There is a rumour that Robin's job is on the line.'

'He's already sold one of his hunters. Anyway, it's back to looking for adverts in the local paper, for me.'

'You don't sound too dismayed,' he said, looking thoughtful.

'No, I'm not. Now that I've worked for local people I'm much happier about my future prospects than I was at first. Besides, well, something'll turn up.'

'Of course it will,' he said cheerfully. 'See you.'

He was about to get into his car when she said, 'If you aren't doing anything for dinner tonight, would you like to join us?'

'That'd be great. Now, must go, I'm late.'

After their meal and once Ash had gone to her room to read, they settled down with mugs of coffee. Harriet found herself talking about Joe – but Felicity's name wasn't mentioned. They talked about their children. 'Jess seems happy where she is,' James said, looking at the bottom of his mug.

'Only seems?' Harriet picked up on a note of doubt. She lifted the coffee pot, offering him another cup.

He shook his head. 'Better not, or I won't sleep. There have been the odd comments made by her teachers. I don't think that she is as confident as she sometimes appears.'

Harriet very much doubted that. Jess had come over as entirely brash not to mention self-centred on the few occasions when they had spoken. 'I expect she is just one of your typical teenagers. Very difficult to read at this age. But you know your daughter best so you are probably right. Goodness, is that the time? I'll never get through tomorrow unless I get to bed soon.'

With a flicker of amusement in his eyes, James agreed solemnly that it was time he was leaving.

She commented tartly that she was a lark, not an owl. 'I'm much better first thing in the morning than late at night.'

'Isn't that a coincidence, Harriet? So'm I. Another time?' He put his arm round her shoulders. 'Thanks for tonight. It's been a hell of a day. Poor Christie was so fed up I had to go and help her and Gordon was even more morose than usual.'

'I thought Christie usually has a sunny nature.'

'She has, but that dratted fox seems to have got in again. This time the chrysanths Christie was potting up for our autumn display were uprooted. Such a mess it left. We were able to save some of the plants but an awful lot had to be discarded.'

And that wasn't good for business. Harriet frowned. That mysterious fox again, she thought. 'You said you were going to look at security, fences and a padlock. Didn't you do anything about a new lock and so on after the previous incident with the fox?'

'Of course I did,' he said a little irritably. 'I guess the wretched animal is cleverer than I anticipated and has already discovered another way in.'

'James, are you absolutely sure this isn't more vandalism?'

'Vandalism? Why do you keep on about vandalism?' He sounded both annoyed and sceptical. 'Why ever should anyone want to damage my garden centre?'

Come on, she thought as her eyebrows shot up. 'Rivalry?' she suggested gently. 'After all, for the first time in what must be years, someone is prepared to work at making a success of the business. That could be construed as a menace.'

'You read too much fiction.'

'Why does anyone, any vandal, do things he – or she – does? Of course, I could be wrong. This could all be put down to a fox.'

'Fox, or dog, or whatever, this was just another accident. Annoying, but an accident. I'm sure you are wrong.'

'Of course these things happen,' she agreed, observing that he looked and sounded rattled. Yet as she uttered the platitude she knew it not only sounded feeble, it was feeble. She had the distinct feeling that James's problems were not over, although why she couldn't say.

'Well, it was really good, being in a normal atmosphere this evening instead of sitting next door, brooding.'

'That definitely wouldn't have been the best idea.'

'So, thank you.' He bent his head and kissed the top of her head.

Without thinking, Harriet lifted her face to his. So he kissed her again, this time on the lips. The kiss felt very sweet.

'See you soon,' he said quietly, and left.

'Yes, James. See you,' she repeated softly, as she closed the front door behind him. Wise or not, she'd liked that embrace. Very much. It had been quite a day for her, too. Of the three jobs that she had counted on to keep herself and Ash only one remained, and she already knew she would be losing that soon. You had to take a gamble in life occasionally, Harriet thought to herself as she lay in bed waiting for sleep to come. She had a skill. It was something to exploit. And a thought had come to her while she was talking to James that evening that she knew exactly where this might best be done. It had been a happy thought, a really positive thought....

Harriet was doing some much needed housework in the cottage when a letter arrived the following morning. What the envelope contained was an offer from the Letts to buy the house they were renting from her. The offer was based on a valuation by a local estate agent. She thought it was worth more, although she knew very well that house prices had fallen in recent months. If she agreed in principle some adjustment could be made, which was probably what her tenants were expecting her to suggest.

She'd had coffee at The Gallery that morning. She had almost confided in Joanne but at the last moment had thought that it was a bit premature. And there was that – atmosphere? – between James and his brother and sister-in-law that at times was less than friendly, so she had desisted.

Yet the timing of the offer was fantastic. Harriet had wondered for some time whether she might persuade the trustees of Ash's trust fund to release some of the capital on the grounds that an investment in a garden centre would be a good one for her daughter. Here was one such, on her doorstep, very run down and with an owner who lacked her credentials. The trustees might very well refuse, considering the state of the garden centre in which she was proposing to invest. But if she could find capital herself, the trust fund would not have to be broached.

Harriet thought about the cottage. James had managed to persuade the owners to sell him Oak Cottage. What were the chances of her doing the same? Sycamore Cottage was not particularly prepossessing when compared with James's cottage but it was weather proof and although the kitchen left something to be desired she had come to like its idiosyncrasies.

Buying property for herself and her daughter to live in had to be a priority, she thought. Rent was dead money. She had no idea what the current value was of the cottage but she was fairly sure that it was considerably less than her house. If she bought the cottage, she should still have a tidy sum to offer to invest in the garden centre and an injection of cash was what that business sorely needed.

She telephoned her own solicitor, thinking that she should consult someone more local in future, and she asked him to write to her tenants agreeing to sell in principle but at a higher price than their original offer. If they were serious, she expected them to come back with an increased offer of fifty per cent of the extra she was asking, which she would accept without further quibble.

So how much of all this was she prepared to tell James? She rang him to suggest a meeting that afternoon.

'Cards on the table,' Harriet said with a smile, when they were sitting in James's shed-cum-office once more. 'As you know, I've lost two of my jobs in the past few days so I wondered if you would like to offer me a job? I know that you already have two employees—'

'Not any longer,' James interrupted. 'I told you that Gordon was becoming increasingly morose. Honestly, it had got to the point when I was seriously considering letting him go. Fortunately he beat me to it. When he came in this morning he gave me his notice. He is over retirement age anyway, but he said something about needing more time to visit his grandchildren.'

Or was it that Gordon was becoming increasingly demoralized by the recent series of so-called accidents? Harriet was convinced that her theory was the correct one.

'The only thing is, I had thought that what with one thing and another I'd try to manage with only Christie. She's a good worker and she does know what has to be done.'

'I can see that, although she's not qualified, is she?' Harriet said gently. 'I'm not sure how you'd manage unless you took on a school leaver, or someone, at least to manage the till. What I had in mind was that you might consider taking me on as some sort of a partner. What I'm offering is an injection of capital.'

'You're offering me money to work here?'

'Not initially. If I became a partner – I mean, with a say in what we do but without overall control – I would be entitled to a percentage of the profits, naturally.'

'You actually assume there will be a profit?' James's face suggested that profit was probably the last best outcome on his mind, although the optimism that had swept over him when Harriet had suggested this meeting surged once more and was apparent in his face.

'There wouldn't be any point in keeping the garden centre open unless we made a profit,' Harriet pointed out. 'So, I've obviously given you a lot to think about.'

'How much of an injection of capital?' he asked bluntly.

'That would depend on several things,' Harriet replied guardedly. 'You'd need to have the place independently valued and give me a price. I'd need to sort out my finances which might not take too long. In the meantime, if Gordon really is going, why don't you take me on in his place and we can at least start tidying up? If we decide that a partnership is out of the question neither of us should have lost anything by working together. What do you say?'

# CHAPTER EIGHTEEN

'Have you fed the kittens?' Harriet asked Ash that evening as she was setting the table. Their roles were reversed for the first time ever. Ash had made a lasagne at school which they were to eat with a salad.

'Not yet, Mum. I haven't had time.'

'Darling, you know you promised that you would be responsible.'

'Yeah, yeah—'

'Ash!'

'I know, Mum. I said I would, and I did mean it, but you wanted me to make the salad and I haven't had time. Honestly.'

'Well, the poor animals are beginning to sound positively pathetic. I think you should stop what you're doing and feed them now. Then wash your hands and make the salad.'

Ash heaved a sigh to show how put-upon she felt, but she stopped what she was doing and fed her pets.

Soon after they arrived at the cottage, Ash had pleaded for a dog but Harriet had vetoed this, reminding her that the animal would be on its own all day. Instead, because she suspected there were mice, she had suggested that they had a kitten. Inevitably there were two on offer through Fiona's mother and not long after Ash's birthday Mish, a tabby, and Mash, a ginger tom, came to live with them, with a cat flap installed in the back door. They were already a much loved addition to the household.

After they'd eaten the lasagne, which had a good flavour even if it was a little stodgy, Harriet told Ash that she had some news for her. 'I start work at Brownlows on Monday.' She told Ash of the proposition she had made to James and the plans she was making for their future. 'I think it's going to be a lot of fun.'

'And you'll sell our old home?'

'I think it's time, don't you?'

'But, Mum. What if it doesn't work out? If you've already lost two jobs, how are we going to manage?'

'Oh, my. I'd not realized how grown up you've become. Darling Ash, I'm not teasing you,' she added hastily, as she saw the mutinous look on her daughter's face. 'You have every right to ask that question and the answer is that I don't know. I think that I would want to have the garden centre's finances settled before I actually bought this cottage. Just in case it didn't work out quite as we expected. But I have a really good feeling about this.'

Harriet began work at Brownlows at the beginning of the following week. From the start the entire atmosphere of the place seemed to have changed, even though parts of it were still shabby. Christie had got over her annoyance over the destruction of the chrysanthemums and now she smiled perpetually while James appeared more relaxed than Harriet had ever seen him before.

She thought how good it was to work with colleagues who not only approved of you but deferred to your judgement and made it plain that they wanted to be with you. James insisted that he was so much more relaxed about the garden centre now because the steep learning curve he'd been on was levelling out, while the rest was down to her expertise. Harriet had enjoyed working on her own. It had given her much needed time to acquire new confidence in her own abilities, but there had been the disadvantage of loneliness. Now this was a thing of the past.

In the middle of the week while they were having coffee together in the shed and Christie was on the till, James said, 'I suppose you haven't thought about buying Sycamore Cottage? Renting is all very well but if we are going into partnership it would be as well for you to know that your future home is secure.'

'I have thought about it, but until I have the funds in the bank there is no point in approaching the agents.'

'I think you'd find that the family would be happy to sell. Word has it that the recession has already hit hard and one of the sons has lost his job. This isn't gospel, you understand, just general gossip.'

'It's interesting, all the same. The timing would be excellent,' she added soberly. But she did need to be cautious, Harriet thought. A lot could go wrong, even now. James could even get back together with Felicity, and on no account could she live next door to that particular couple.

Harriet's luck was holding. A few weeks later the sale of Box House had been agreed and she told James that, if he still wanted to go ahead with their partnership, she would be very happy to set the legal wheels in motion.

'We'll get Adrian Goff to check everything out and set up a contract,' he said, his eyes alight with pleasure.

'I can't think of anything else that I would rather be doing,' Harriet smiled, too. 'But in the meantime what we must do is to make a business plan, decide what our priorities are. Even with an injection of money we obviously can't do everything at once.'

'Christmas,' declared James. 'Holly wreaths, Father Christmases, tinsel, baubles and glitter. That'll pull in the punters.'

'Naff stuff! Do we really have to?' Harriet groaned.

'We'd be fools not to. I've been sent a couple of trade catalogues. Some of the "stuff", as you call it, is quite attractive. Suppose I go through the catalogues tonight and work out a list. You can have right of veto, if you hate anything very much. I know we'll probably be one of the last garden centres to have their Christmas stock for sale but if we get an order in quickly we could have it all on display by the beginning of November.'

'December.'

'Mid November, or we'll definitely lose out on sales.'

'All right. But no carols until December!'

'You're on.'

Another letter arrived, not long after the contract had been signed. Harriet looked at the writing on the envelope and sat down quickly, her heart thudding. There was no mistaking the thick, black pen strokes. It was from Paul.

*Dear Hari,*

*I hear that you have recently sold Box House. You must be pleased that the sale went through comparatively quickly, given the difficulty in the housing market at the moment. All the same, I am surprised that you have been beguiled into a dubious business venture with the market garden in Cennen Bridge.*

Now, I wonder just how he discovered that? she thought to herself. A chill ran down her spine. It sounded as though all his protestations that he never wanted to see her again, or have anything to do with her, were hollow. But that was nonsense.

*I am not going to try to persuade you otherwise since I know how stubborn you can be and I imagine that Ashley's trustees are not encouraging you to imperil her funds, so what you do with your money is your own affair.*

*Nevertheless, I have to point out that during those years when you were living with me as my common law wife I was keeping the two of you. Now that you find yourself in the happy situation of having money in hand, I think it only right and just that you reflect on what you owe me for those years.*

*I suggest that a lump sum in full and final consideration of the benefits the two of you received under my roof would be the fairest means of recompense. Therefore, I am awaiting your cheque for the figure of £170,000.*

He signed it, *Yours most sincerely.*

*

Recompense between two people who had been lovers? Harriet threw down the letter in disgust. The sum he wanted was one third of that which had been agreed between her and her former tenants. They must have been in contact with him, was her next, outraged, thought. Then she reasoned that you can find out what a house fetched from the internet so it was probably unfair of her to imagine that they had talked to Paul.

Acceding to his demands would jeopardize any chances of buying Sycamore Cottage. Which was probably what he intended should happen, she thought indignantly as she picked up the letter to read it again. She knew that, as yet, there was no such thing as being a common law wife in British law. So she and Paul had lived together. She had bought food. She had cooked and cleaned, washed and ironed his clothes and gardened. Did she have proof of her financial outlay, bills? Of course she had not.

Harriet was almost certain that Paul did not have any right to demand anything from her but she would need to make absolutely sure before she used any more of her money on improvements to the garden centre in case she needed it for legal fees. Although surely this had to be merely another example of manipulative bullying on his part?

Later that day Harriet found herself telling James what had happened. She had not meant to pour out her troubles to him but James had guessed that something was worrying her.

'Wretched man!' he said forcibly.

'I can't make up my mind about going to see my solicitor,' she ended. 'It's unreasonable and yet so stupidly trivial. I mean, how can he demand that I pay all that money for living with him?'

'I don't imagine that he can. He's just out to rile you. And, to look at you, he's succeeded.'

'That's what I think, in my heart of hearts, but what if I'm wrong? What if a court rules that I have to pay him all that he asks?'

'What if pigs have wings? I'd treat the letter with the contempt it deserves but I can see that it's difficult for you, having received it. I think you shouldn't concede to his blackmail – for that's what this is. Sheer blackmail. Write him a dignified letter that tells him in effect to go to hell. Keep a copy of that along with his letter as evidence. In other words, call his bluff.'

'What if he counters that with another demand?'

'I'm sure that would constitute blackmail. My guess is that he can't imagine that you will no longer be bullied by him, but once he discovers that he has misjudged you he'll give up and find someone else to attempt to control.'

'James, that's a terrible thought.'

'Or maybe someone else will start bullying him.'

'You're laughing at me.'

'Dear Harriet, nothing could be further from my mind.' He put his arm round her shoulders and gave her a little squeeze, and her heart lurched at the contact. 'If Paul were here, within touching distance, I'd wring his neck, certainly give him a black eye for the worry he's causing you. The man is a monster.'

'Control freak,' she agreed. He was not always so, she thought sadly, remembering all the good times – for there had been good times – all the kindnesses she had received from Paul in the beginning, after Joe had been killed. 'I disappointed him,' she added soberly, 'because I couldn't love him as he wanted me to.'

James huffed, 'So because he can't have what he wants Paul has a hissy fit. Dear me.'

Harriet smiled, remembering that Florence had said something similar about Paul. It was comforting to have someone who was on your side, someone who believed that you were not at fault. 'Very well, I'll do as you suggest, write to him and then forget all about it.' Or try to forget all about it.

# CHAPTER NINETEEN

Harriet was so sane. What he felt for her was a lot more than admiration. Lying in bed, a picture came to James, not as a flashback, but as a daydream in which she was in his arms. How he yearned for a relationship with her, a proper one, not just in the way of business. He knew, unfortunately, that no sane woman was going to want to take on a man with the problems he had.

Inheriting the garden centre had seemed a lifeline until he realized just how limited was his knowledge of gardening. Then, at his lowest ebb, along had come Harriet. With her beside him, he didn't see how Brownlows could fail. Harriet.... Look what life had thrown at her. No sooner had she coped with one problem than another cropped up. She had reason enough to complain at the cards dealt her. You never heard her moan.

He supposed you never could tell with a woman. One might be sympathetic, another was the opposite. He had concealed the true nature of his problems from Felicity, certain that she would scorn the deficiencies in him, but he had definitely underestimated her tenacity. He had thought that, after all this time, she would have moved on, found someone else. It was uncomfortable, sensing that she wanted him back. It wouldn't do, of course. Apart from there being no physical attraction left for him, there was more: he could never trust her again.

His sister-in-law was another woman who complained constantly. True, Gareth had always expected to inherit Brownlows – although whether his brother would have been able to run the place any better was another matter. James supposed it was because their parents had died only recently and Gareth had inherited the haulage business, that their uncle *had changed his will and given Brownlows to him and a fair sum of money to Gareth. Which he and Joanne had frittered away. Not James's fault.*

*He thought that he could trust Harriet with anything.*

One evening the phone rang at Sycamore Cottage. Harriet was doing accounts at the kitchen table. 'Can you get that, Ash?' she called. 'If it's James, I'll take it. If it's anyone else, say I'll ring them back. I don't want to leave this at the moment.'

'It might be Matt. He said he thought he and Jess were coming over this weekend.'

Ash took the call upstairs. After a while she came downstairs to stand beside her mother. 'That was Paul,' she said, her voice expressionless.

'Paul. What on earth did he want?' Harriet put down her biro and asked without thought. Then she remembered that she hadn't told her daughter about the letter she'd received from Paul. She had done what James suggested and politely declined to send him any money at all. She'd not mentioned blackmail, or what she would have to do if he persisted in his demands.

'He said he hadn't heard from you. Mum, you're not thinking of getting back with Paul, are you?' Her voice was tight.

'Of course not,' Harriet began indignantly.

Ash relaxed visibly. 'Because I don't think I would want to live with him again,' she declared in a voice that was absolutely determined.

'That is never going to happen,' Harriet said firmly, her eyes fierce with the denial. She observed her daughter relax. It was almost imperceptible but Ash was plainly relieved. Then Harriet said, 'Paul seems to think that I owe him money. He wrote to me. I said I wouldn't pay him anything. Did he mention that to you?'

'No. He just said he was waiting to hear from you. I told him you were busy. Did I do right?' Harriet nodded. 'He asked me about school. Did I like it. Had I made any friends. You know.'

'After that scene ... you know, when he attacked me. I thought

115

he'd never want to speak to us again. He even said so, when James took me to fetch our things. I certainly have no intention of going back to him. Ever. But he is a strange man. Did you have any sort of a conversation with him?'

''Course not,' the girl said scornfully. 'I was polite. I listened. Then I just said that I had to go.'

'That was definitely the best thing to have done. Um … Ash. If Paul does phone again, it would probably be best if you didn't even listen politely. Come and get me. He's a bit like a dog with a bone. Can't let go.'

'I don't think I like being compared to a bone.'

Harriet smiled. 'No? I did mean a big, juicy one. Sorry.'

''S OK, Mum. I get the message.'

Harriet was glad about that. The whole episode niggled, though. She couldn't get it out of her mind that Paul wouldn't leave them alone. She didn't know how to handle the situation. In the end, a couple of days later when they were in the office at the end of the afternoon, she told James what had happened.

He thought about it for a while and she sat opposite him, not saying anything. In the end he said, 'I know I said just to write to him and tell him you wouldn't pay him anything. Now I think maybe you should phone him, after all. Tell him in no uncertain terms that you won't submit to blackmail and that if he contacts you again you'll go to a solicitor. Or the police. Going to the police would probably be the better threat.'

'Phone now?'

'Why not?'

Harriet could think of all sorts of reasons why she should not phone Paul at all. On the other hand, having James by her side would give her moral support.

'I thought it might help,' he said diffidently.

'You're right,' she agreed, after a moment's reflection. 'It is a good idea.' She smiled resignedly. 'It would be good to have someone hold my hand. Metaphorically,' she added hastily, as he reached out to do just that. He grinned, not in the least abashed. 'I need both of them, just now.' Gently she disengaged her fingers and reached into her pocket for her mobile phone.

Harriet was aware of the sound of classical music in the background the moment Paul answered his own phone.

'Hello?' His clipped greeting sounded impatiently in her ear.

'Paul. Hello.'

'Hari? It's taken you long enough to get back to me, Hari.'

He still recognized her voice. There was no civilized inquiry about her welfare. So she plunged headlong into her reason for calling him. 'You phoned me two days ago. I said all that I had to say in my letter. There will be no money, Paul.'

'And that's your final word?'

'Absolutely. Leave us alone. No more attempts at blackmail or I go to the police.'

'Blackmail is a strong word, Hari.'

'What you seem to be doing is nastier. You know very well that I owe you nothing. You had as much from me as I ever had from you. Perhaps you'd better read up about the position of common law wives. I owe you nothing,' she repeated emphatically. 'And I demand that you have nothing more to do with Ash. I won't have it. Do you understand?'

'Ash and I always had a good relationship. I was her father figure,' he said. He even sounded defensive.

'You were,' Harriet agreed, 'until she saw you attack me.'

'I'm sure that Ash is old enough to understand that a relationship between a man and a woman can have its difficulties.'

Harriet held the receiver away from her ear and looked at it as though something particularly nasty was emanating from it.

'I always thought that Ash was a singularly astute child,' Paul continued, as though the conversation they were having was perfectly normal. 'She was not always polite, considering the benefits she received under my roof. I remain fond of her, even after her appalling behaviour when I called to bring you home.'

'Enough.' Harriet rallied her resources. This had not been a good idea. It had exposed her once more to Paul's hectoring, and even if that was less painful than his manhandling of her, it was not pleasant. 'This was a stupid notion, that you would be open to reason. But I repeat. No money from me. Leave Ash alone.'

'I'm back, Paul. The train was delay—'

Harriet heard the clearly enunciated tones of an unknown woman before she was cut off abruptly.

'I regret I cannot help you. Thank you for calling.' Paul rang off without another word being spoken.

Harriet looked at her own mobile for another long moment, as though it did contain a serpent inside its workings. Maybe it did, she thought fancifully, maybe it did.

'That was interesting,' she said, at last.

James was regarding her strangely. After a moment he said, 'I'm sorry, Harriet. It didn't sound a very comfortable exchange. It was a bad idea of mine.'

'It wasn't comfortable, but it was interesting.'

'You mean that Paul admits that he was wrong?'

'No. Not that. Paul never admits that he could ever be wrong. It was interesting because there was a woman there. It means he's moved on. It means that I don't have to worry myself about him, ever again.'

'Poor love,' he said, thinking that although he could cheerfully strangle the man for what he'd put Harriet through, at least some good had come out of this situation. 'Harriet, you mustn't worry. If there is another woman in his life, I am sure that you are right and that now he knows he can't blackmail you, he will just drop the whole thing.'

'Promise me?' she asked, a trembling smile on her face as she heard the genuine concern in his voice. Love, he'd called her love. It was probably just an expression but it sounded so good.

'Of course I'm right,' he said firmly and hoped that he had spoken with sufficient conviction to make her believe what he only half believed himself. 'Paul is an ass, but not that much of a one. Must get on,' he added, after a pause, 'or we'll never finish the staff accounts.'

*After a while he almost forgot the wound. It was there, when he show-ered, but after six months or so the pain had left him. The nightmares had gone, too. At least, that was what he thought. Until they returned worse than they'd been before. He supposed you couldn't call them nightmares because they happened at any time. Utterly without warning. As if he entered a tunnel and at the end of it there was the noise again, men falling, men screaming. There was the flash of an explosion, the sensa-tion of pain that followed, as it always did, even though he knew that he was no longer in pain.*

*When he jerked awake this time, sweating profusely in the dead hours of the night, it took James several minutes to come to himself. He'd not had the flashback for several weeks. So why....*

*It was his concern over Harriet, of course. He had suppressed those thoughts of Paul standing over her, his foot poised to kick her. Again. But nothing had happened since. Nothing was going to happen. He turned over. There was a knocking in his head that was not usually there, not a usual element of the flashbacks. He struggled with the entangled sheets and sat up....*

# CHAPTER TWENTY

He sat up, but the knocking persisted. After a moment James began to realize that it was someone pounding on his front door. Matt! His son! Jess! Something had happened to the children.

He disentangled himself from the sheets that were their usual mess after he'd had a nightmare. Then, grabbing a towelling robe but not bothering about the state of his nightwear, he leaped downstairs, knocking his shin on the banisters as he reached the bottom step although the pain was as nothing to his terror. He threw open the door to find Harriet Finamore on the step outside. 'Harriet? Harriet! What's happened. Is it Matt? One of the children?' He caught hold of her arm and pulled her inside, shutting out the night air that struck coldly on his overheated body. 'Tell me,' he urged.

'No. Nothing has happened.'

She sounded calm, but puzzled. She was also looking at him quizzically. He registered her expression and fumbled with the belt of his towelling robe.

'At least, nothing has happened to me,' she amended. 'It's you. I mean … there was such a noise. Shouting, banging on the wall. Our bedrooms must be side by side. I-I was a bit …' Petrified, she wanted to say, wondering what on earth was going on, but with him in front of her it seemed too much of an exaggeration. He seemed entirely normal, except for tousled hair and a sheen of sweat that glinted on his bare chest, visible through his towelling robe that he had put on inside out and only partially closed with its belt. She also saw that his feet were bare. She swallowed, panic subsiding as a new emotion surfaced. 'I was concerned that something was happening to you,' she ended, avoiding his eyes.

'Oh, God,' he said simply. 'I've always been afraid something like this was going to happen.' He saw that she was looking mystified, but through his anguish that now it was all going to have to come out into the open, he was aware that she did not seem frightened.

'Tell me,' was all she said.

James took hold of Harriet's hand and gently pulled her further into the room. 'Come and sit down. I knew I'd have to tell you sometime. You see, I suffer from post traumatic stress disorder. Have you heard of it? Do you know what it is?'

'I've read about it, although I've not known anyone who's suffered from it. And Gareth mentioned—' She shook her head as she saw him frown. 'Flashbacks, isn't it? Very distressing for the sufferer.' So that was what all this was about. She relaxed visibly.

He sighed. 'Distressing. Yes, I suppose that's as good a way of describing it as any. Shall I tell you?' When she nodded emphatically, he went quiet for a moment, gathering his thoughts. 'It all began in Helmand Province.'

'When you were wounded.'

He told her about the incident when the improvised explosive devices had gone off under their transport. He described it simply, not wanting to distress her with grizzly details. He told her that by no means everyone who was wounded suffered subsequently from PTSD. No one really knew who was going to succumb to it, or why. 'They say it's what the men in the trenches must have had happen to them, post traumatic stress disorder.'

'And we all know what happened to men in the trenches who refused to go back after their leave.'

'They were denounced as cowards and shot,' he said bluntly.

'I always thought that was grossly unfair.'

'There probably were some malingerers. But a lot more were

suffering from something they were powerless to control. And for those men, no one could predict when a flashback was going to occur, or how frequently.'

'So you are saying it's like a waking nightmare?'

'That's exactly it. You see it all happening again, sometimes in slow motion. You know what is going to happen, but you cannot stop it. You see everything sharply delineated in colour – just like in real life. At first it was like one of those silent movies; now I hear everything, just as it happened.'

'That's dreadful for you! Do you feel the pain?'

He thought for a moment. 'Not exactly. You anticipate it, so you know what is going to happen and how it is going to hurt. Then, just as it happened at the time, everything goes black and you are back in the real world.'

'Scary. Is it getting better, James?'

'The attacks are less frequent.'

'Will you go to the doctor tomorrow?'

'Heavens, no. My next appointment isn't for another four weeks. I shall just make a note of this episode. I'm supposed to note the frequency and the intensity of them. We talk it through. Talk therapy seems to work better for some people, like me, than any drugs. Harriet, I am so sorry you were dragged into my mess. I was so glad I'd bought this cottage because it meant I'd not disturb a neighbour. And then you came.'

'I suppose you must have been a bit put out when we arrived. That's understandable.'

'In some ways. But afterwards I found that the thought of having neighbours was a comfort.'

'I've left Ash on her own. She probably won't wake up but I should go.' All the same she stayed where she was.

'Thank you for coming over.'

'Shall you sleep now?'

'I ought to. I'm tired enough.'

Harriet could see that he was also beginning to relax but she sensed that he was reluctant to see her leave. 'Shall I make you a cup of tea?' She went into the kitchen and opened cupboard doors until she found his dry goods. There was a jar there of local honey. She made a mug of tea for them both and put the honey jar on a saucer with a teaspoon and went back into the sitting room. The honey was the runny sort. 'I remember that you don't like sugar in your tea so you'd better have the honey separately. It's therapeutic. You'll have to eat it quickly or it'll drip.'

He licked the spoon carefully then handed it back. They drank their tea in a comfortable silence. Harriet tried to suppress a yawn and failed.

'I'd like to ask you to stay longer.'

'But that would mean leaving Ash on her own.'

'What would she do if she woke up and found you not there?'

'I scribbled a note to say that I had heard a noise and had come next door to see what was the matter.'

'Wouldn't that alarm her more?'

'Knowing Ash, she would come to investigate herself. It wouldn't be a problem. There's a torch by the front door in case of emergencies.'

'Do you have emergencies?' He was alarmed for them, two women living on their own (and one of them only a child, if a resourceful one).

'Not the sort you are thinking about, although Mash already has a habit of wandering off. We thought we were getting two female kittens but I have a feeling this one is all male. As for Ash, I expect that she'll be fast asleep until breakfast time as usual.' If it did not mean leaving Ash on her own, she would have stayed, she was thinking. 'You could come next door yourself.' She made the suggestion without thinking through the consequences. What consequences?

'And sleep on the sofa?'

'What?' She looked at him, startled. 'Not a comforting thought.'

She hesitated. 'I wake early. If you left before Ash woke you could sleep in my bed. It is a large double.'

His face was non committal. 'Could I, Harriet?'

'I've got a very comfortable mattress.' She put the lid back on the jar of honey and picked up the empty tea mugs. 'I shouldn't be here for much longer. Because of Ash. It's your call, James. If it would help, you can sleep in Sycamore Cottage tonight.' It was an impulsive suggestion, one she did not expect him to agree to. She couldn't take it back. She didn't want to take it back. She yawned again.

'You're exhausted,'

'We're both exhausted. Come to bed.'

There was a spare pillow in her airing cupboard. She put a clean pillowcase on it and he took it from her without comment and got into her bed – thankfully her sheets were clean that morning. Harriet went to the bathroom and by the time she got back to the bedroom James was asleep, or making a very good exhibition of sleep.

'Sleep well,' she whispered, and turned off the light.

He grunted once. Then all was quiet.

Tired as she was, Harriet found that she could not fall asleep. She turned over cautiously, but that didn't help either. It was strange, having a man in her bed again. In the darkness she blushed. That was not what she meant at all! James was only sleeping beside her because there was no other bed in the cottage for him to use. Then, that was not right, either. James was there for comfort. She was human comfort for him in his distress. Once more she turned over. This time James moved, too.

'I can't sleep,' he said.

'Neither can I.'

'It might help if we had a cuddle.'

To her amazement, Harriet found herself chuckling.

'That was not meant to be a come-on,' he whispered, as indignantly as a murmur could make it sound.

She stroked his face gently. The rasp of a beard was beginning to emerge. 'I know,' she said quietly. 'I think it's just the strangeness of all this. But I'd quite like a cuddle, too.'

He put his arms round her and she settled her head in the crook of his shoulder. It was a comfort, she thought as she began to drift. Joe had never been a man for cuddles. When they had contact in bed it was for sex, quick, sometimes satisfactory sex. She did not remember Paul ever cuddling her for her emotional satisfaction.

She felt James's lips on her hair, his hand gently smoothing it away from her forehead. He kissed bare flesh. She thought: *This is not what I meant to happen.* Then she thought that she could do with emotional release. She lifted her face to his and he kissed her mouth.

What followed was as natural as breathing, as right and as inevitable as living. They came together sweetly, tenderly, with gentle sighs and murmurings.

She woke as a greyness was beginning to seep through the edges of the curtains. She was held close to James's hard body by his arm which was lying across hers. But he was not asleep. His hand was stroking her, touching her, playing with her so that the fire that he had ignited before flared within her again. She stretched languorously and he turned her towards him. This time it was hot and fierce, deeply passionate and all-consuming and only the knowledge that they were not alone in the cottage prevented Harriet from vocalizing a union that was triumphant and quite unlike anything she'd experienced before.

When it was over, once more she fell into a deep, refreshing sleep.

# CHAPTER TWENTY-ONE

When Harriet next woke, it was at her usual time, just before seven o'clock. She stretched, feeling wonderfully at ease. Then the events of the night flooded back. For her it had been fantastic, magical. For him…? She tensed, and turned her head cautiously.

The space beside her was empty, the pillow gone. She sat up and blinked, blushing furiously as she realized that she was naked and recalled total abandonment. She had certainly not imagined the events of the night, for apart from a certain soreness in places that were unaccustomed to prolonged and ardent activity, the pillow lay innocently on the floor, as though she had thought to use it herself and then changed her mind. She showered and got dressed in the usual manner and went downstairs.

James had let himself out – but he must have returned, for on the kitchen table there was a jam jar full of late rosebuds, still with the dew on their petals. Not from her rose bushes, but from James's garden. There was a note accompanying the flowers. 'Busy, this morning. Will the two of you come to supper?'

It was a message that could have been read by Ash without compromising her mother. The rosebuds said something different.

She touched one of the flowers with a soft finger. Part of her, the old, wounded, tentative, scared part, considered throwing away the roses as if to deny that anything had happened – or might again. The new, more confident Harriet smiled at their brave beauty. No, she did not know where this relationship would lead and for the moment it did not matter in the least. They were in unknown territory and without a map but the prospect of what she would find there with James was both intriguing and exhilarating.

During the course of the morning, Harriet went to see her new bank investments manager. She explained her circumstances: that she had sold her house; that she intended investing in the local garden centre as a partner with a part of the money, keeping a good portion with which to buy a house locally. She told the woman – who was younger than she was herself – that she wanted a short-term loan of £8,000 to begin the urgent repairs and to invest in a selection of Christmas goods.

'The bank would need a business plan, of course.'

'I expected that.' Harriet handed over the required document.

'We'll get back to you.'

Already the garden centre was beginning to look as though someone cared for it. Gone were the weeds in the gravel paths. All the broken decorative pots had been removed and in their place were the newly potted chrysanthemums, bright yellow, vibrant bronze, gorgeous deep pinks and brilliant white that were flying off the shelves. 'We are selling them at a very good rate,' admitted James, 'but people are also buying other things. Think what it'll be like once we introduce poinsettias and our Christmas lines.'

Harriet had also suggested that it might be a novel idea to have a corporate image. 'I was thinking about a sort of uniform for the three of us.' Christie was now an enthusiastic member of the team and had taken on a new persona almost immediately after Gordon had left.

'What's wrong with jeans? I think you look great in jeans. Mind you, I think you look greater without them.'

'James!' she hissed, her face pink. 'You shouldn't say such things.' He cocked his head and grinned. It was almost lascivious, she thought, a fluttery feeling in the pit of her stomach.

'I shouldn't say such things, or I shouldn't say such things here?'

She thought, *How stupid to be coy after what was happening between them. She had not been coy that night, nor the following night, or that time in the afternoon when he had insisted that they had something to discuss at home. Discuss? She supposed you could call it that.*

'There's nothing wrong with jeans in the right place, James!' Harriet continued, a half-smile on her face. 'We all wear serviceable clothes, but mine are definitely more suited to working on my own in a private garden than working where the public sees me. What if we had sweatshirts with Brownlows' logo on them?'

'Brownlows doesn't have a logo. Ah. Maybe that isn't such a bad idea at that. The logo, I mean.'

'Quite. We could order a batch of green sweatshirts. If the logo was a fun one, or a purposeful one – like crossed spades – we might even sell them to locals. I think we should make sure that our working trousers at least start the day clean. The staff could have an anorak for rainy days, also with the logo on. What do you think?'

'I think that's a brilliant idea. Who could we get to design a logo?'

'I'll ask Florence.'

'Why not approach one of the local primary schools and ask them to design something for you?' Florence suggested. 'Do it as a competition. Offer a prize of child-size garden tools, or something like that, with a deadline to be ready for the Christmas rush.'

'That's brilliant. Thanks, Florence. I'll mention it to James.'

'Today, at teatime?' Florence asked mischievously.

'If he comes round,' Harriet answered austerely. Then she smiled. 'He usually drops in sometime after we've cleaned ourselves up after work.'

'So I'm told. Lucky you. He's quite a dish. Although they do say that the willowy Felicity isn't quite out of the picture. Just a word of warning, you understand.'

Harriet forced her face to remain unconcerned. It was not possible, she was thinking, not after those nights they had spent together. At first she had worried about Ash's reaction but the girl was already fond of James and she seemed only too pleased to find him at the breakfast table on those occasions when he spent the night at Sycamore Cottage – which did not happen all that often.

Yet, Felicity still a force to consider? She would have to think about that.

'Florence set me off on yet another tack,' she reported to James the day after. 'We don't have child-size garden tools. And we should. They would also make good Christmas presents. And gardening gloves in different sizes and weights.'

'And wellie boots.'

'Coloured ones. Fun ones.'

'You and fun,' he smiled indulgently. 'It comes into all your conversations, did you know that?'

'But I am having the most enormous fun. Working on my own was satisfying but it had its disadvantages. Now I have such a lot to be grateful for.'

'And I can't imagine what I should have done without you.'

She went into his arms, quite determined not to permit fears about Felicity to spoil what was becoming a precious relationship.

Two days later, the Christmas delivery, which they had ordered so late, arrived at Brownlows. James had a meeting with his bank so Harriet was in the office when the lorry appeared. There was a large number of boxes but all appeared to be in order. Now Harriet looked forward to making as spectacular a display as possible to lure their customers to spend money.

Halfway through the morning another lorry drew up. Harriet was at the far end of the garden centre; Christie was working in the shop.

'Special delivery for Brownlows,' the driver said, handing over his delivery sheet for a signature. 'Christmas goods. The usual.'

'But we had a delivery this morning.'

'Did you check it? Always best to be absolutely sure, love. Did the boss send in a second order? They often have to, you know. Can't always trust the bosses to get it right first time.'

'They ordered all that we thought we could sell.'

'So what am I supposed to do with this, then?'

'Leave it here?' said Christie dubiously.

'Right, then. Course, it'll cost you, if I have to come back to fetch it,' he said kindly. 'Boss around to check first?'

'One is out, the other is out at the back. I could call her.'

'Haven't got time to hang around, love. I've got three more deliveries miles apart before I finish and the traffic's something awful today,' the man sighed heavily. 'D'you want me to leave it or reload?'

'I guess you'll just have to leave it.'

'OK, then. Sign here.'

'He couldn't get away fast enough,' Christie explained miserably to Harriet when she finally tracked her down.

'Good grief. It looks as though our order has been repeated.'

'I thought I was doing the right thing.'

'Of course you did,' Harriet comforted her, thinking they must set up a better system of communication.

'Anyway, we probably will be able to shift whatever else has come. I did wonder if James was being super cautious.'

Once he had returned and finished expressing total horror at the double order that had been delivered, Harriet defended Christie. 'She thought she was doing the right thing.'

The suppliers were less than helpful. 'We could take it back, I suppose. It'll cost you.'

'Don't bother,' James gritted his teeth. 'No doubt the extra discount for a large order will apply?'

'I guess we think twice about using that company next year,' Harriet said as cheerfully as she could. 'They don't seem very efficient.'

The following morning another lorry appeared. This time James was on the till and the lorry load was turned away. The supplier was defensive, insisting that they had only sent out what had been ordered. They had never had any trouble with their orders before.

He was still talking to the supplier when a fourth delivery appeared....

After supper that evening, James came round for coffee. 'Have you got to the bottom of it, yet?' Harriet asked.

'I guess it must have been a glitch in their computer ordering system,' he answered. 'It's something that they can't disprove so at least they have agreed not to charge us for anything other than the second delivery which we had already started to unpack.'

'So you don't think it was some kind of practical joke?' she mentioned casually. It was something that had been preying on her mind ever since the last order had arrived.

'Come on,' he scoffed. 'A practical joke? Who'd play something like that on us?'

'A rival firm? After all, Brownlows is doing so much better than it was this time last year. You've only got to take a look at the books to see that. We must have taken profit from other garden centres.'

'That sounds a bit paranoid. I can't really imagine established firms round here being as devious as that.'

'No,' she agreed dubiously. 'But it does seem very strange. Let's just hope nothing else happens to us.'

James shrugged and changed the subject by putting his arm round her shoulders and pulling her into his side. His kiss had the desired effect of making her forget her anxieties.

'Will you stay?' she asked tentatively.

'I thought you'd never ask.'

# CHAPTER TWENTY-TWO

James wondered if he was coming out of the PTSD at long last. The drugs had been almost as bad as the flashbacks until they decreased the dose. It had been the wooliness, the feeling that there was a damp muslin curtain between him and the rest of the world for months that had been so demoralizing. His counsellor had told him that sometimes there is nothing to do but embrace the isolation.

There used to be a constant dread. He had known what was going to happen to him each time, and each time it had happened he was powerless to do anything about it. Yet that had gone now and he felt more alive than he had since he had been wounded, which was wonderful, and he was sure that it all stemmed from loving Harriet Finamore. Far from embracing isolation, what he wanted to do was to embrace her as frequently as he could!

Counselling, they'd told him that counselling was the thing. At first it was the probing that he hated, the stripping bare of his life, his assumption that he was one of life's failures. The doctors told him bluntly that it took on average two years to get over PTSD. Two bloody years. They assured him that people were cured. Eventually.

He was beginning to believe them as the interval between the dreams/nightmares was getting longer. He'd not had a flashback for several months. That was Harriet's doing, giving him the gift of positiveness and his luck with her was holding. He prayed fervently that it was and that her mind could be coaxed into being as in tune with his as it was obvious that she gave her body both willingly and joyfully.

*

It was Saturday evening. Harriet and Ash had been given supper by James. The adults had sent Ash home to finish some homework while they cleared up after which they would have coffee at Sycamore Cottage while she watched TV. As they put the last of the supper things away there was a knock on the door. James sighed, but he went to answer it.

'I need to talk to you,' Felicity said abruptly, pushing past her ex-husband as she entered the room. 'I see you're here. Again,' she said as her eyes swept over Harriet, taking in the unfinished bottle of red wine on the coffee table.

'Thank you for the meal, James,' said Harriet. 'I must get back to Ash. I expect she's finished her homework by now.' She picked up her jacket and went to the door.

'I'll be round as soon as she's gone,' James said quietly as Harriet smiled at him, and he closed the door behind her reluctantly.

In spite of his promise, she did not see James again that evening. He met her in the driveway after breakfast the following morning. 'Sorry I didn't come round. It got a bit late.'

'I expect you had things to discuss.' In spite of herself her tone of voice was guarded.

'I also think I should apologize for Felicity last night.'

'There's absolutely no need. I get the message that I'm not her favourite person, loud and clear.'

'And I came round to tell you why she appeared so dramatically yesterday.'

'You don't have to.'

'Are we having our first quarrel?'

Harriet was about to give a quick and caustic retort about ex-wives who expected an instant response from ex-husbands. Then she grinned weakly. 'I don't know. Are we?'

'I'm an idiot. And of course I don't have to tell you what went on between Felicity and me,' he replied, sounding exasperated, so that she bit her lip. 'But I want to. Matt's being bullied at school.'

'That's horrible. It happened to me, for a time. I managed to sort it, but not without a lot of anguish.'

'So what do we do about it?'

'This is for you and Felicity to sort out, not a total stranger.'

'I thought that you and I had progressed far from the total stranger mode by now.'

'Well, yes. Of course we have,' she said. It was dreadful, being at cross purposes with him. She went closer to him, reached up and kissed his cheek.

Immediately he pulled her close and kissed her back. Deeply.

After a while she murmured without pulling away, 'Where were we? Ah, yes. James, how you deal with the problems your son is encountering at his school really has nothing to do with me, has it?'

'Absolutely not. So what would you do? The person on the sidelines has a much better overview of what is important.'

Harriet said reluctantly, 'What Matthew needs is a coping strategy.' She was looking at his face and she saw how his eyes widened when she mentioned the coping strategy. 'You see how carefully I was listening to you when you told me about your PTSD.'

'You're brilliant. Do you know that?' She shook her head and impulsively he hugged her tightly and said, 'Why didn't I think of that? Of course you are right.'

It was not until the evening when she found herself staring blankly at the TV screen that she knew she needed to take stock. She had drifted into the affair with James, but now? There was something about the man that she found more than a little endearing: his smile that melted her insides not to mention his lovemaking that was mind blowing; the habit he had of looking into her eyes and making her feel that there was no one else he wanted to be listening to; the way there was a lick of hair that stuck up at the back of his head – just like a small boy's. Just like Matthew's.

Harriet might dislike the woman intensely but that was her problem, not Felicity's. Could she be, was she, just plain jealous of the woman? The night James had told her about his PTSD had ended so fantastically that it had seemed to herald a new future for him as well as her.

Harriet freely acknowledged that her track record with men was disastrous. She had loved Joe, yet he had proved to be anything but an ideal husband. Then there was Paul. She would so much rather there had been no Paul. How stupidly foolish it made her appear to have so obviously succumbed to the weakness of wanting to be looked after. Now it would appear that she had fallen for James. Where that would end was anyone's guess.

There had been a concert at Windcote at which Matthew was the unexpected star turn. James had driven Harriet and Ash there and on their way home Ash discovered that Matthew had left his sheet music with her.

'Are you sure that he'll want it immediately?' Harriet asked in dismay, for they were almost back at the cottages.

'He has a lesson after school tomorrow.'

'Then we'll turn round and take it to him,' said his father, with only a small sigh. 'It's just as well you discovered it now, Ash.'

It was James who took the music to the door of the house where his children and their mother lived. The door was opened by Felicity who, when she saw who was standing on her doorstep, put her hand on James's arm to pull him inside. James obviously explained the situation – that he had Harriet and Ash with him and, having handed over the case of music, turned to go. Felicity said something and he stopped to look back at her. She laughed, a musical sound that carried as far as the car as she dropped the music case on the doorstep and took a pace towards him. Placing her hands on either side of his forehead, she drew his head down to hers. Then she kissed him on the mouth.

Harriet discovered that she could not manage to wrench her

eyes away from the scene, deliberately and flagrantly public though it was.

'Cor, Mum,' exclaimed Ash, her eyes on stalks. 'Did you see that? She kissed him. Do you think Matt's parents are going to get back together? How could he when you and he … well, you know.'

'It's rude to stare, dear,' said Harriet, continuing to do just that.

Felicity had initiated the embrace. But James had not pulled away. Perhaps he had been unable to, logic said. Most likely he had not wanted to pull away, her heart acknowledged painfully. Look how he had put his hands on her waist – to steady her, to prolong the embrace? – and he had left them there for far too long.

'It would be nice for Matthew and Jessica if their father and their mother did get back together,' she said then, as evenly as she could, trying to sound as though she meant what she said.

'It wouldn't be nice for you and I'm not sure that James would be very happy,' commented Ash, with a censorious note in her voice.

Would he? Harriet asked herself. She had no answer.

Ash had fed the kittens before they went to the concert. Now she called them to make sure they were safe for the night. Although the kittens had learned to use the cat flap quickly, the girl liked to know where they were before she went to bed.

Mish came immediately. Mash was nowhere to be found.

'Never mind, dear. I guess he's out hunting.'

'Probably. He caught a small mouse yesterday.'

'I know. It was my early morning present. Ugh! Go to bed. He'll be back for breakfast.

But he wasn't.


Work at the garden centre had increased to such a furious pace that James had suggested that it might be worth while engaging someone for the busiest days of the week until after Christmas. They were able to find a young lad, called Stewart, who was amenable to being told what to do, and who then actually did what he was asked. He was particularly adept at working the machine they had hired to enclose their Christmas trees in a plastic netting for buyers to transport home in their cars. But a week before Christmas Stewart announced that he was leaving at the end of the day. 'So I'd like me wages when I go.'

'Excuse me?' asked a bemused Harriet.

'I'm not stopping 'ere. I got a job at the garage the other side of town. Good money, too.'

'I'm glad to hear you have somewhere to go to, but what about giving us notice. It is usual, you know,' she said mildly, wondering frantically who they would be able to find to take his place so near to Christmas.

The boy shrugged. 'This job come up, see.'

'I had the feeling you enjoyed working here.'

He scuffed the ground with his working boot. 'I did,' he admitted.

Harriet looked at him closely. He looked as though he had not slept properly. Drugs? She had never come in contact with the problem and so she had no idea what she ought to be looking for. All the same, something wasn't right about this and drugs seemed to be the likely explanation.

'Are you in some sort of trouble?' she asked. 'You're a good worker and I'd like to help, if I can.'

''T'ain't me what's in trouble,' he said, after a pause.

Harriet frowned. 'What's that supposed to mean?'

'Nothing. Nothing at all. So I get me wages this afternoon. All right?'

'I can't force you to stay. And, of course you'll have what's due to you, Stewart, but I wish you'd tell me exactly what's wrong.'

# CHAPTER TWENTY-THREE

It was plain that Stewart would say no more to her. Harriet set him work to do in the potting shed since he seemed reluctant to work outside near the Christmas trees. Then she went to find James.

'I'll speak to him later,' James said. 'He seemed to be happy with us. It does seem a bit odd.' But afterwards he admitted that the boy just clammed up and would say nothing.

'I've made your wage packet up,' Harriet told Stewart when she saw him hovering outside the office at the end of the afternoon. 'We're going to miss you.' She hesitated. 'I don't suppose you've changed your mind?'

He would not meet her eye but shook his head.

Harriet sighed. 'Oh, well. Look, why don't you pick one of the Norway Spruces to take home to your mother?'

'Can I, Miss? I'd really like that. Me mam said it were silly us two havin' a tree this year. I've always loved the trees, lights 'n all.'

'Then you must definitely take one home. And, don't forget, if you should decide you want a job here later on, we might have a vacancy. It'd be worth asking.'

He kicked the dirt with his booted foot. 'I do like it 'ere. But I gotta go. And you want to watch your back, Miss. There's people out there who don't like you. Me mam said she'd 'eard I'd live to regret it, if I didn't change me job. Said me car'd get bashed, if I didn't finish 'ere. An then it got a scratch down one side, didn't it? Looked like they used a screwdriver. Left a typed note under the wipers, too. It were parked outside my 'ouse, so they know where I live 'n' all.'

They all knew that Stewart's newly acquired banger was his pride and joy. 'Where did she hear that?' Harriet asked sharply.

'Said they was talking about it in the local.'

'Have you told the police?'

'What use would that be? So that's why I'm going. Merry Christmas.'

White-faced with shock, Harriet went to find James. 'It wasn't just a new job. Stewart was warned off us.' She related all that she had been told. 'What are we going to do?'

'Manage on our own, I suppose. It'll die down, you'll see.'

'What'll die down? Vindictiveness? A local vendetta? And you won't go to the police, either?' she asked bitterly.

'What could they do? Question Stewart? I don't suppose he knows any more than we do, and he'd clam up, anyway.'

'He had a note, an unsigned, typewritten note.'

'Which, naturally, he threw away.'

'The police are supposed to be there to help us when we need them,' she said stubbornly.

James hugged her. 'I'm quite sure that we'd be asked for a lot more proof than the tale of a local lad who's changed his job.'

'James. This is yet another event that we can't explain away. Do you realize that? The so-called storm damage, the trashed pots, the ruined chrysanths, the repeat orders, now an employee who has been scared off. And I was forgetting your flat tyre.' The plum tree? She shivered. That was a bit too close to home. Her home.

'Come on. The flat tyre could have happened to anyone. And don't you think Christie would be the more valuable employee to scare off, if that's what's happened to Stewart.'

'Perhaps we'd better ask her, then,' she glared at him.

Christie admitted reluctantly that she had received a vague threat. 'A stupid note. Do you think I can be intimidated like that?'

'And was your car damaged, too?'

She gave them an old-fashioned look. 'You know it's got so many dents and scratches already, one more wouldn't show.'

That was true enough, Harriet acknowledged. 'So you won't go to the police?' she asked James again, when they were locking up.

'No. But I am making a record of these events. Dates, times, consequences. If … if there is anything else, I might think again. For now I prefer to believe that the Stewart business is no more than a spat he's having with an ex-mate.'

She was unconvinced. But although she had now invested heavily in it, the garden centre was James's, not hers.

They had not seen Mash, the kitten, for several days. Ash was extremely upset, although Harriet had done her best to console her by saying that toms were notorious for wandering.

'And we already know that Mash likes his freedom.'

It was James who found the little body one evening, lying in the middle of the road in front of his drive, rigid and foul-smelling. He had arrived at the cottages first as Harriet had stopped off to go to the supermarket. Hurriedly he fetched a bin bag, wanting neither Ash nor Harriet to see the mangled remains. A car driven carelessly, he supposed. But by the state of the corpse it was obvious this had not happened that day, or even the day before. Yet another unexplained incident? he thought at first. It was sufficiently nasty for him to decide then and there to bury the body without showing it to Harriet. She and Ash – especially Ash – would mourn, but not be overly worried about what had happened.

Had it got anything to do with what Stewart had told them? As he dug the small grave he decided that it was paranoid nonsense. He did not believe in terrorism. Then he laughed, a hollow laugh. He, if anyone, should be well aware of terrorism, and its effects.

As he had feared, Ash was inconsolable. Harriet was so glad

they still had Mish. 'She is a homebody, love. I doubt if anything will happen to her, and at least we do still have her. But it was kind of James to bury Mash, wasn't it?'

'Could we have a headstone?' Ash hiccoughed.

'I think that would be a very good idea. We'll take a look at the cat plaques at the garden centre at the weekend.'

Harriet and Ash had asked Florence to spend Christmas Day with them. 'We owe her so much,' Harriet told her daughter. 'I don't like to think of her being on her own.'

'What are we giving Aunt Florence for Christmas?' asked Ash.

'I have seen some gorgeous long cashmere jackets. Do you think she might approve?'

'If it's the right colour.'

Ash was to have a new bicycle. Harriet had thought long and hard about this. It seemed to her that the country roads were generally unsafe, with drivers driving dangerously fast and often too close to verges when they rounded bends. She only had to remember what had happened to Mash to know that. But Ash's new friend Miranda had a bicycle, which she used when she visited Ash on a Saturday and there were no buses as an alternative.

James's Christmas arrangements had also been concerning Harriet. 'Either you or I will have to go over daily to check on things – the automatic watering device and the air vents. Do you have plans, James? We'd love you to come to us, unless you have already arranged to be with Jess and Matt.' She knew how important his children were to him and that their own relationship, however intense it was, had to take second place at such an important time of year. Deliberately she avoided the use of Felicity's name. There had been no sign of the woman anywhere near Sycamore Cottage for some time. 'Or do you spend Christmas with Joanne and your brother?'

'I can't think of anything I'd like more than to spend Christmas with you.' He sounded so enthusiastic that Harriet glowed inwardly. 'Gareth and I prefer to maintain a certain distance, as you've probably guessed and most years they go to Joanne's parents. They still both tend to blame me for their lack of funds, which is stupid because Gareth has always had grandiose ideas – hence the new house – and Joanne's gallery hardly pays its way.'

'I wouldn't know about Gareth's business but I think the gallery's doing really well. It looks very impressive when you go in and Joanne works extremely hard. I've even bought a couple of things there myself recently.'

'Have you? That must have been a relief for her,' he said drily.

'Anyway, Christmas with us is a date, then,' she said, with no special emphasis although her heart was singing.

'I'll be taking Jess and Matt's presents over on Christmas Eve and the three of us are going to a pantomime on Boxing Day, but I was preparing to hole up quietly on Christmas Day itself after the church service.'

'We'll love having you. Florence is coming, too,' she added. She had already decided that it wouldn't be a problem. Florence had warmed to James since Harriet had made it plain that she wasn't going anywhere else by investing in the business. What she thought about their feelings towards each other she was not saying.

It was the day before Christmas Eve. Harriet was walking home through the village when a car swept past her, then pulled up abruptly. Felicity Ormston switched off the engine and got out of the car, slamming the door behind her.

'How dare you try to take Matthew and Jessica's father away from them on Christmas Day!' she stormed at Harriet without any preamble.

'Excuse me?' Extremely taken aback, Harriet stood stock still.

'You heard me. I think it's absolutely diabolical of you to inveigle yourself into James's life and totally spoil his children's Christmas at the same time.'

Harriet shook her head. 'I think you must be mistaken.'

'Oh, no. It is you who are mistaken, Harriet Finamore.'

Harriet sighed. She could see by the way Felicity had roused herself into such a temper that it was unlikely she would be able to make any sense of her complaint, let alone put in her side of the matter.

'James should be spending Christmas Day with his family.'

So that was the problem. 'That may be true,' Harriet conceded. 'He told me he is calling to see you on Christmas Eve and he is taking the children out on Boxing Day. He also told me that he was intending to spend Christmas Day itself on his own. I assumed, not unnaturally, that you and the children had other plans. That he was to be on his own seemed a pity, considering that we live next door.'

'So you insisted that he should come to you. Being a kind man, James wouldn't have wanted to sound ungrateful. But that he is disappointing his children is just so unfair on them.'

'I hadn't realized …' Harriet began.

'Well, you do now. Shall you tell him, or shall I?'

'You—' Harriet began, then she thought, hang on a moment. Wouldn't that be just what Felicity wanted, to be able to couch a change of plans to make it seem that neither she nor Ash wanted James to be with them? If it were true, that there had been a mis-understanding about how Christmas Day should be arranged, this should be made clear. 'Thank you,' she said decisively. 'I'll speak to James myself.'

'Then see you make it clear where his priorities lie,' snapped the other woman before she turned abruptly and got back into her car.

'And a happy Christmas to you, too,' murmured Harriet. The car shot off, spraying her legs with dirty water from where it had gathered in a puddle by the side of the road. 'Wretched, careless driver!' she hurled after the car. It relieved her feelings. She very much doubted if Felicity knew what she had just done – or that she would care in any way, if she did.

# CHAPTER TWENTY-FOUR

'So, of course I understand that you should be with your family,' Harriet said to James, as brightly as she was able to, later on Christmas Eve.

'I see.'

His reply had come with absolutely no intonation. Harriet was torn between asking him when the arrangement had been made with Felicity and demanding why on earth he had not mentioned it before. She made a small, helpless gesture and said, 'I'm sure the children will be pleased to have you with them after all.'

'Felicity and I are divorced. They are well aware of the situation.'

'Yes. I see.'

'It's lucky that I live near enough to walk and not to have to take the car out. At least I can have a drink.'

So he wouldn't be staying the night, Harriet thought, with something akin to a blaze of joy. Although minds could be changed. Minds probably would be concentrated, she thought, and wondered which mind would have the final say. She sighed. 'I'm sure you'll have a splendid day with them.'

'Are you?'

'Of course I am, and of course you will,' she answered bracingly. 'So, happy Christmas, James. We'll both look forward to seeing you after the festivities are over.'

'I was going to play Father Christmas to Ash, and you,' he said, and Harriet thought he sounded truculent. At least, that was what she would have called the sound, if it had come from Matt.

'I'm sure that Jess and Matt will love having you at home. After all, you weren't with them last year, were you?'

'I was staying with friends. Felicity brought them over on Boxing Day for a couple of hours. It was all right but I'd not long been out of hospital and I got tired quickly. She went off to friends. So this year all I have to do is to try and curb Jess's avarice and her mother's insistence that she's worth it.'

'That sounds a bit harsh. Aren't all girls a little selfish at that age? The one when you are firmly convinced that the world is your oyster.' Deliberately she made no mention of the selfishness of his wife.

'I suppose you are right. It's a difficult age, all the same.'

'And everyone loves presents, don't they?' she said brightly.

'Of course they do.' He was sounding more cheerful. His eyes were glinting in the light cast by the garden lamp as he caught hold of her hand. He pushed back her glove to reveal a small amount of exposed flesh on her wrist. Then he drew her hand to his lips and kissed it. 'No mistletoe. No excuse, except that I want to kiss you. Happy Christmas, dear Harriet. I would so very much rather I was with you and Ash tomorrow.'

Would he? Would he really? Harriet wondered if she would ever understand the relationship James appeared to have with Felicity.

In the morning, when they were leaving the house to go to church, Ash discovered two small packets wrapped in Christmas paper and tucked behind a bush by the front door where they were out of sight from the gate.

'Look, Mum! One's for you, the other is for me. Shall we open them now?'

'I don't think we have time. It'll be more fun to wait until later.'

'I s'ppose. No, not really. If I run on ahead, I'll be in plenty of time to robe for the service.' She had recently started singing in the church choir. 'Please let's open them, Mum. Who do you think left them? Was it Aunt Florence?'

'It's definitely not Florence's writing. It looks more like James's.'

Ash tore the paper and dropped it on the ground. 'It is from James. Wow, it's a bracelet. It's ever so pretty,' she said admiringly, slipping the jewellery onto her wrist and twisting and turning her arm to admire the effect. The bracelet was encrusted with enamel flowers and set on a gold band. 'Hurry up and open yours so I can see that. Do you think James has given you a present, too?'

'The writing on the card is the same. But you know I like to unwrap presents slowly, savour the moment,' her mother said, only half teasingly. The box felt uncannily like a ring box. She didn't see how James could possibly give her a ring in such an impersonal way. She had to be mistaken.

'Ohh. *Really* gotta go, Mum. See you after church.'

'Fine,' Harriet answered vaguely. She picked up the discarded wrapping paper and went inside, taking Ash's jewellery box and her own present. She sat down in the sitting room and opened the parcel slowly. She was right; there was a box inside it. The box was old and shabby. She opened the note that went with it.

*I found this quite by chance, Harriet my dearest, and thought immediately of you. It's old, at least one hundred years, and it's called a regard ring.*

She opened the box and there, nestling in rubbed velvet was a ring with six small stones set in gold. The note continued:

*Ruby, emerald, garnet, amethyst, ruby, diamond. They spell regard, which is a very small portion of what I feel for you.*

*Forgive me for not giving this to you in person as I wished to but I do so want to think of you wearing it today.*

*James*

How could she resist wearing it? Harriet slid the ring onto the fourth finger of her right hand. It fitted perfectly. It was a pretty sentiment, she thought. And, after all, it was merely a dress ring. Unless you happened to know better. Somehow she knew that most people would not even have heard of such a thing. A regard ring.

It put her own gift to him, which she had put behind a similar bush in his garden first thing that morning, crushingly into perspective. Harriet had bought James a sweater. It was cashmere and silk, and in the colours she knew he preferred, but it was only a sweater.

As she expected, Ash was suitably impressed, although she did say the choice of stones was peculiar. 'I mean, Mum, two rubies and no sapphire. It's a bit odd. But it will go with anything.'

'And it's very pretty,' said Florence, who had also been pressed into admiring it. 'I often think that old jewellery is much more interesting than modern stuff. R.E.G.A.R.D.,' she spelt out under her breath while Ash was distracted by another parcel. 'An interesting way to express feelings. An unusual design,' she added more loudly, regarding Harriet steadily. 'I'm sure it's Welsh.'

'Is it? There can't be many of them around nowadays.'

'Is that because it's very old?' asked Ash, who had unwrapped some paint brushes from Florence. 'Thanks, Aunt Flo. They are just what I would have chosen myself,' and she gave her godmother a hug and a kiss. 'Do you think my bracelet is old?'

'Not as old as your mum's ring, and certainly not as fragile.'

Then Florence duly admired her long cashmere cardigan and urged Ash to open her other present, a pair of fashionable jeans. Harriet was given a pair of good quality secateurs.

'Thank you so much,' Harriet enthused. 'I've almost worn out my cheap pair. Quality always wins out in the end.'

'So I suppose Brownlows will go for the quality end of the market in future,' Florence teased her.

'Oh, I think it will pay us to provide a few inexpensive tools.'

Harriet had not told her friend about Paul's demand for money. Florence would have been horrified. But it appeared that James must have been right, too, that Paul's demand was not truly serious, for neither had he written to her again. But he had sent Ash a present, a first edition of a *Harry Potter*. Without comment the girl held it between two fingers and dropped it into the wastepaper basket. Wisely neither of the women made any comment.

Later, doing the washing up in the kitchen while Ash was watching TV, Florence said, 'I do hope that you know what you are doing.'

Harriet raised her eyebrows as if she were about to deny that she knew what Florence was talking about. Then she set her mouth. 'If you are referring to James, I know exactly what I am doing. But thanks for being concerned about me.'

'Hari, you lost your husband in dreadful circumstances. You left Paul in circumstances that were almost as awful. And thank heavens that you did leave him,' she added hastily. 'But although this man is divorced, I'm not sure that anybody in Cennen Bridge believes that the marriage is over.'

'I know that Felicity would like to think that it isn't,' Harriet murmured quietly. 'She's being perfectly obvious about that. I believe that Matt would love to have his dad back home, too. But Jess? I have no idea about her. As for James, I truly don't think that I'm being set up as a bit on the side, if that is what you fear.'

'A crude way of putting it, but yes, that is what I fear.'

'Flo, we may have the beginnings of a relationship, but that's all it is, early days.' Was it? Was it, really? She did so hope that she was wrong. She crossed her fingers for luck as she went on, 'You know that James wasn't well when he came home from Afghanistan? He's definitely better but in the same way that I'm recovering from Paul, so he is recovering from war. It's all too soon for anyone to know where it will end.'

'But in the meantime you have his regard ring.'

'Yes, I have,' she said defiantly. 'And I'm willing to bet that it's something that he never gave to Felicity.'

Florence hung up the tea towel on its peg by the stove and squeezed Harriet's shoulder as she passed her.

'He's a nice man and I've always thought you are a nice lady. I hope it all works out for you, I really do.'

'I must go. Chores to do. See you both later.'

Harriet changed into old trousers, pulled on her boots and put on her waxed jacket, woollen hat, scarf and gloves. Then she picked up her keys and called out that she would be as quick as she could.

All was quiet at the garden centre. Harriet spent some time checking the heating system and adjusting the automatic watering device that they had installed for some of their more exotic lines. Everything was in order, except that when she was preparing to leave she found she had a flat tyre.

'Drat!' she exclaimed, and kicked the offending wheel.

Then sighing resignedly, she set about changing the wheel. *At least she wasn't wearing her Christmas finery*, was her one consolation. It was when she found a huge nail in the tyre that she remembered how James had picked up a nail that had caused his slow puncture, the one that had made him slew into the ditch. It had been just one of the unexplained incidents that so beset Brownlows. Had someone deliberately hammered this nail into her tyre?

If so, it meant that it must have happened while she was working inside. She had not seen anyone around. But she would not have been alone.

Harriet shivered at the thought of a stranger damaging her tyre. Another thought intruded. What if it had been no stranger?

That would be far worse. 'Madness,' she said aloud, crossly. 'Idiot woman. This was an accident.'

She finished the job and put away her tools. On her way out

she pinned a note on the gate for Christie, who had offered to go in first thing on Boxing Day, to watch out in case another nail had been dropped. Then she locked up carefully and left.

# CHAPTER TWENTY-FIVE

The following morning Harriet discovered an envelope on the doormat when she came downstairs for breakfast. The letter inside was from James.

*Dearest Harriet,* he had written, *Thank you so very much for the sweater which I really like and will wear a lot (though not when I'm working). Weeks ago when I was buying the tickets for the pantomime I bought an extra one. Would Ash like to come with us? Please don't think that the children would consider this an intrusion as I did my fatherly duty by them yesterday.*

Once again he signed his note simply – *James*

Harriet went upstairs to rouse her daughter. 'Would you like to go?' she asked.

'Yes, please, Mum,' Ash said enthusiastically.

'You are so good to have written me a thank-you note,' Harriet told him, after they had discussed his plans for the day's outing over the phone. 'You make me feel guilty that I haven't thanked you properly for my ring.' He gave a small chuckle and she could almost hear him think that there was plenty of time for expressing proper gratitude later.

'Selfishly I wanted to give it to you myself,' he told her 'I wanted to watch your face as you unwrapped it and discovered its meaning.'

'It fits perfectly,' Harriet said. 'It is a most unusual and delightful Christmas present, one that I would never have thought of. I shall treasure it.'

'Mu-um… I've got nothing to wear!'

'I heard that.'

Harriet could sense the smile breaking on his face at the eternal female complaint. 'I must go. I'll give you a drink when you bring Ash home.'

Not long after Ash had been collected by James and the other children for their trip to the pantomime, there was a loud hammering on the front door. Not Felicity, was Harriet's immediate, dire, thought as she went to answer it.

'Harriet, you have to come. Immediately. It's dreadful!' Christie could hardly contain her anguish, bursting into tears on seeing her employer at the door.

'Christie! Don't tell me you had a puncture, too. Are you hurt?' It must be worse than a flat tyre. Harriet put her hand on the younger woman's arm and drew her into the cottage.

'Not me,' she hiccoughed. 'It's the garden,' she ended in a wail.

'Sit down and tell me. What on earth's happened?' Harriet guided her to the sofa, pressed her back against the cushions and sat down beside her, taking hold of her hand.

'Someone's – someone's....'

'Take a deep breath, and then tell me.'

The tale emerged slowly. It appeared that between the previous afternoon when Harriet had left the garden centre in good order and when Christie had arrived to check on it, the pots of spring bulbs and the rosemary and thyme that were displayed near the tills had been sprayed with some powerful chemical.

'They're all dying, those that aren't already dead that is. It's such a mess! Something must have gone wrong with the watering system. They're all dead, or as near as. It looks awful.' She sniffed, fumbled for a tissue and blew her nose violently.

Harriet went cold. It was she who had adjusted the watering system. She had watered some of the pots herself, by hand. Could she have caused massive destruction herself?

'Give me a moment to change and I'll come over with you,' she said as calmly as she could over nausea that lay heavily on her stomach. 'Would you like a cup of tea or something while you are waiting?' Sweet tea, she thought. That's what you gave someone who had had a shock. She was in shock herself.

Christie shook her head. Then she said tentatively, 'I think I would like a cup of tea, if it isn't too much trouble?'

Harriet put the kettle on. 'Do you think anything can be saved? If we drench everything with water, would the chemical wash off?'

'I don't know,' Christie answered helplessly. 'I suppose we could try with the evergreens, but we couldn't sell the herbs now and the bulbs have definitely had it. No sugar, thanks. I don't take it,' she added, as Harriet dropped two heaped teaspoonsful into the mug. She omitted the sugar in her own.

'You do, today. You look as though you need it.'

Christie was looking much calmer when Harriet reappeared, dressed in an old pair of jeans and a sweatshirt that had seen better days. She picked up her purse then checked that she had her mobile and her keys. 'I'll use my car in case I need it later.'

The destruction was as Christie had described it. Neither the pots nor the stands had been disturbed but what they contained was heart-breakingly destroyed. Flowers and tender leaves were blackened or shrivelled. It was obvious that nothing could be done to save anything. There was also a whiff of chemicals in the air.

'Leave the door open,' said Harriet, as Christie was about to close it. 'I don't want either of us keeling over in here.'

'I'll get on with clearing it up, then,' Christie said bravely, and turned to fetch a barrow.

'No,' said Harriet slowly. 'I think we'll put a closed notice on the gate and wait until James has seen this.'

'Are you going to ring him and get him to come over?'

'He's taken the children to the pantomime. There's no point in spoiling everyone's day. I think we are going to leave everything just as it is until we decide what is best to be done. In the meantime, we'll turn off the new watering system.'

'That may not have been the problem,' Christie said. She lifted up one of their large watering cans. 'Smell it.'

The watering can reeked. It had plainly contained the chemical that had done the damage.

'You're not wearing gloves,' snapped Harriet, badly shaken. She had not been alone when she changed the tyre. She had been watched from the shadows and when she had left this had happened.

'I don't always, especially when I'm not expecting to get filthy,' Christie said, defending herself.

'Well, you should. We both should. Wash your hands at once and leave that can well alone. Although I don't suppose there will be any fingerprints on it.'

'Fingerprints? You mean this wasn't a terrible accident? This was done deliberately?'

'None of us could possibly have made such a dreadful mistake. I mean, look at it! So much has been destroyed. More than one canful of liquid was used here. If James, or I, or you, had watered with a chemical, don't you think we should have smelled it? Of course we would, the moment we poured it onto the first pot. Most chemicals make the water look milky. They all smell. There is a possibility that one of us could have made a single mistake, but not gone on to repeat it. This was done deliberately.'

'By the person who smashed the good pots? I never believed it was a fox, you know. They kill chickens, yes, for the fun of it, because chickens are alive and try to run away. A fox might knock a pot over, might even knock over several. Not a whole stand.'

'And I never did buy into the theory that the supplier's computer had gone haywire. So, for now we take a look around, do what we have to do in the greenhouses.'

'Change the lock on the gate?'

On Boxing Day? 'Good thinking. One of the big centres is bound to be open on the ring road,' Harriet said optimistically. 'I'll go immediately, leave you to lock up as usual after you've finished here. Hopefully I can find a stout padlock and install it before it gets dark.'

'Are you telling the police about this?'

'I think that this time we have to. But I will wait for James to decide what to do first.'

'I had a new mobile for Christmas. It takes photos. Should I take some now?'

'Christie, that's a brilliant idea. Just a few, to show the damage. And the watering can. Then at least we have proof of what we found. I'll go now. Talk to you later.'

As she had hoped, Harriet was lucky enough to find a multiple open. She bought the largest, strongest padlock she could find along with a suitable chain. Then she returned to the garden centre and exchanged it for the one they had thought would protect the source of their livelihood. But for how much longer? It was chilling to have to confront a hatred – or fear – of them that could go to such lengths to put them out of business. For she was positive that this was what it was all about.

James was feeding the children at lunchtime. Harriet was sure that ice cream and chocolates would appear during the course of the afternoon. She made a plateful of turkey sandwiches, covered them and put them in the fridge. She placed a bottle of red wine on the table in the sitting room with two glasses, then she settled down with a book.

Ash was bubbling when James brought her home. 'Ace' and 'cool' figured largely in the lengthy description she gave of the performance while Harriet poured a glass of wine for James. But when she produced the turkey sandwiches Ash declined them.

'We had fish and chips on the way home. I couldn't eat a thing.'

'I don't expect you can,' Harriet smiled indulgently. 'But I'm sure James could manage something and I'm hungry.'

'I hope you don't mind that we're later back than expected,' said James. 'Matt insisted that he was starving and even Jess ate a portion of chips.'

'What's on telly?'

'Oh, no. You've had enough stimulation for one day, young lady. I think a nice, long read in bed is the thing, after you've had a bath. Besides, I need to talk to James.' Something in her voice must have given him cause for thought for he raised his eyebrows. Silently she shook her head.

'Oh, all right.' Ash smiled and gave in graciously. There wasn't even any need for Harriet to prompt her, for immediately she turned to James and said, 'Thanks a million for taking me, James. I had ever such a good time. It's the first proper panto I've been to. Night, night.' She bent over and kissed his cheek. Then she gave her mother a hug, yawned and left the room.

'Oh, dear. Have I deprived you of a first? I'm so sorry. You should have said.' James was contrite.

'It's not the first time she's been to the theatre but I've always managed to find something like *The Wind in the Willows*. There'll be other years for us to go to adult pantomimes. Are you sure you won't have another sandwich?'

'They're good, but I won't.' He put his glass on the table and sat back on the sofa, making himself more comfortable. 'Now, what's happened? I can sense that something has. Tell me. Is it Felicity? What has she done?'

'It has nothing to do with Felicity. I—' She had not meant to lose control. She had meant to tell him quietly, discuss what they should do rationally. Instead, Harriet burst into tears.

# CHAPTER TWENTY-SIX

'What on earth is wrong?' James demanded, alarmed by Harriet's obvious distress. 'What's happened?'

She took a deep breath, scrabbled in her pocket for a hankie and blew her nose. 'I'm so sorry. I'd intended to be entirely rational about all this. I've something to tell you.'

'Something I'm not going to like?'

'I'm afraid so.'

Harriet told him what had happened at the garden centre. She spelt it out plainly, omitting nothing, none of the awful destruction. She stressed that she thought it was a vendetta, that quite likely someone was doing his, or her, best to destroy what was becoming formidable opposition. She also told him about her flat tyre, the huge nail that she had found in it, reminding him about his own puncture.

'Are you serious? Are you seriously suggesting that none of this is pure coincidence?'

'Neither Christie nor I believed in the fox theory, you know. And the computer glitch always seemed to me a bit strange. As for the rest?' she shrugged.

'I'm not sure that I believed in the fox theory,' he replied wryly. 'But anything like a vendetta sounded far too outlandish.' Had they, whoever they were, believed the kitten belonged to him? 'And the repeat deliveries, well, that could have happened,' he added defensively. 'So could your flat tyre.'

'The chemical damage? Stewart's warning? I don't think so,'

she said defiantly. 'The destruction of the stock couldn't just have happened, James. We have to go to the police.'

'Yes, I'm very much afraid that we do. But not tonight. They couldn't do anything tonight. We'll wait until morning.' He sighed. 'It's going to take time to come to terms with all this.'

'Do you think I'm crazy, suggesting a vendetta?'

'That's what is so hard to take, the fact that someone, somewhere, could contemplate such actions just to get me out of business. For goodness' sake, there's room enough for more than one garden centre in Cennen Bridge. I must go and see it.' James declared, getting up.

'It's late and we can't do anything. Leave it until tomorrow.'

In the end he calmed down. 'Oh, God. Let's forget about troubles. We'll sort them out. But no more tonight. Harriet, you are wearing my ring.'

*My ring?* Still, she did not pull away. 'Of course I am. It's so pretty,' was all she said, although her voice was soft and warm. She knew he was going to kiss her and she went into his arms willingly. Her lips were warm, wine flavoured, and her body was pliant and welcomed his seeking hands under her cardigan. This time the tension was sexual and she let the feelings envelope her.

It was a long kiss and it told her even more explicitly than the ring had done that spending Christmas Day with his ex-wife had been for the sake of his children and not to please Felicity. Eventually they moved apart. He smoothed her hair and kissed the top of her head.

They gazed into each other's eyes and he ran his hands down her arms, picked up her right hand and brought it to his lips. 'Nice.'

'Very nice,' she agreed, and both knew that they were not talking about the ring on Harriet's finger.

'You'll let me stay? And not only for the comfort it brings to have someone near you in the middle of the night when you are troubled.'

'Please stay.'

The following day Harriet phoned Florence to tell her what had happened and, as she hoped, her friend insisted that Ash should spend the day with her. 'You won't want her around while the police are there and there's no point in subjecting her to anything so distressing as heedless vandalism.'

'Thank you, Flo. You're a star.'

Harriet and James were at the garden centre early. If anything, the destruction looked more comprehensive than when she'd first seen it. The police were non-committal, though appreciative of the offer of copies of the photographs that Christie had taken. They promised to send someone over to dust for fingerprints.

'Leave everything as it is until this afternoon. But it's unlikely there'll be anything of significance. What about your employee. Christie, is that her name? Does she have any reason for wanting your business harmed?'

'Not a chance. We've always got on so well. She couldn't possibly have acted so distressed when she came to see me if she had been involved. Besides, she has a job here. Jobs aren't that easy to find in this business.' Stewart, she was thinking. But no, it was Stewart who had left them. There was no reason to suppose that he had anything to do with all this. 'An employee who decided to leave just before Christmas told me he'd been warned off. He didn't know why. He left, all the same.'

They asked for his details which Harriet gave reluctantly. 'He's a good lad. I'm sure he had nothing to do with this.'

'We'll need to interview him. Let us know if anything like this happens again.'

'Which means they have more pressing matters on their hands,' James said bitterly, as they watched the police car drive away.

'That sounds cynical.'

'And in the meantime we're losing money by remaining closed.'

'Which might be all that the perpetrator wants,' she said reflectively as she watched him walk away from her, outrage in the very set of his back.

In spite of everything, the world turned towards the New Year. James had dinner with Harriet and Ash. He was to be away for a few days and it was all low-key. Harriet began to wonder if he was missing his children.

Of course he must be! Whether he was missing Felicity was another matter altogether. Because James had gone to visit old friends, Harriet was left in charge of the garden centre which fortunately, considering all that had happened recently, was not likely to be busy at this time of the year.

Harriet was invited to a New Year's Eve party at Gareth and Joanne's. Joanne was too busy to talk for long but as Harriet said her goodbyes Joanne hugged her. 'I'm so sorry you're having all this bother at Brownlows. Such rotten luck for you. I do hope you don't lose too much by it. It was always a risky business. Still, I'm sure you're a great comfort to James.'

So she also knew about their relationship. 'We comfort each other.'

'Of course you do. We're happy for you both.'

Harriet and Ash also followed the foxhounds by car and foot on the New Year's Day drag hunt after the meet had gathered outside the village pub for hot toddy and sandwiches.

It was a crisp, sunny day with the ground perfect for hunting, and they found the event exhilarating as they sought a good vantage point and watched twenty or so huntsmen and their pack of hounds jumping two fences and streaming over fields between as they followed a scent laid some twenty minutes earlier.

Vicky Heard had suggested that they might be interested. 'Robin's taking out his hunter,' she had told Harriet, when they met outside the church on Christmas Day. 'He says this is probably the last time as he's having to sell the horse. He used to talk of the time when the twins could ride with him but that wouldn't be for years, anyway. When you're drag hunting, you have to be able to handle cross-country jumping properly, for the fences can often be four feet high and you also need to be able to maintain a gallop all the time, which is pretty strenuous unless you are an experienced rider.'

'Think you'd like to do that some day?' Harriet asked Ash, as they waited until some young riders had passed by on their way to the next line.

'I'd like to ride. I think I'd be scared riding to hounds, though. Jess and Matt both ride.'

'We'll think about riding lessons for you in the spring.'

'Look, there they go again!'

Harriet and Ash arrived home as James was unloading his car.

'James! You're back. We've just been to watch the hunt. It was ever so exciting.'

Ash hurled herself into the man's arms and hugged him. He hugged her back. Harriet was touched. She couldn't remember ever seeing Ash so demonstrably happy at seeing Paul, while she knew that her daughter's memories of her father were of a shadowy man who, although she had been assured time and time again that he had loved her to bits, were tempered by the fact he was not there.

Then James released his hold on Ash and walked over to where Harriet was standing. He took her into his arms and, in front of Ash, he kissed her lingeringly.

'You're back earlier than you said you would be,' murmured Harriet, snuggling her face into his shoulder.

'I didn't want to outstay my welcome. If you'd been there it might have been different but after one day I knew where I'd prefer to be.'

At that moment Harriet became aware that in the background there was the sound of horses' hoofs striking the metalled road. She lifted her head and there, over James's shoulder, she met

Jessica's shocked gaze. The girl kicked her pony's sides, the animal skittering as though protesting at unfair treatment, then they trotted off smartly.

'That was Jess and a friend. Do you think she saw you two kissing?' asked Ash unnecessarily.

'I suppose so,' said James easily. 'Never mind, eh?' Then, as if to make it evident that he had meant to kiss Harriet the first time, he kissed her again.

'Wow,' said Ash, impressed. 'You look as though you enjoyed that more than when Felicity kissed you.'

'Ash! Teatime,' said Harriet weakly, when she had managed to extricate herself from James's arms. 'Come and have a cup of tea.'

Later that evening, after they had all eaten in Sycamore Cottage, Harriet asked James, 'Did you mind that Jess saw us this afternoon?'

'Given a choice, I suppose I would have preferred her to have known about us before she saw the evidence with her own eyes, but no, I am perfectly happy that she, and everyone else, should know that there is a marvellous woman in my life.'

'Am I in your life?'

'Most definitely,' he declared. 'That is,' he added anxiously, 'provided that you want to be in it. Do you?'

'I am very happy to be so, James. But I think that this is very new and that I want to take things slowly. I don't need to tell you that I'm a bit of a disaster area when it comes to men. I wouldn't want you to become one of my mistakes.'

'Neither would I,' he declared. 'I do think, though, that it'll be fun persuading you that I'm a good prospect and not a mistake, as you so elegantly put it.'

Harriet giggled and, because Ash was upstairs, he kissed her again.

Nevertheless, she was sufficiently a pessimist to dread that inevitably there would be a reckoning.

# CHAPTER TWENTY-SEVEN

Although James had previously decided not to tell Harriet about the state in which he had found Mash, the kitten, after the chemical vandalism he decided that he had no option. 'It had to be deliberate,' he told her soberly. 'At the time I thought that, just maybe, whoever had run him over had thrown him in a ditch and then had second thoughts. Now I'm not so sure.'

'You think that Mash was targeted because he belonged to us?'

'Or because they thought he belonged to me,' he interjected.

'James, that's a frightening suggestion.'

'Don't look so stricken, my love.' He was filled with compunction and furious with himself for hurting her so. 'You see now why I buried him before I told you and Ash. I couldn't let her see the state he was in. I would never have told you, only—'

'There have been too many unexplained events.'

'It's probably coincidence, but I do think that we all have to be careful, about locking up, taking note of strangers, peculiar incidents. At least until we discover who is behind this, and for what reason.'

A week later Harriet was just going out of the supermarket when she met Felicity at the door.

'Ah. The marriage breaker,' Felicity said scathingly. Her cut-glass accent was piercingly clear.

The woman who was at the head of the nearest checkout queue turned to the woman behind her, whom she apparently knew, and the two of them gazed avidly at what was turning into an altercation.

This was what Harriet had been expecting, and it was just as awful as she had imagined. But she had vowed that she was not going to continue to consider herself as one of life's victims. She could not permit Felicity to have the last word.

'I'd rather not have a row in such a public place,' she said, as evenly as she was able. Deliberately she pushed past Felicity and started to walk smartly towards her car.

'I'm sure you don't want the world to know.' Felicity followed Harriet out of the building and into the car park. 'How dare you kiss my husband in public,' she screamed – like a fishwife, thought Harriet, the humour of it giving her a boost of self-confidence. Felicity caught up with her by her car.

'Jess told you. If you want the absolute truth, it was James who kissed me. Admittedly I did kiss him back,' Harriet said candidly, and instantly wished that she had kept that morsel of information to herself. She put down her shopping bag and shoved her hand into the pocket of her coat to find her keys.

'That's not how Jess saw it.' Where Harriet was pink from embarrassment, Felicity was white with fury, her eyes flashing.

'It was very nice, being kissed by James.' Again Harriet permitted her foolish side to utter the words best kept unsaid. What was she thinking about? she thought, appalled by her behaviour. She shouldn't be goading the woman. Although it was true, it was not a tactful admission and Felicity looked as though she might attack her.

'You deliberately flaunted yourself in front of his daughter. You cow! How dare you try to steal another woman's husband.'

'I didn't know that Jess was there. But as for stealing another woman's husband, you've forgotten that you are divorced. You are no longer James's wife. He is a free man, was a free man long before I ever met him. You are both free. And there is nothing to stop me from falling in love with him.' Harriet caught her breath.

She had never envisaged making such a declaration, certainly not to James's former wife.

'Husband stealer.' Yet Harriet's declaration appeared to have shaken Felicity for, although she spat the epithet, her voice was suddenly uncertain. 'Of course James is free to have some fun on the side,' she said then, 'but I am the one he loves and very soon we shall get back together. You won't be so smug then, will you!'

Fun on the side. Was that all...? 'Oh, go away, Felicity. Your marriage was over long before I came on to the scene. For your sake I regret it, but for my own.... Whatever you think, it is all very new and who knows where it will end? In the meantime, I would prefer it if you did not attack me like a fishwife whenever you see me, because I am not going away.'

With that she turned her back on the woman, opened the boot of her car and put her shopping into it. It took considerable nerve, for Harriet was expecting … what? More invective, a blow? When she looked round, Felicity had gone. Harriet sat in the front seat for a couple of minutes, trembling with reaction.

Then she realized that this was the very first time in her life that she had not been the victim who had slunk away. It felt good. It was definitely empowering. She started the engine and manoeuvred the car out of the large car park and drove home. At that moment she did not care whether James remained her lover – or became something more significant. She was no longer one of life's victims.

As they all suspected, time went by and there were no tangible results from the police inquiry. This time the insurance company paid out and James pointed out gloomily that their premiums would be astronomical when they had to be renewed.

They had done better over their Christmas promotions than they had anticipated. Joanne Ormston was one of many who had come into the garden centre to buy pots of the newly acquired bulbs. 'My aunt loves hyacinths and these look really healthy.'

Harriet and Joanne tried to meet once a week, to have a quick lunch or a coffee. The gallery owner was knowledgeable about modern art and Harriet was beginning to appreciate trends that previously she had not understood. She was aware, though, that Joanne's stock was not moving as fast as she would have wished.

Brownlows now had pots of early white snowdrops that were coming into bloom and the early narcissi were also beginning to show their colour. They had chosen *Grand Soleil d'Or* especially as it had rich, golden petals and a tangerine trumpet with several flowers to a stem, and they had also managed to find more *Minnow* which had clusters of four rounded flowers in a creamy yellow with lemon trumpets. They were Harriet's choice because both these had a very sweet perfume.

'I've noticed that you always insist on fragrance,' said James. 'Personally I don't see its importance.'

'Do you really not have a good sense of smell?' she asked curiously.

'I've never given it a thought. But since I've come into this business, I've noticed that you're not the only woman to comment on smell. Some of them even mentioned the smell of our Christmas trees as they walked round the display.'

'There you are, then. It's a woman thing.'

With tiny conifers to give added substance and moss for the greenery, the bowls they were selling promised a splash of cheerful spring colour in the darkness of winter.

Outside, they displayed prominently pots of evergreens which now made a stately display with their varied coloured needles, and they interspersed these with the hardy varieties of daffodils that they hoped would tempt their customers for the following year. Now was the time for them to overhaul the greenhouses where they would do what propagating they would have the time for in the spring, having already decided that they would have to import most of their new stock. Except for the new glasshouse, there were also several panes of glass that needed replacing, these having been damaged in a January storm, and the woodwork required a lick of paint.

They had instructed an architect to draw up plans for a building that would be their new entrance and he had recommended a local builder. This was to be where they might display their new lines – garden furniture and indoor ornaments that would appeal to their customers. There was also to be a light, airy coffee shop, with the inevitable loos.

'That'll please the local punters,' said James.

Sometimes, as Harriet was drifting off to sleep, she wondered what the local opposition was really thinking about all these improvements that they were making. Could the vendetta be at an end? Ash had been miserable for weeks over the death of her pet but Mish, homebody that she was, was also missing Mash and the two of them were managing to find consolation in each other. Harriet did so hope that this really was to be the end of it all.

'I'd like us to sell as much local produce as we can get hold of,' said James, as they watched the foundations of their new buildings rise. 'Honey, cheeses and so on. As soon as our new building is up and running.'

'It's a splendid idea. I'll do some research and we might even persuade some local concerns to support us right from the start,' agreed Harriet enthusiastically.

Both Harriet and James had poured over catalogues as they decided what garden implements, seeds and bedding plants and herbaceous plants they would stock in the spring.

'We should also think about new pots and garden ornaments.'

'Not gnomes!'

'Not this year,' James concurred. 'Just a few bird baths and perhaps some small fountains? So long as you don't decide to pull out. You wouldn't, would you?' he asked, for the first time in weeks sounding apprehensive.

'Certainly not. I'm having far too much fun.'

*

It was late afternoon; a grey, overcast day it had been and Harriet was looking forward to a good fire and the sustaining casserole that she had left all day in a very low oven. Ash had made a another new friend in the village, a girl called Suzie, and often both girls went home to Suzie's house to start their homework. Harriet accepted that on dark winter afternoons Ash found the cottage dreary, so when it was not convenient for Suzie's mother to have her, Florence did. That day Ash was going to Suzie's house from where she would make the short walk home as soon as her mother, coming from the opposite direction, phoned her to say that she was home.

For once, James was also arriving home at the same time as Harriet. They both parked their cars, then approached each other, James bending to kiss her when they met, his hands on her shoulders drawing her close, as though they had not been working together all day.

When they broke apart, Harriet's nose wrinkled and she sniffed. There was a strong smell of smoke.

'Have you been having a bonfire?' she asked. 'I do so love the smell of bonfire smoke.'

'Certainly not,' declared James. 'After your lecture I recycle, take green stuff to Brownlows and other rubbish to the tip,' he added righteously. 'I can't smell anything.'

'I haven't had a bonfire, either,' said Harriet. She glanced towards her cottage. From where she was standing she could see right into the sitting room. The curtains were open and through the window she became aware of a flickering light.

'Fire!' They both exclaimed together and immediately ran towards Sycamore Cottage.

## CHAPTER TWENTY-EIGHT

As she got nearer the cottage this, Harriet realized, was no bonfire smoke that she was smelling. It was more acrid, catching the back of her throat. Curls of black smoke were coming from the open chimney but from where they stood the flames seemed to be concentrated in the kitchen. 'The cottage is on fire! What do we do?' she screamed.

'Where is Ash?' James demanded. 'Has she come home?'

Harriet's instinct was to run into the house and search every room for her daughter. She moved towards the front door but James held her back. 'Leave me be!' she yelled at him. 'I have to find Ash.'

'Of course you do but the last thing you should do is to go into the house until you know that she is there,' he panted, wrestling with her frantic struggles. 'The draught from the door will fan the fire.'

Common sense agreed with him. She went limp and he let her go. 'I'll phone Suzie while you call the fire brigade.'

'Ash left half an hour ago,' said Suzie. 'I told her it was too early.'

James was already giving crisp, urgent details to the fire brigade. 'No, we don't know if anyone is inside.'

'Ash, where are you?' Harriet was becoming distraught having discovered that, no, Ash had not gone to see Florence. As she spoke her eye was caught by a movement at Ash's bedroom window. 'Oh, my God! It's Ash. She's upstairs.'

'Stay where you are, Harriet!'

James's voice stopped her in her tracks. 'Ash ...' she moaned.

'I need a wet towel. Stay exactly where you are,' commanded James, running to his own cottage.

'Bring a fire extinguisher,' Harriet yelled after him.

'I don't have one,' he called back tersely. He emerged almost immediately with a dripping towel round his head then, calling Ash's name loudly, he opened the door. Almost immediately, as he had warned, there was a *whoosh*. Flames engulfed the doorway into the kitchen and began licking at the sitting room wall.

There were agonizing moments of waiting. Harriet heard herself uttering a monotonous chant, 'Ash, Ash, James, James, Ash, Ash.'

She heard what sounded like the miraculous note of salvation, the blaring klaxon of a fire engine's siren. Then flashing blue lights appeared. 'Thank God!' she breathed, and ran towards the first appliance.

'Is there anyone inside?' the senior fire officer asked.

'My daughter is in her bedroom,' she shrieked. 'James, the man from next door, has gone inside to bring her out.'

Hoses from the appliances were already being laid out efficiently, and a ladder was positioned to give access to Ash's bedroom. Then James staggered from the cottage with a bundle in his arms. Two of the firefighters ran towards the door. James had taken no more than three steps when he began to collapse, caught by the firefighters, one of whom relieved him of his burden while the other guided him away from the cottage.

Harriet ran forward. 'Ash,' she cried, her voice trembling.

The bundle stirred. 'Mum?'

'She's alive. Thank God,' murmured Harriet, sinking to her knees and taking her daughter into her arms. Ash coughed weakly. 'Are you all right? Are you burned?'

One of the firefighters pulled her away. 'Let me see,' he urged, kneeling on the ground by the girl, but it was immediately apparent that Ash had not been harmed.

Harriet scrambled to her feet and ran towards James who was now lying on the ground, wrapped in an emergency blanket. She knelt beside him.

'So there you are,' said James weakly. 'At least you had the sense not to follow me into the cottage.'

'Oh, James. You are so brave,' said Ash, her voice full of admiration. She was wrapped in another emergency blanket which trailed behind her as she came to stand by James and her mother. Miraculously she was cuddling her kitten. 'Mish must have been outside all the time.'

'Such a relief,' agreed Harriet fervently. She knew how devastated Ash would have been if anything had happened to Mish.

'James ran upstairs and grabbed a blanket and totally covered me in it. It was ever so scary when I saw the fire. I didn't know what to do. Then I remembered you saying it was safest on the floor by a window. So I stayed there.'

'You could have been killed,' agreed Harriet fervently. 'Why didn't you get out when the smoke alarm went off?'

'I didn't hear it.'

'You could both have been killed.' The enormity of that fact was a revelation. Then, without warning, Harriet burst into a flood of tears.

'I can't get at my hankie,' James said. 'If I could, I'd give it to you. Don't cry, darling Harriet. I am all right, you know.'

'I've got one of my own. It doesn't matter. Nothing matters now that you are both safe.' She took his hand and he winced. 'You're hurt,' she exclaimed.

'Just a small burn,' he told them, so Harriet held his arm instead.

The three of them continued to sit on the ground in silence, trembling from the reaction, hardly feeling the cold as it seeped into their bones. The men, knowing that now there was no one who needed rescuing, were concentrating on ensuring that the flames did not spread to the cottage next door. As water played on the roofs, a choking smoke drifted towards them.

'James's cottage is going to be in a bit of a mess,' observed Ash, unnecessarily. 'I bet that water goes down the chimney.'

'Oh, my God, James. I am so sorry. What will you do?'

'I doubt if there will be much actual damage, except what is left of the smell,' he said, attempting cheerfulness.

'Mum! Our kitchen roof is falling in,' said Ash. 'We won't have anything left, will we?'

It was indescribably dreadful. It might only have been a rented property but everything of value that she had salvaged from the time she had lived with Paul was in that cottage. Harriet's mind flicked over the possessions that they could be losing: clothes, jewellery, books, papers, photographs....

'Don't worry, Ash,' said James, attempting to comfort her. 'It can all be replaced, you know.'

'Mick can't,' the girl said, in a small voice.

'Mick?'

'Her bear,' said Harriet briefly. 'Elderly, but much loved. But do you know the worst thing? It's the irreplaceable photos.'

'Don't you have anything on disk?'

'Yes, but the disks are in a bookcase.' There did not seem much to add, after that.

An ambulance drew up. James insisted that he was fine, but the paramedic who attended advised that he should be checked at A&E. 'Smoke inhalation,' he told Harriet briefly. 'Your daughter, too. Let's get you both in the ambulance.'

'I'll follow in my car,' said Harriet. 'In you get, Ash. You must look after James and I'll see you in a bit.'

But before she was able to leave, the firefighter in charge wanted to know if Harriet had any idea how the fire could have started.

'I did leave a casserole in the oven,' she admitted, 'but it was only on at 110 degrees.'

'Old appliance, madam?'

'Reconditioned, I think, but it came with the cottage.'

'We'll need to investigate, for insurance purposes. Obviously we can't do that tonight. We'll leave the site secure and no one must enter until we have declared both cottages safe. Understand?'

'I doubt if there's much to be salvaged in Sycamore,' Harriet grimaced.

'You'd be surprised, madam. Anything solid, in a cupboard, for example, should have survived. Did you have papers in a firebox?' Harriet shook her head. 'Pity, that.'

'Are we able to go next door? James – Mr Ormston will want to go home. Tomorrow definitely, even if they keep him in tonight.'

'We'll need to check everything tomorrow, madam,' he said tactfully. 'Be in touch with the station before you try to do anything.'

'Thanks for coming so quickly,' she said tremulously.

'All in the day's work.'

Harriet picked up her bag and fumbled inside it for her car keys. As she opened the car door she was aware of a figure standing opposite. An interested bystander, a nosey local, she thought scornfully. He – or she – might have come forward to offer some assistance. Even if it were only to offer a cup of tea for the firefighters. Then she laughed at herself, fighting hysteria. That had been the whole point of renting Sycamore Cottage. It had no neighbours. Except for James. Who was now in hospital.

First of all, though, she needed to phone Florence. 'You must be getting so tired of me, Flo. Here I am, yet again, asking for shelter.'

'No problem,' insisted Florence. 'I'll see you just as soon as you have made sure that they are both fine.'

'Um … Do you think that I should get in touch with Felicity?'

'Mm …' Florence's hesitation echoed Harriet's.

'Damned if I do.'

'Damned if you don't. I suppose you could wait until you

know exactly how he is. I mean, if they are going to keep him in tonight, perhaps you should let Jessica know. If they discharge him, it's entirely up to James, isn't it?'

'As always, what would I do without you?' replied Harriet.

Ash was checked over and it was established quickly that she was not hurt in the least. 'I doubt if there is any smoke inhalation damage, either, because she says that her head was covered, so she can be discharged. Take her to your own doctor tomorrow if you are in any way worried,' Harriet was told.

It appeared that James's burn was superficial. 'I was an idiot and caught hold of a metal door handle with my bare hand. My hand should heal quickly, though I should have known better. I'm just being kept under observation for twenty-four hours for smoke inhalation.' He coughed. 'If you see what I mean.'

'Then stop talking,' Harriet said sternly. 'I'll ring in the morning to see how you are and either come and fetch you, or come and see you. If that's all right? I'm sorry I couldn't bring you your own pyjamas. Those hospital gowns are so ghastly but they wouldn't permit me to go anywhere near either cottage. Said they'd got to do an investigation for insurance. I'll never, ever leave a casserole in the oven again while I'm out,' she declared.

'Don't make rash promises,' he grinned. 'It might have been faulty wiring. And I shall buy a fire extinguisher as soon as I get out of here. Now, what I could do with is a goodnight kiss,' he said, suppressing another cough.

Harriet put her head on one side and waited, one eyebrow raised. She handed him a wipe, then she bent forward and kissed him gently on the mouth. 'I'll see you tomorrow.'

On her way out of the ward, she collected Ash who had been talking to one of the nurses. 'Just wait by the door, love. I'll be with you in a minute.' The charge nurse was by the desk. 'I'm probably worrying unnecessarily, but I think you ought to know that Mr Ormston has been in Afghanistan. He's been seeing someone for PTSD. I don't suppose—'

'I'll make a note,' the man said. 'Thanks for mentioning it. I doubt if Mr Ormston would have done.'

'I'm sure he would not,' agreed Harriet. 'Goodnight.'

# CHAPTER TWENTY-NINE

Florence was waiting for them with eggs ready to scramble and bacon already sizzling on the stove, the fragrance of which greeted them as they entered her cottage, making Harriet's stomach rumble.

'It'll be ready in five minutes. You've just got time to have a glass of wine and wash. You too, Ash. Without the wine. I've a can of Coke for you. I don't suppose your mum will mind too much, for once. Will you?' she nodded in Harriet's direction, as she passed a can to Ash and a glass of red wine to her friend.

'Not in the least. This is good,' Harriet said fervently. 'I'm exhausted.'

'You two are going to have to share my spare double bed again, I'm afraid, but it's made up and the electric blanket is getting it cosy.'

'What would we do without you?'

'I'm sure there would be other offers of help,' answered her friend. 'but before you say anything more, just remember that my life would be a lot more boring without your small dramas.'

'Small dramas be damned,' said Harriet. 'I think we've lost everything.'

'I expect they told you it might not be as bad as it seems? Just wait until morning and you find out for definite before you succumb to melancholia. What are you doing about Felicity?'

'I'll ring Jess. James has a burn on one hand and a bit of a cough. From the smoke, I imagine, but otherwise he seems fine.'

It was Jess who answered the phone. 'So they're keeping your father in for observation,' Harriet concluded. Jess, shocked, asked questions about the fire – how fierce was it, how long had it been before the firefighters put it out, did the roof really cave in completely? Of course she'd tell her mother.

'But you won't be allowed to see him tonight, Jess,' Harriet broke in, for this was all too painful to dwell on and the girl seemed to be relishing the gory details. 'I'll ring you in the morning.'

'And that will greatly endear you to Felicity,' commented Florence, 'refusing to speak to her at all. Not that I blame you in the least.'

'I'm sure Jess will remember everything I said.'

Over the meal they discussed what had to be done in the morning. 'I can lend you some clothes, Hari, but I've little that Ash could have. Give me your things before you get into bed and I'll put them in the washing machine. At least we can get rid of the reek of smoke from them.'

'After we've eaten I'll have to phone the estate agent. Heaven knows whose insurance pays out on a thing like this. We'll have to go shopping, Ash. You'll need a day off school to do that.'

'Great!' Ash yawned.

'Go to bed, love. I'll try not to disturb you when I come up.'

'By the looks of her she'll be dead to the world. And that was insensitive. When I think what might have happened.' Florence shook her head as Harriet shuddered.

'That wretched casserole.'

'You don't actually know that it was your fault, do you? After all, if everyone thought that way, no one would ever leave anything quietly simmering for an evening meal.'

'I suppose not, but what else could it have been?'

First thing in the morning, Harriet phoned Christie and told her what had happened. 'I'm sorry to be such a nuisance, but I'm not sure how much you can rely on either of us for the next few days. Do you know anyone who could give us emergency help?'

'I have a couple of friends who came back from an extended trip to Australia only last week,' she replied. 'They were looking for temporary work. I'll ring them straight away.'

'Even if they are still available, I don't suppose either of them would have any experience in gardening,' said Harriet wistfully.

'That's where you're wrong,' Christie replied triumphantly. 'One of them trained as a plantswoman and both of them worked in a garden centre in Melbourne to help with their finances.'

'How fantastic. If they're good we might even use them again. See what you can do to talk them into coming to see me.'

Having ascertained that James had slept well but that he had yet to be examined by a doctor and also that she would not have the results from the fire service that morning, Harriet left Ash with Florence and drove to the hospital. She arrived to discover that Felicity was pacing the corridor outside the ward. 'They won't let me in. He won't see me.'

'Are you surprised? I imagine he is tired of your histrionics. That is precisely why I spoke to Jess and not to you last night. But I won't have another row with you. Just be thankful that James is alive. He could have been killed in that awful fire.'

'They are saying that it was all your fault. You caused it, leaving the stove on. Such a tragedy.' There was a strange glitter in Felicity's eyes and a smile almost of triumph on her face that seemed to contradict her words of sympathy.

'It was a very low oven. And nothing has yet been proved,' insisted Harriet. It was not Felicity's words, it was her attitude. As though she was glad that it had happened. As though.... 'I'm expected,' she said firmly and pushed open the door.

'They won't let me leave until tomorrow,' said James, after he had pulled Harriet down to his embrace.

'How is your cough? Did you sleep well?'

'Not very, but the cough is a little better.'

'Take your stay here as respite care. You can't get into the cottage yet. The firemen are still investigating the cause of the fire. James, Felicity is outside—'

'I won't see her. She'll demand that I go and stay with her and I really could not do that.'

'Florence hasn't any more room.'

'And I certainly can't oust Ash from your bed. Unfortunately. I've already phoned the local pub. They can put me up until I am allowed back into Oak Cottage.'

She would have liked nothing better than to be able to stay with him. 'I need to go. I have all sorts of people to see. You can't begin to imagine.'

'Thank goodness, no. Take care. Don't overdo things.'

'How did you really sleep?'

'Not a flashback to be experienced,' he replied cheerfully. 'Nor will there be.'

'I'm glad. Only—'

'How can I be so sure? It's all right. I've worked it out. It's simple, really. You see, in Lashkar Gah there were casualties. I was the senior officer. That meant that I was the one who was responsible for two deaths. Last night there were no casualties. So why should I worry about a thing?' He grinned at her, and tried unsuccessfully to suppress another cough.

'Moreover, you were the hero of the hour, saving Ash's life,' she said fondly. 'Yes, you did save her life. If you hadn't gone into the cottage, Ash could have been suffocated, if not burnt to death.' She shuddered. 'When I think what might have happened.'

'Don't think about it,' he said forcibly. 'It didn't happen, and the fire brigade was there so quickly they would have rescued her. Don't forget that they were clad for the event, and experienced.'

'Which makes your rescue all the more fantastic.'

'Such praise,' he teased her. 'Carry on, I'm loving this.'

Her eyes narrowed and she looked at him closely. Apart from the cough, that she supposed was not too worrying, he seemed

179

more relaxed than she had ever known him. Perhaps James was right and that, at last, the PTSD would no longer trouble him. 'But you are still feeling the effects of the smoke, so I'm sure that you should be resting. I'll see you later.' She bent and kissed him again.

Felicity had gone by the time Harriet left the ward. There was to be no more hounding of James, then.

Next she went to the bank to ensure that funds were available to replace the essential things that she and Ash would need. Insurance would probably cover what she had to pay out, but it would all take time to resolve. Insurance again, she thought resignedly. Would there be anyone prepared to take her on in the future?

Then she went to see Matthew John. He began by commiserating formally. He was less than forthcoming when she then asked about another rental. 'I am so sorry, Mrs Finamore, but I have nothing on my books at present that would suit you and your daughter.'

'Nothing?' She recalled the choices that he had presented her with not so very long ago. Her chin lifted defiantly. 'You believe that the fire was my fault?'

'The wiring was not faulty. I had an electrician go through the place and check it thoroughly before you moved in. There were smoke detectors and a fire extinguisher. Your young daughter should not have been there on her own.'

'Ash usually stays with a friend,' Harriet said tightly. 'I do not believe that an oven – even a reconditioned one – could be responsible for that fire. Not at the temperature I was using it.'

'Nevertheless, I regret that I have nothing to offer you. At present. Of course I will keep in touch. The owners will, naturally, need to know your exact position as far as the insurance cover is concerned.'

'Mr John.' Harriet nodded curtly and left his premises.

Joanne rang, full of sympathy. 'I'd love to offer you a home.'

'But you haven't yet done up the attic rooms. Thanks, but don't worry. I'm sure I can sort out another rental.' She crossed her fingers for luck.

'So awful, losing everything. I can't imagine.'

'It might not be as bad as I feared,' she said cautiously.

'I do hope not. You must let me help as much as I can.'

People were so kind. All the same, a niggling feeling that she was missing something persisted.

There was a message from the fire station on her mobile. She was required to attend the police station in Cennen Bridge that afternoon. She was to let them know if this was convenient.

Present at that meeting was the station officer from the local fire station and the DI whom she had met before. They greeted her warmly, offering her tea or coffee.

'Mrs Finamore, the fire would appear to be arson,' the station officer told her, without a preamble.

'Arson! Are you sure? It wasn't my fault? The oven—'

'The integral smoke detectors were dismantled. There was petrol just inside the back door. The back door was unlocked.'

'I would never disarm a smoke detector and I always make sure the back door is locked.'

'We believe you. Where do you keep the key?'

'I keep it in the lock.'

'Unwise. It's not that difficult to get the key out of a lock. Even a child could do it. It's best to leave a key several feet away from the door. And out of sight.'

Then the fact of petrol hit her. 'So it wasn't the oven.'

'No, Mrs Finamore. It was definitely arson. Now all that we have to discover is the identity of the arsonist.'

# CHAPTER THIRTY

The detective inspector asked her if she had enemies. At first Harriet denied categorically that she knew anyone at all who would wish her harm. The very word was pejorative. An enemy implied dislike bordering on hatred. She faltered. The station officer persisted. 'Is there anyone in Cennen Bridge who wishes you harm?'

Harriet took a deep breath and reminded them of the recent events at Brownlows.

'I should have made the connection,' the inspector replied ruefully. 'I think I'd better talk to my colleagues. But, let me get this straight. You have a financial interest in Brownlows?'

'I have. I've put in an injection of capital. Once the sale of my house was finalized a proper partnership agreement was drawn up.'

'Even though you have had these problems?' The station officer made it sound as though her financial acumen was not particularly acute.

'James thought the problems were circumstantial,' she tried not to sound defensive.

'And now you aren't sure?'

He was quick to pick up on her suspicions, she noticed. 'I had a few doubts. When chemicals were used to destroy the potted plants I was sure it was vandalism. It was then that James agreed with me. Which was why we went to the police.'

'And now we have a fire at your cottage. So, do you have enemies, Mrs Finamore?' the inspector repeated.

Felicity Ormston. Reluctantly she mentioned James's wife. 'But Felicity wouldn't – couldn't – set fire to my cottage. The fire might have spread to James's cottage. What would be the point of destroying that and everything he possessed if she wanted to rekindle their relationship?'

'It would make him more dependent on her. Why did you choose to come to Cennen Bridge, Mrs Finamore?'

Harriet went cold. 'To get away from an abusive relationship.'

The men looked at each other. 'Would you care to elaborate?'

Reluctantly Harriet described the abusive relationship with Paul that had blighted her recent years. She was also forced to admit that there had been another incident of violence, foiled by James Ormston's providential appearance. That James had subsequently gone with her to Paul's house to fetch her belongings.

'Many of which are now destroyed,' pointed out the inspector.

'But Paul could not, would not, be so vindictive.' Even after all the episodes of violence she could not believe that she had lived with a man who was capable of setting fire to her home. Not only that, but of endangering the life of a child for whom he professed to care.

'And is there no one else?'

Two was more than enough, she thought resentfully. 'Of course not,' she declared.

They thanked her politely and each man said that he would be in touch if there were developments. She was free to make arrangements to visit Sycamore Cottage to see what might be salvaged. James was free to return to his property when he was discharged from hospital.

It was as she drove back to Florence's cottage that Harriet had her own flashback. She remembered the day of the drag hunt when James returned home unexpectedly. Jess had ridden by to see her father embracing her. She distinctly remembered how uncomfortable she had felt to be discovered in his arms by his daughter. More to the point, she recalled the look of venom that had crossed Jess's face.

Was it possible that a fourteen-year-old could be so consumed by hatred that she was capable of obtaining a can of petrol then pouring it over a door to set fire to someone's home, regardless of the damage done? James's daughter? On the other hand, the back door had been locked. She was sure of that. Felicity might have had the ability to get the key out of the lock. Paul certainly would. But Jess? Yet the police had said a child could do that.

Harriet thought that she might have to mention her misgivings to the police, but not until she had slept on it. Even imagining that Felicity was sufficiently vindictive to relish this misfortune was one thing. To accuse James's daughter of such a crime would put paid to their relationship forever, irrevocably damaging James's feelings for her that were new enough to be fragile.

It was a total mess.

Yet, it had been arson, not an unfortunate fire. It had not been the oven that had caused such damage. She could cook as many casseroles as she wished, she thought, attempting wry humour. When she had a kitchen again.

But, arson? Felicity, or Paul? Or Jessica? Could you really so hate a person that you did more than wish them dead?

The next few days passed in a blur. To Harriet's relief Christie had been able to arrange for Julie and Isobel, the friends who had been travelling together, to help in the garden centre for the couple of weeks that Harriet was taking off to sort out the aftermath of the fire.

'They are real assets,' James commented after he had seen them at work. 'I'll be sorry when we have to let them go.'

'We might rethink staffing for the next few months, then?' replied Harriet. It was all very well, having grand plans for expansion, but without good staff she was well aware that they could not hope to compete with other garden centres in the vicinity.

Fortunately, although Sycamore Cottage was damaged, it was

the extension – kitchen with a bathroom over it – that had been demolished when the roof caved in. The remainder of the cottage was relatively unharmed. There was a cupboard in the sitting room that had completely survived the fire and although a sideboard had been scorched, its contents were still intact. Two of Harriet's pictures were too badly damaged to be restored but the contents of a glass-fronted bookcase had also survived not only the fire but the water the firefighters had used to douse the flames in the kitchen extension. Upstairs it was mainly smoke damage, so that clothes in wardrobes that could be washed or dry cleaned would be wearable, while possessions in chests were essentially unharmed.

So far as James's cottage was concerned, there was also less damage than they had feared at first, and that was mainly confined to a part of the roof that abutted Sycamore Cottage's kitchen extension. A tarpaulin was thrown over it and builders were booked to replace some tiles. A firm of local house cleaners was engaged to wash walls, clean carpets and generally eradicate the smoke damage, and, within a short time, the cottage was habitable again.

The problem of who had started the fire in the first place remained to be solved.

During an interview with a woman detective constable, Harriet had mentioned the figure she had seen watching the fire at a distance. 'At the time I thought he, or she, was an inquisitive bystander. And, after all, I suppose you wouldn't necessarily want to advertise your presence in case you were thought to be ghoulish.'

'Particularly if you had started the fire in the first place.'

'That's what I am wondering now,' Harriet admitted. 'The figure I saw was fairly tall, wearing trousers, and a heavy jacket – which was why I didn't know if it was a man or a woman.' Did that rule out Felicity? 'Felicity Ormston wears jeans.' But then, so did Jess and she was almost as tall as her mother.

'Was this person wearing a hoodie?'

'Probably, because their head was certainly covered, but I can't see Felicity even trying on a hoodie.'

'It was a mild night. A bystander, unless it was a hoodie, would have been unlikely to have been wearing anything on his head. After what you told us about his behaviour, Paul Marsh was the prime suspect. But he has an alibi. A Mrs Mona Cooper, who lives with him, says he was with her. Felicity Ormston was at home.'

She remembered the woman's voice she had heard when she had been persuaded to phone Paul after Ash went missing. This woman was actually living with Paul. As she had thought, it meant there should be no more hassle from him, no more letters demanding money to which he was not entitled. It was an enormous relief. 'So who was it?'

'We are hoping that the results of forensic tests will help there.'

There was an almost inconceivable problem. If James hadn't already guessed the difficulty, how did Harriet tell the man she had fallen in love with that his wife was suspected of arson? She had told him as soon as she was informed that it had not been her oven that caused the fire.

'Such a relief,' she ended fervently.

'But arson is appalling to contemplate.'

'It is, if it's personal. It could have been a total stranger, though.' In the night when she woke up, which she was doing frequently, she lay rigid, wondering if the rustle she thought she could hear was leaves in the tree outside Florence's spare bedroom window, or something more sinister. Then she told herself firmly that there was no one out there with feelings of vindictiveness towards her. She had been in the wrong place at the wrong time.

That was all. The rest was imagination.

Matthew John might have had his misgivings about renting a property to Harriet and her daughter, but a furnished property in the centre of Cennen Bridge unexpectedly became vacant through another agent and Harriet snapped it up. James seemed a little put out when she told him, enthusing about her luck. 'Two bedrooms and a modern kitchen and bathroom. The rent is a little more than Sycamore Cottage, but it's well worth it.'

'Good.'

'Oh, James. You don't sound very enthusiastic. Why? You know that we can't possibly live in Sycamore Cottage without a kitchen, even if Matthew John were prepared to continue the rental.'

'I had thought that maybe … well, you know.'

'No, not really. Tell me.'

'I had wondered if you and Ash might come and live with me.'

'You never said. It never occurred to me.' Of course it hadn't. James had never told her that he loved her. If actions were supposed to speak louder than words she could very well persuade herself that he did love her. Yet he had not told her so, not spoken the words aloud. Her feelings towards him were intense but still there was his family in the background and the fear that if James was seen to be too close to her she could be putting Ash in danger.

'I'd like it very much, if you did both come to live with me.'

She thought for a moment. Then she put her arms round him. 'I'd like it very much, too. But it wouldn't do. Not at all.'

'Why do you say that?'

'We couldn't possibly come and live with you until the matter of the arsonist is sorted.'

'Because one of the likely suspects is Felicity.' He said it bluntly, looking her straight in the eye as he spoke.

There. After all, it was out in the open.

# CHAPTER THIRTY-ONE

'James, I don't know who to suspect,' Harriet answered him wearily. 'Mostly I believe it would solve all sorts of problems if the arsonist is a total stranger. Until the police get their forensic results we just have to wait. But until everything has been settled Ash and I, and you, are better living apart. Please say you understand.'

He shook his head. 'I'd like to know you were both where I could protect you.'

'And I love you for that, but it wouldn't be right,' she replied.

He cocked his head. 'Do you think you could repeat that? Did you mean what you said, or was it merely a figure of speech?'

'Why, what did I say?' She opened her mouth. 'Ah,' was all that emerged. She could feel the heat rising in her face. But surely he knew that she loved him. She'd shown it a hundred times. Or did he think she was willing to sleep with him just for the sake of sex?

'You don't think I thought you came to bed with me without it meaning something special, do you?' He was smiling but he managed to sound offended.

'Certainly not. I knew you knew it meant something.' For heaven's sake, she was sounding positively incoherent. It was true; she did love him. She had loved him for a long time.

'Do you really love me?' Now he was looking at her tenderly and her heart turned over because it was something she should have been saying often.

'Yes, I do. I love you so very much,' she said, and went into his arms.

After a while he said, 'Then please come and live with me.'

'I will,' she said, and pushed against him.

He let her go immediately. She wondered if he was offended but he was merely sitting there, looking at her enigmatically. 'Why do I sense a caveat?'

'Ash and I will come and live with you just as soon as the arsonist is caught. James, don't you see? The fire was set in my cottage. How could I possibly come and live with you, even though I love you – especially because I love you – and put your life in danger? Let the police find out who it was and then we'll have this conversation again. If you still want me,' she added sombrely, wondering if that could ever be, if what she feared was true turned out to be so.

When they came in, the results of the forensic tests were inconclusive.

'I'm sorry. This happens more frequently than you might expect,' the DI told her. 'Your insurance can be told that it was definitely arson. We just don't know who the arsonist is.'

'Will you ever find out?'

'Sometimes a pattern of arson is set.'

But that would mean that someone else had to go through what she had suffered before justice could be seen to be done.

Harriet composed herself, set her mind on spring in the garden centre and tried not to feel too dismayed that yet another relationship was ultimately doomed to failure. Although James was more tenacious than she had given him credit for. If they did not have supper together, he phoned her last thing at night. Several nights a week, now that they had extra help in the garden centre, he came over and they sat together, sometimes watching TV, sometimes listening to music, close and companionable. They also spent part of the weekends alone together, sometimes with Ash. It was a relationship that was becoming as delightful as it was intense.

Harriet was also relieved to find that Felicity was no longer harassing her deliberately. Florence told her it was common knowledge that Harriet and James had become an item – 'Such a ridiculous way of putting it' – so she supposed that was the reason.

Then Ash, who continued to see Matt regularly, reported that he had mentioned that his mum was seeing a man from Cowbridge. 'Matt told me that this man has been over to Cennen Bridge several times for a meal. Matt says that he's all right, he supposes, but that Jess doesn't like him one little bit.'

It was a weekend in late spring. Ash was spending the night with Miranda and Harriet was looking forward to staying with James. She arrived at Oak Cottage to find evidence of activity next door that she had not expected, for Sycamore Cottage had been demolished in the week since she had last been there. The party side of Oak Cottage was now shored up; there was a pile of old bricks stacked neatly in one corner of the garden ready for re-use and new foundations were in the process of being dug.

'What's going on?' she asked, as she encountered James.

'Looks interesting, doesn't it?' he said smugly. 'Want to come and have a look?'

'Absolutely. I never thought the owners would bother to do a complete re-build,' she said, as they tramped round the building site where she had spent happy times and where she had hoped to build a new life. 'I thought they'd just repair.'

'It's turned out cheaper to start again. Besides …' he looked sheepish. 'I have a sort of confession. I bought Sycamore.'

'I thought the owners couldn't agree about a sale.'

'I think that minds were concentrated once they realized how much money they would need to get it into a state to be lived in again. Selling to me was much easier.'

'I suppose that eventually it could be an investment,' she commented doubtfully.

James shook his head. 'Not in the way I think your mind is

working. I'm re-building it as an extension to Oak Cottage. Now, that will be an investment.'

He was thinking of moving. Of course he was. Who would want to remain next door to a building site? she thought.

He turned and took her into his arms. 'You have the most expressive face. I can see exactly what you are thinking.'

She turned in his embrace. 'What am I thinking?'

'That I should kiss you.' Which he did.

After a while she said, 'That isn't what I was thinking at all. Even if it was nice.'

'Nice!'

'You know what I mean. As in deliciously seductive. So, what was I thinking?'

'If you look at me so provocatively I shall have to finish this conversation somewhere less public.'

'Mm.… What were we talking about?'

'That you thought I would dislike living next door to a building site.'

'That *was* what I was thinking. Am I wrong?'

She looked so serious that he was compelled to kiss her again. 'About living next door to a building site? I guess there are better places to be, but that's not the point. I'll be on hand to make sure everything is done just as I want it to be.'

'And that is?' she prompted him.

'Let me tell you. It'll be fantastic when it's finished,' he said enthusiastically. 'Most of the ground floor will be a kitchen diner. There will be a downstairs cloakroom, and upstairs a master bedroom with an ensuite. Then, when we break through into Oak – the really messy bit – we'll make my kitchen into a utility room, and add a study, leaving the sitting room much as it is. Upstairs will also remain the same except for another bathroom, giving it four bedrooms. What do you think of that!'

'I'm envious,' she said.

'You sound forlorn.'

'No, as I said, I'm envious that you have the means and the foresight to do all this.'

'And is it interesting enough for you to help me with all the details, and then come and live in it with me?'

'You don't give up, do you?' she said fondly. 'James, I shall consider myself privileged to be consulted about your new home. What will you call it?' Deliberately she glossed over his suggestion that it was time she moved in with him.

'I don't know. What do you suggest?'

'You can hardly call it Oak and Sycamore.' She reflected. 'I suppose you could call it The Cottage in the Woods.'

'A mouthful, but I quite like it. We'll have a formal ceremony when you move in. So, when will that be?'

He was more persistent than she had given him credit for. 'How can I possibly say I'll move in when we still don't know how this all happened in the first place?' she said, gesturing towards the rubble that remained to be carted away. She looked at him helplessly. They were back to square one.

'I'm not giving up,' he replied softly. He took her in his arms and said softly into her ear, 'And I'm a stubborn man. You don't get to lead men and women in the army, Harriet Finamore, without learning a thing or two about human nature. I may have been down, recently, but one of these days you will not only admit that you love me as I love you and that nothing, nothing will keep us apart, but you will have the courage to show it openly by marrying me. You mark my words.' And then he kissed her.

'Um … yes,' she murmured, as he let her go and her eyes were wide, and she was not sure what she was saying yes to. 'Are you asking me to marry you?'

'I most certainly am. Don't you think I want to make an honest woman of you?'

She looked amused. 'I didn't think that men used that expression nowadays. An honest woman. Whatever next?'

'That I love you more than words can say?'

He had said that he loved her, her heart sang. He had said it and it sounded so good.

'You look strange,' he said.

'Somehow I never thought.... Marriage. James, you know that I never wanted a child with Paul? I doubt if I even could, now.'

'Do you honestly think that matters to me?'

'It matters to a lot of men.'

'I already have two children of my own and you know how fond of Ash I am. She, of me, I like to think.'

'And that is enough?'

'Idiot, it's you I want, not another baby. You still look perplexed.'

'You've just told me you love me.'

'But you knew that. Surely?' He sounded incredulous, almost cross that she had not known. 'Have you forgotten my regard ring?'

'Regard, yes, but you never actually said that you love me. Women like to have these things spelled out.' She smiled at him, to take the sting out of her complaint.

'I am a fool. I love you. There,' he said triumphantly. 'Do you believe me now? I've said it.'

'Say it again,' she whispered.

'I love you.' It was so true that he wanted to shout it from the rooftops. He almost did. Then he thought that saying it quietly, with emphasis, would sound better. So that's what he did. 'I love you.' It sounded good. He thought he might like to repeat it, often, if she looked at him in the way she was, the way that made him feel ten feel tall and very potent.

'Harriet—'

'Soon ...' and there was a longing in her voice that he heard as if it were a clarion call.

# CHAPTER THIRTY-TWO

Joanne Ormston had designed The Gallery with a small seating area where she dispensed coffee to potential purchasers. Harriet had considered it wasted space when she first saw the sofa, easy chair and coffee table but she had seen a hesitating buyer make up her mind to spend money just as she was finishing her last mouthful of coffee and she was full of admiration for Joanne's ability to clinch a sale.

Harriet was in The Gallery one Saturday morning – for coffee, since she usually called in to see Joanne when she was passing by – when they both observed Jess Ormston crossing the road. It was a chilly morning and the girl was dressed in regulation jeans and a floppy sweater and she was slouching, her hands tucked up inside her sleeves.

'Amazing, isn't it, how dress sense bypasses generations. You'd never guess that she is the elegant Felicity's daughter,' said Joanne. 'Whatever I may think about my sister-in-law, she's always exhibited excellent dress sense.'

'I haven't seen Jess for ages. Before the fire, of course, she and her brother were regular visitors to James's cottage.'

'Dreadful little madam, if you ask me.'

There was positive dislike in Joanne's voice. Harriet was a little taken aback. 'Whatever has your niece done to upset you?'

Joanne laughed lightly. 'Well, nothing, of course. It's just her attitude. If you come face to face with her she looks through you as though you are as common as muck. Gareth may not be the world's best business man, but he is still her uncle."

Harriet recalled their own first encounter when Jess had been extremely uncivil to her. 'I suppose it's her age. Although I can't imagine us getting away with that sort of behaviour, can you?'

'Never in this world. She probably gets it from the fair Felicity.'

'Ouch. I didn't realize Felicity is one of your pet hates?'

'I used to get on well with Felicity. We saw quite a lot of each other when she and James were first married. Then, when she was furnishing her house, she bought several things from me. Now?' Joanne shrugged. 'She has far bigger fish to fry.'

'Whatever do you mean?'

'Don't tell me you haven't heard that Felicity has set her sights on a husband with a lot more clout than James?' Joanne mentioned the name of a nearby wealthy landowner, recently divorced, whose house was a gem set in a delightful valley. 'She wants a new husband and it seems that he is smitten.'

So this was the man whom Ash said that Jess disliked. 'Play your cards right and you never know, Felicity might become a customer again,' said Harriet, with a smile. She saw the sour expression on Joanne face. 'Best of luck to her, anyway,' she added and hastily changed the subject.

The weeks passed and the new house took shape. Ash was excited and seemed to take it for granted that one day she and her mother would be living in The Cottage in the Woods – for the name had stuck – with James.

'He loves you and you love him. What's so difficult about that?' she maintained, so firmly that her mother was hard put not to comment on her daughter's match-making skills.

There was nothing difficult about it at all, Harriet thought, if you forgot that there was a strong possibility that someone hated you so much that they had put your daughter's life in danger and that a second assault could harm James even more than he had been hurt already. The fire was far worse than the damage that had already been done to their shared business venture. There were still times when she woke in the night alone, shivering with the disturbing thought that he – whoever he, or she, was – might be out there, now, waiting for the moment to do – what? She was hard put, then, not to scream; she could well have succumbed to the temptation, if it had not been for Ash, sleeping in the room beside hers.

Was this how James had felt when he was suffering from PTSD?

Harriet was shopping in Cennen Bridge one morning when she came face to face with Jess. The girl had lost weight, her face was pinched and her wrists, protruding from the cuffs of the long-sleeved shirt she was wearing in spite of the humid day, were stick-thin. Whatever her mood or whatever she might – or might not – have done, she looked wretched.

'Hi,' Harriet said. This was, after all, James's daughter. How had Jess been allowed to reach this state? 'You don't look as though you have been very well.' The sympathy in her voice broke what barrier there was between them.

Jess's eyes welled. She turned away, her sandalled foot scuffing the pavement.

Harriet could not bear to see such misery. 'Hey. Come and have a cup of coffee.' She put her arm round the girl's bony shoulders and guided her into a nearby coffee shop. Somewhat to her surprise, Jess did not resist but allowed Harriet to guide her inside although she was trembling visibly. 'Why don't you sit down here,' Harriet manoeuvred their way to a table for two that was in a corner – reasonably private. 'I'll go and fetch the coffee. What will you have? Latte, espresso, something more exotic?' she smiled lightly.

'Just black. Please.'

Harriet fetched the coffees, smouldering with irritation at the time it was taking because the girl behind the counter was too busy gossiping with a friend to pay attention to any service. She did so hope that Jess would not take it into her head to run away to avoid what seemed to be some sort of a confrontation.

Jess had not run away and eventually they were both seated with coffees between them. Jess deliberately pushed away the little cartons of cream that had come with her black coffee.

'Are you sure you won't have something from the pâtisserie counter as well as the coffee?' Harriet asked. It had seemed so long since breakfast that she had taken a croissant for herself. 'I can easily fetch it for you.'

Jess declined, with a slight but unmistakeable shudder of distaste. 'No, thanks. I couldn't.'

'Now, tell me what's wrong.'

To Harriet's surprise, it all came out in a rush of confidences: Jess was missing her father. 'Mum is seeing a man. She's with him all the time. He's rich and thinks so much of himself. I hate him,' she ended vehemently.

'What does Matt think of him?'

'Matt's been sucked in. You know. He takes Matt shooting. Says that he's going to buy Matt an air rifle for his birthday. It makes me sick, it's so obscene.'

Jess wouldn't even use his name. But by all accounts Matt was happy enough. And Matt was a level-headed youngster. 'What about your father? What does he say?'

'Dad never comes to visit us any more. Mum says he doesn't care about us now, only you and Ash, and that we've got to make the best of things.'

'I know that your dad still loves and misses you.' Harriet was thinking that she would definitely have to mention this to James. He was not the sort of man to be deliberately unkind, certainly not to his daughter. 'He talks about you a lot, Jess. But you, you rarely come to see him now yourself, do you? And you never seem to want to talk to him when he phones. I know, because I've been in the cottage with him when he's phoned you.' There was no point in pretending that there was nothing between herself and James. She thought that it would be unfair to Jess to pretend otherwise. 'Is there any reason why you don't come round?' Was it because she could not bear to be anywhere near the cottages she had almost destroyed, or was it trepidation of being near the father she had caused to be hurt?

Jess shrugged. 'I don't know how to talk to him any more. I just feel so helpless all the time.'

Which was why she was anorexic. You didn't get to this state in a matter of weeks. These problems must have been brewing for ages. Maybe even longer than the time that had elapsed since the fire. Harriet took a deep breath. What she was about to do might have unforeseen consequences, mostly bad ones. Nevertheless.... 'You had nothing to do with the fire in my cottage, did you, Jess?'

There was a pause. It was infinitesimal, but the pause was there. 'Of course not! How could you think I'd do such a thing?' Jess said weakly, not looking at her but playing with a spoon. 'It could have destroyed my dad's cottage, too.'

Which was what Harriet herself had thought originally. 'Perhaps you know who did cause the damage?' she suggested gently.

Again there was that pause. After a moment Jess lifted her eyes. There was confusion, pain, guilt – yes, guilt – in their depths. There was also defiance, a hint that the old Jess still lurked there.

'Maybe,' she said guardedly.

'But it wasn't actually you, was it?' And suddenly Harriet doubted very much if it had been Felicity, either. If Felicity had her sights set on another man she would never waste her energies on a vendetta with her first husband. Which left Paul, Harriet was thinking. Or maybe the police were right, that it was a local arsonist who thrived on the sight of flames and the destruction he had caused. 'Was it a local boy? Someone who likes setting fire to things?'

'I don't know anyone like that. Besides, it wasn't anybody young.'

Then Harriet remembered that Stewart's mother had been warned in the pub that her son should leave his job. Paul....

'Where did you see this person?'

'By the cottages. I-I was just passing.'

'Do you do that often? Pass by?' Harriet asked gently.

'Sometimes,' Jess answered defensively, after a pause.

'And this person – who wasn't a boy or a girl – was there that night?'

'Whoever it was standing there, was just looking at the cottages. I don't know if it was to find out whether they were occupied, or what. It was a bit spooky. I didn't stop.'

Harriet began muttering soothing words to Jess who was suddenly pouring out all her troubles, to do with school and her mother, as though all the pent-up emotions were too hard to bear. 'No one understands,' she muttered in the end. 'No one cares about me at all.'

She had the self-centredness of the typical teenager, of course. But it was worse than that. Harriet took Jess's hand, which was still cold, even with the temperature hovering around twenty-seven degrees and even though the girl had been clasping the hot coffee cup in both of her hands, and had still not drunk from it. 'I'll talk to your father,' she promised, as eventually they got up to go. 'We can all sort out something together, now we know how you feel.'

It dawned on Harriet that nothing was insuperable. Jess needed professional help, but it could be forthcoming. In the meantime her own problems could be resolved, if only someone could prove that it was Paul who was responsible for the fire although, given that he had an alibi, for the moment she did not see how this could happen.

# CHAPTER THIRTY-THREE

It was a few days later. Harriet, who was back working at the garden centre full time, felt her mobile vibrate. When she saw the identity of the caller she said to Christie, with whom she was working, 'I'd better answer this. Back in a minute.'

The caller was an Evelyn Shortland. It took Harriet a moment to register that this was a neighbour of Paul's, an elderly widow who kept herself to herself. Harriet had never been on more than nodding terms with her, mainly because her own problems had left her too embarrassed to meet people socially in case she was compelled to confess what was being done to her. How did a woman admit to being abused? All the same, she had felt instinctively that this particular woman was sufficiently astute to know what was happening between Paul and herself.

'Harriet, dear,' Mrs Shortland said, when Harriet answered the phone. 'It is so good to talk to you again. I have a favour to ask you. Would you be kind enough to come and see me. Tomorrow?'

She would not say why. In the end Harriet agreed as graciously as she was able. 'It's such a nuisance, after all the time I've lost in the garden,' she told James that evening. 'But I really felt that I couldn't refuse.'

'And you are intrigued?'

'Of course I am. But it's probably nothing more than a request to witness her signature to a will, or something like that.'

'A long way to go for you to be a witness. She could ask at her bank or go to her solicitor.'

'Which would cost.'

'The miserly sort.'

'No. I'm being unkind,' Harriet insisted uncomfortably. 'The trouble is, I don't know the woman well enough to know why she wants to see me. So I think I ought to go and see her. I know it's Saturday tomorrow and bound to be busy but Evelyn sounded so insistent. Do you mind very much?'

He scrutinized her face for a long moment. 'It's as good a reason as any for seeing Paul,' he said, at last.

She did not try to deny it but lifted her shoulders. 'I have no choice. Ash will stay with Florence in case I have to stay over.'

'I should come with you. Just say when you want to leave.'

'No, James. It is dear of you to suggest it.' She raised her hand and touched his cheek tenderly. 'But don't you see? You have slain your dragon, the one that caused your illness. Now it is my turn to slay mine. He is still there, Paul is still very much there, in my mind, and if I can't get rid of him there is no hope for us.'

'Is that why you wouldn't come and live with me?'

She considered that, as if she had not already thought about it many times. 'Partly, I suppose,' she confessed. 'At first it was because I was afraid for you. Then I suppose I realized that there was a block, a barrier between us. Not of your making,' she added hastily. 'As I said, it was all in my mind. Paul, and what he had done to me, remains in my mind, still, and I know I have to exorcise him.'

His sigh was resigned. 'What will you do?'

'Confront him, after I have seen Evelyn Shortland.' Strangely, it did not appear that James connected Paul with the outrages at the garden centre, nor with the fire, and therefore he would not imagine that there could be physical danger in a confrontation that hovered in the back of her mind and would not go away.

He kissed her then and his kiss was hard and compelling. 'Take the greatest care, my dearest love. I'll ask both the girls to do a few hours extra to cover, so you take all the time you need. Go, but take care of yourself because my life would be worth nothing if anything were to happen to you.'

There was something else lurking at the back of her mind as Harriet drove east out of Wales. It niggled all along the M4. Something that she was missing. Something significant. It had first come into her mind soon after the fire. Then, when she had failed to solve the enigma, she had forgotten about it. It was not until she was taking a break at Reading Services that the penny dropped. All the dreadful things that had happened to her and James in Cennen Bridge had happened at a weekend.

So? What was so very significant about a weekend? She wasn't sure. There was more time to perpetrate horrors at the weekend? You could drive further at the weekend? Christmas was different. It was a holiday, anyway. Paul would be free to travel to Wales at the weekend. She could think about the implications of that again, later.

It was strange, driving along the avenue where she had lived for several years. Some of them had been happy; some of them were sufficiently bad to bring her out in a cold sweat even as she parked in the driveway of Evelyn Shortland's house. She rested her forehead on her hands for a moment, taking deep breaths. Then she thought that she had better move in case Paul saw her, which made her feel even more uncomfortable. But it was a Saturday and Paul always played golf on Saturdays. She hoped that she'd be away long before he was due home.

Was that the solution she had been looking for? Was it possible that Paul, himself, had been away from home occasionally at the weekends? Doing something other than playing golf?

'Won't you come in?' Evelyn Shortland held the front door wide open. 'It is so good of you to come all this way, and today especially because there is someone here I think you'd like to meet. Someone who really wants to meet you. You see, I am looking after Mona Cooper. I don't know if you've heard that she's Paul's new partner?'

Harriet nodded. 'I had heard. Is there a reason why she isn't at home?' she asked cautiously.

'Unfortunately there is, my dear. Try not to look too horrified when you see her.'

Mona Cooper was sitting in an upright chair with a plastered leg on a footstool. Her face was a mess of bruising that was all colours of the rainbow. Harriet's ribs ached in sympathy.

'You poor thing,' she whispered, and sat down abruptly.

'She'll mend,' said Evelyn Shortland briskly. 'Now, you two start talking while I fetch the coffee.'

'I take it Paul did this to you,' Harriet said gently, her mind a mixture of horror and guilt. Even when he assaulted her at the cottage, Paul hadn't left her in this state. Because Ash had interrupted them. Because James had saved her. Could she have prevented this if she had gone to the police? After Paul's attack, James had been adamant that she ought to go to the police. Once more Harriet felt so stupid that she had succumbed to being a victim of Paul's and that she had refused stubbornly. She supposed that James had felt then that he didn't know her sufficiently well to insist. 'Would it be too intrusive to ask how this happened?'

'Evelyn said that I needed to tell you. That's why I agreed that she should phone and ask you to come. I suppose that like you, in the beginning Paul and I were happy together,' Mona told her, mumbling through a badly swollen mouth and a broken front tooth.

Evelyn Shortland snorted as she put down the tray on which were two cups and saucers and a mug from the same pretty bone china Wedgwood set. There was a straw in the mug that she handed to Mona. 'You can drink it straight away, dear. I put some cold water in it to cool it down.' Mona took the mug with a grateful grimace of a smile. 'Quite soon he began to be controlling, though, exactly as he was with you, dear,' Evelyn said, nodding at Harriet, emphasizing that she had always known what was going on.

The story emerged haltingly, then more fluently as Mona fought the pain of her torn mouth. 'Some weeks ago Evelyn urged me to go to the police after she saw me with a black eye; although I said it was just a stupid accident, she guessed the truth. Fool that I was, I didn't report it. It was the usual thing. I'm sure you know what I mean. Inertia. His promise never to let it happen again. He even cried that time. I mean, real tears. How could I not believe him?'

'I remember all that very well,' Harriet said. Although Paul had never wept with regret after he had assaulted her.

'I was idiot enough to believe him, even though I was beginning to think that I'd made a mistake coming to live with him. There were phone calls. I'd even found a woman's handkerchief in the car. Circumstantial, I know, but I did wonder if he was getting tired of me. Then he did this to me. I knew that I could never go back to him. You see, yesterday we had a real row. I answered him back. Paul boasted that he'd used me as an alibi to prove that he could not have set fire to your cottage. It was a lie. I challenged him that even if he'd not committed arson, he'd been with another woman. We were upstairs after breakfast. He hit me. I fell and he kicked me viciously as I lay there. I was too near the top of the stairs. I sort of toppled all the way down.'

'My God. You could have been killed!'

'I rolled. Then, when I got to the bottom I was stunned.'

'I'm not surprised,' Evelyn muttered acidly.

'I lay there, waiting for Paul to attack me again. He came downstairs and – and I—' she gulped, put down her mug with a hand that trembled.

'Did he touch you again?' whispered Harriet, remembering that the sight of a helpless woman lying on the floor at his feet had often initiated another attack. With Paul's feet.

'He walked round me. He didn't say a word. I didn't, either. I didn't even cry out. I just lay there.'

'This has to be the very last time he does anything like this, to any woman.'

'Oh, it will be,' Evelyn said confidently.

'So what did you do?' asked Harriet huskily.

'I managed to stagger round here and Evelyn took me in. She drove me to the hospital and then brought me back here and this morning she persuaded me to phone the police.'

'That was very brave of you. Braver than I had ever been.'

'Not true,' said Evelyn Shortland firmly. 'You were brave enough to leave him before he did you any real harm.'

'Except set fire to my cottage and endanger my daughter's life.' Briefly she told them what had happened and they exchanged looks of disbelief and horror.

Evelyn went to get more coffee for Mona. Harriet was thinking that attacking women must definitely not be the only crime Paul had committed. She had to be right. It must have been Paul who had set fire to Sycamore Cottage, even though Mona believed that he'd been with another woman. He had endangered Ash's life. The shadowy figure that first Jess, then Harriet, had seen in the road on the night of the fire had been neither some local arsonist nor a pervert. It had been Paul. He had just not been able to leave her alone.

She got up, spilling some of the still hot coffee into its saucer. 'I have to go,' she said abruptly.

'Go? Go where, dear?' asked Evelyn curiously. 'You've only just arrived. I thought that you and Mona could have a longer talk than this. I'm sure there are things you have to say to each other,' she added meaningfully.

'I need to see Paul.'

# CHAPTER THIRTY-FOUR

As Harriet declared that she had to see Paul, Evelyn's coffee cup rattled on the saucer and she put it down unsteadily on to the mahogany table. 'Go and see Paul? My dear, I don't think that would be very wise.'

'Maybe not. But it is something that I have to do.' She stopped in the doorway. 'He's not playing golf, is he?' she asked Mona. It wouldn't matter, she thought then. She'd hunt him down wherever he was, golf course, nineteenth hole. Wherever. In fact, she thought maliciously, wouldn't she just love it if she could confront him in the bar with all his golfing cronies around him.

'Paul's at home. He sprained his ankle on the golf course on Wednesday,' Mona told her.

'Paul plays golf in the middle of the week?' Harriet asked in surprise.

'He's done so ever since I've known him. He plays at the weekends as well. Sometimes he plays away.'

'Does he, now.'

'Not always, but he likes to play on a Wednesday to keep up his handicap, he says. Anyway, he put his foot in a rabbit hole this week. He was furious that his game was ruined. He said terrible things to the groundsman. He had a letter from the secretary warning him that he'd be banned, if he didn't apologize. He did, of course. He apologized to the groundsman immediately. Bullies only stand up to the weak, don't they?'

Bullies never stand up to people who refuse to be bullied. Not like the two of them, who had both caved in under all the bullying. Except that Harriet had broken free, in the end. Because of Ash, and also because James had shown her how to stand up to his bullying. Now it seemed that Mona had also gained the courage to defy him. 'I have to confront him,' she insisted. 'But I'll be back.'

Harriet left Evelyn's house and walked determinedly next door, ignoring the little, cowardly voice that said as soon as she reached the garden gate that she was being a fool and wouldn't she rather stay with Evelyn and drink some more of her delicious coffee from the cup decorated with pink roses? Of course she would, but it was exactly as she had told James: unless she confronted Paul she would never be able to live in peace with herself.

The large gate was firmly closed. Harriet went through the little wicket gate at the side and walked steadily up the drive to the front door. Then she rang the bell, which had a different ring tone, she noticed, a ding-dong chime. Mona's choice, she thought. Paul had always preferred something sonorous. The door was opened almost immediately, as though he had been waiting for her.

'Oh, it's you,' he said, as if she were the last person he expected to find there, looking over her shoulder as he spoke, appearing almost relieved that there was no one else behind her. 'What do you want? I thought I told you I never needed to see you again.'

'There are things I need to say.'

He looked her up and down as though she were of no possible consequence to him. Then he sighed. 'I don't suppose it's that important but you'd better come in, then.'

Harriet had not really planned what to say to him. For a moment the old, familiar apprehension washed over her as she took in the furniture in its usual place, the silver salver placed just so, saw the look on his face, that gentle, concerned expression that so often had presaged violence in the past. Almost she ran away. Bullies only attack the weak and vulnerable, she reminded herself. She was no longer vulnerable, and, where Paul was concerned, she would refuse to be weak ever again. She took a deep breath. 'Why did you target the garden centre, Paul?'

For once he was disconcerted, doing a double take on her face as though this were the last thing he'd expected to hear. Then he frowned. 'What on earth are you talking about?'

'Brownlows, the garden centre that I have put money into. You know, the business you wanted me not to invest in because you'd have taken my money.'

'Hari, I'm sure I don't have the least notion what you are talking about. As for the money, I still believe it is only my due.'

'Due! Oh, never mind all that,' she said impatiently. 'I am talking about the upturned pots, the destroyed plants, the extra deliveries. It was all you, wasn't it? Except for the extra deliveries, done at the weekend when you had time to drive over and wreak havoc on my new enterprise. Those weekends when you were supposed to be playing golf away.'

'I like playing golf away. You often get a better class of player. But, upturned pots? I haven't a clue what you are talking about.'

'And what about the kitten, Ash's kitten?' Only then did she remember that. 'You killed Mash, didn't you, and the following week you left him where you thought Ash would find him. Except that it was James who found the creature and buried him before Ash could see his poor, broken body.'

'What is all this nonsense about pots and deliveries and kittens? You know I can't abide cats. Hari, I really haven't got time for this.'

Paul had always had the capacity to block out the things he had done. 'You get a buzz out of seeing broken bodies, don't you, Paul? You contemptible coward! Why did you set fire to Sycamore Cottage?'

'Set fire to— How dare you come here and accuse me of these things, woman! I think you'd better go before I call the pol—' He stopped abruptly.

And then Harriet remembered that Mona had been persuaded only that morning to call the police. Because he had assaulted her. Paul assaulted women when he needed to vent his anger. She went cold. Paul was obsessive about fire safety. Neither could she remember a single instance when Paul had damaged objects. He had even carefully wrapped her paintings in one of his blankets (a good one) before storing them in the garden shed.

Had she got this wrong, after all?

'You didn't come over to Cennen Bridge on various occasions and create havoc in the garden centre? You weren't the man who set fire to my cottage?'

'Set fire to your cottage! Why would I do that? Ashley could have been in it. You know I have always loved Ashley.'

She had always thought that was the truth. 'Ash was there when the fire was started. James saved her life.'

Paul grunted. Then he said, 'I know children nowadays are badly brought up. I always thought that we were making a good job of bringing up Ashley. I was extremely disappointed that she never wrote to thank me for the *Harry Potter* first edition I gave her at Christmas.'

'She threw it away. Ash said she could never again accept a gift from you.'

'She threw it away! Such a waste.'

The conversation was becoming surreal. 'Where is Mona Cooper?' Harriet asked abruptly, as though she did not know the answer. 'I've really come to see her, not you. I thought you'd be playing golf,' she added snidely.

'I sprained my ankle,' he muttered, flexing the joint of his right foot. 'Mona's not here.'

'When will she be back?'

'What's that to do with you?'

'There are things we have in common. Things we need to say to each other.'

'I don't know what you mean. Stop looking at me like that.'

'As if you were dirt? You are, Paul. You are.' She waited for the explosion that must surely come. Paul would never have permitted an insult to go unpunished, before.

He said sullenly, 'There was an accident. Mona broke her ankle and decided to stay with her sister for a week or so.'

Harriet was gazing at him in assumed disbelief. 'Are you trying to tell me that another woman has had an "accident" in your house? Accident? Or did you hit her, like you hit me?'

'Of course it was an accident. She tripped and fell going downstairs. It was her own fault. Don't look at me like that. What do you take me for?'

'A bully, a monster.' But, she was beginning to suspect with a degree of cold certainty, not an arsonist.

'Get out. Get out, do you hear me? Get out before I—'

'Before you do what, Paul? Hit me?' She was not afraid, Harriet realized. It was bluster. It had only ever been bluster, and bullying. She should have stood up to him from the very beginning. If she had…. It was her luck, her immense good fortune that had taken her out of Paul's influence to the haven that was Florence, and James.

Paul did not have a chance to touch her. There was a loud knocking at the door. He went pale at the sight of the policeman taking up the entire space of the doorway, a second man standing to one side, the police car parked in his driveway that could be seen clearly from the road.

'Paul Marsh? I am arresting you….'

Harriet stayed only long enough to watch as Paul was guided into the back seat of the police car and to give her own details to one of the policemen. Then she walked back to Evelyn and Mona.

'He won't be doing anything like that again,' declared Evelyn, as she poured out fresh coffee and handed a silver cream jug to Harriet.

'At least let us hope he never hurts another woman again,' mumbled Mona.

Except that leopards never changed their spots….

Harriet was persuaded to stay for a lunch of a sustaining soup. 'You need something to keep you going before you do that long journey home,' Evelyn insisted. Harriet was glad to agree. There was a lot of thinking she had to do and hunger and distracting thoughts did not go well with motorway driving.

When she left, Harriet put her arm round Mona's shoulders and squeezed her gently. 'Keep in touch,' she urged her. 'I'd like to know how you are getting on.' She hugged Evelyn more robustly. 'I have a lot to be grateful to you for,' she said huskily.

'Not really. You have already turned your life around yourself. Think of this as an act of generosity towards another broken woman on your part. But she'll mend, as you have.'

She had got it wrong, Harriet thought with chagrin, as she drove westwards. Paul was definitely a control freak. He had behaved monstrously towards both her and Mona, but he had not targeted the garden centre, nor had he set fire to Sycamore Cottage.

So if it were not Paul, who was it?

# CHAPTER THIRTY-FIVE

As she drove home, Harriet made a mental list of the suspects who were left now that Paul was excluded. Felicity had been her first thought. But she had already discounted her because of the new relationship she had begun. Harriet still believed that she was right to do so. Felicity had the opportunity all right, but she had absolutely no motive.

Jess, by her own admission, had been in the vicinity of the cottages. She also had the opportunity. The motive? But Jess had already told her that she could never have damaged her own father's cottage, which Harriet believed. Besides, Harriet was convinced that Jess's illness – for that was what anorexia was – would have taken away the girl's strength of mind, let alone cunning. To have been able to obtain petrol, take it to Sycamore Cottage and pour it through the back door cat flap was just beyond the capability of Jess in her present state of mind, let alone dismantle the smoke alarms.

So all the obvious suspects were eliminated. Someone once said that when you have eliminated the possible only the impossible is left – or words to that effect. Who was left?

There was James himself. Harriet's foot slipped off the accelerator as the face of the man she loved came into her mind's eye. Conveniently there was a motorway service station sign on the side of the road. Coffee. She needed coffee, she decided, and drove into the car park, parking away from other people, under a tree. Back by the car with a takeaway coffee and an egg and cress brown bread sandwich, she delved into her bag for a pencil and an old envelope.

Feeling a pang of intense disloyalty, *James,* she wrote on the back of it. James had had his problems. PTSD could have led him down devious routes. She believed not one word of that. Besides, James had not had a single occurrence of his flashbacks since he had rescued Ash. He loved her, she was as sure of that as she was of anything. As for the fire, James could have obtained the petrol but he had no opportunity, for she, herself, was his alibi. They had been working together all afternoon. No need even to think of the other incidents. Harriet scored out his name vigorously.

*Christie,* she wrote then. Harriet remembered defending Christie to the local police. Motive? None that she could think of. Opportunity? Plenty, for some of the incidents. But the girl was transparent. Christie would have had to have been a consummate actress to have wept as she'd done when the pots of chrysanthemums were destroyed with chemicals. She had also been at the till all the afternoon of the fire.

*Florence.* Come on. She and Florence were best friends. Florence was always there for her – look how she had come to their rescue several times since she and Ash had arrived in Cennen Bridge. She and Florence went way back. If Florence had done all this, Harriet just wouldn't want to live.

*Gordon.* An old man's revenge on an unsympathetic employer? It was possible, but she thought it unlikely, given that she'd heard that his back was still bad.

There was no one else. The Smithsons and the Heards remained friends, even though she no longer worked for them. Of course they were not even suspects. There was no one else in Cennen Bridge who disliked her so much.

Was the problem that it was James, not herself, who was so hated by the perpetrator? She had focused solely on herself, yet when you thought about all that had happened, most of the incidents had been directed against James.

Harriet had crossed the Severn Bridge before she remembered Gareth. He was a weak and not a particularly nice man. Look how he persisted in blaming his own brother for the things that had gone wrong in his life and were continuing to do so, but could he really be so evil as to destroy his own brother's livelihood?

Logically, and then there was Joanne. Joanne was her friend, her mind objected vehemently, and she was James's brother's wife.

Come on, Harriet said to herself. You put James's name down on the list first. Just to eliminate him, she countered. She had never truly believed that he could be involved. So, first eliminate Gareth and then eliminate Joanne.

Both Gareth and Joanne had the motive, Harriet thought as she drove homewards. They both needed money. They always seemed to need money. It was a twisted way of thinking, but by harassing James into selling the garden centre, they could have believed that Gareth would finally get the inheritance they thought he deserved. They both had the opportunity to inflict damage. Gareth definitely had the ability. Admittedly she had always thought that Gareth was all show and bluster but he was in the haulage business. He must have considerable knowledge of both chemicals and fire hazards. Harriet was not quite so sure about Joanne, who had refused to do any work in her garden that involved getting dirty. She remembered her friend's nails with a smile. Recently she had taken to displaying a pattern on the little fingernail of her left hand (a nail which wasn't all that little, come to think of it).

So, both of them had the opportunity. As for cunning, did either have enough of that?

It was all circumspect but the more she thought about it, the more Harriet became convinced that, at the very least, she first had to confront the man who was James's brother.

It was early evening when she reached Cennen Bridge. She drove through the town in the direction of the old house that

Gareth and Joanne were slowly renovating. She parked the car, got out and strode towards the front door, lifted her hand to the old fashioned knocker, and hesitated. What was she doing? How could she possibly walk into someone's home and accuse them of causing malicious damage and arson?

'They ain't 'ere. Either of 'em.' A harsh male voice behind her left shoulder made Harriet jump.

'What's that?' she exclaimed. The man who had come up behind her without making a sound on the tarmacked driveway was obviously one of the men working on the house, for he was wearing plaster-splattered overalls and carrying an ancient tool box in his right hand.

'If you was expecting to see Mrs Ormston, she ain't 'ere. Never is, until after I've gone 'ome. An' I'm goin' 'ome now. You'll prob'ly find 'er at that galley of 'ers in town.'

'I never thought of that,' Harriet answered, half in chagrin, half relieved. 'Mr Ormston?'

'Who knows?' the man shrugged. 'Don't give me a breakdown of 'is whereabouts, do 'e?'

'Right. I'll go, then,' Harriet said weakly.

He nodded and walked away without checking to see that she was leaving. Harriet got back into the car. What on earth had possessed her to come here? Then she thought, perhaps after all she would go to The Gallery. Not to confront Joanne, of course. But just maybe she would get a feeling, a reassurance, that having slain one dragon she had not conjured another; that neither James's brother nor his sister-in-law had a vendetta against him.

So Harriet drove to The Gallery, parking at the back in the courtyard beside a Land Rover that she recognized as Gareth's.

It was only as she passed behind the other car that she realized the car was not empty. She raised her hand in greeting but the figure in the front seat ignored her. *Be like that,* she thought crossly, a little guilt ridden as she remembered from where she had just driven. But there was something about the posture of whoever it was that didn't seem quite right. Adding foolish to guilt ridden, Harriet went back to the car. To her surprise, it was Gareth in the passenger seat. He was sitting with his head back against the seat, his eyes closed and his mouth open slackly. There was a trace of dribble on his chin.

There was no signal on her mobile. She knew that Gareth drank but in the middle of the day, in charge of a car? The man was an idiot, she decided. On the other hand, there was no need to disturb him. Much better let him sleep off the alcohol in peace.

She tried the side door of The Gallery but that was locked so she went round to the front entrance. The old-fashioned bell jangled as she opened the door and she went inside. The showroom was empty. She waited for a moment and when Joanne did not appear, Harriet stood on the second stair and called up, 'Hi, Joanne, are you there?'

Joanne's head appeared over the banisters. 'Hey, Harriet. Have you just got back from Guildford?'

'How did you know I was in Guildford?'

'I saw James this morning. He told me where you had gone. Hey, I suppose it isn't Paul who's done all those ghastly things at the garden centre? Did you think to confront him about them? It would seem to fit.'

'It would also have been a neat solution. But, no. It wasn't Paul. I accused him and he denied it. To my surprise, I believe him. But he has attacked another woman – which is why I went over there – and he is now in police custody. I hope he stays there.'

'So the mystery still hasn't been solved?'

'I wouldn't say that, exactly. I've parked in the courtyard. Is that all right?'

'The courtyard? Fine.' She hesitated. 'Did you see the state Gareth's in?' When Harriet nodded slowly, Joanne went on, 'Stupid man. I told him he'd have to stay there until I was ready to drive him home.'

'Did you take the keys?'

'Of course. What do you take me for?'

She sounded odd. Then, having even a friend discover your husband in the state Gareth was in must be embarrassing. 'I'm not here for anything important. I guess you are busy. I'll see you some other time.'

'No, come along up.'

Harriet mounted the stairs. 'If you are taking Gareth home, what will you do tomorrow without your car?'

'I wouldn't have had it anyway. It's at the garage.'

'I thought you'd had it serviced last week.'

'I did. Someone obviously didn't do a proper job on it.'

Harriet did so hope that the incompetent job had nothing to do with Stewart. He never looked terribly happy on the occasions when she'd been filling up at the pumps and had seen him at a distance.

When they were both upstairs Joanne looked at Harriet appraisingly. 'I must say, you don't look as though you are about to declaim mission accomplished. You seem a little fagged.'

'Perhaps dispirited is the better description. I've slain one dragon, so to speak, as in I now know that Paul had nothing to do with any of the incidents that have been plaguing both James and me. Unfortunately like the monsters of old, this particular dragon seems to have grown another head. So I need to think things through. Then I suppose I'll just have to go to the police.'

'That sounds serious,' Joanne said lightly. 'Let's have a drink and you can tell me all about it.'

# CHAPTER THIRTY-SIX

They went into the office that had been furnished with a sofa bed as well as a desk and inevitable cupboards and filing cabinets. 'Sorry I've no wine,' Joanne said. 'I must do a big shop tomorrow now that a cheque should have cleared. Gin and tonic? Oh, drat, I'm even out of tonics. Gin and bitter lemon?'

'Just so long as it's alcoholic. I'm exhausted, but I can walk home from here.'

'I'm not surprised, driving all that way.' Joanne went behind the kitchen counter and brought out a bottle of gin and two bitter lemons. She poured for both of them, handing one to Harriet. 'Cheers,' she said, raising her glass. 'Ah, smell that scent. James brought me that bunch of lily of the valley on the desk this morning. That's when he told me that you were sure it was Paul who must have been responsible for all the attacks on Brownlows. So if it wasn't Paul, who was it?'

'I'm not entirely sure,' said Harriet, swallowing the gin and bitter lemon. 'Strange flavour this bitter lemon has.'

'Does it? I hadn't noticed. I think it's a supermarket brand. The gin's all right, though. Why have you changed your mind? If you don't mind telling me, that is.'

'Paul is a complete bastard when it comes to women. He isn't an arsonist. Nor was he responsible for the attacks on Brownlows.'

'It wasn't Paul? Are you sure?'

'It wasn't Paul. I think it could have been Gareth.'

There was a moment's pause. Harriet swallowed the last of her drink. Dutch courage? Possibly. She felt she needed it.

'Now you are being absurd. Gareth? Whatever makes you think Gareth tried to harm James's business? His own brother! Come on, Hari, you have to be joking. You'll be blaming me next.'

'Unfortunately I'm not joking. Motive: Gareth is so bitter about not inheriting Brownlows he'd do anything to damage both it and James, who did inherit.'

'That's a convoluted argument. Why on earth would he want to damage a business that should have been his, ours by rights? Gareth is the elder brother. He should have inherited it. He didn't. But that doesn't make him, or me by inference, a saboteur.'

'He wanted James out, however he managed to accomplish that. You both had the opportunity, the skills and the determination. All the other suspects have been eliminated and I just don't believe it was random.' Harriet frowned, then she shook her head, rubbed the back of her neck and winced at the sudden pain in her gut.

'Are you feeling all right?' The question seemed to come from far away. 'Are you feeling all right, Harriet?' Joanne repeated her question, her voice oozing sympathy.

She was not feeling all right. She was feeling … 'No. I'm—'

'Would you like to lie down for a moment? I expect it's the effects of the alcohol on top of the long drive. I did pour you a stiff drink. I'm sure you'll feel better soon.' She took Harriet firmly by the arm. 'Perhaps you'd better sit by the window while I find a blanket,' she said, guiding Harriet to an upright chair with a padded seat that stood near the low, sash window opened wide from the bottom. She pushed her on to the chair. 'I'll fetch you a glass of water.'

Joanne went behind the chair. Harriet sat there, wondering if she was going to be sick, wondering what she could have eaten that was making her feel so ill. It must have been the sandwich that she'd picked up at the service station. She remained slumped in the chair, willing the world to return to normal.

Instead of the water, Joanne produced a coil of rope. As if she had done this before – had she practised it? Harriet wondered afterwards – Joanne flung it round Harriet's upper body, hauling her upright before tying her to the chair. Then, with the other end, she began to secure Harriet's feet to the chair's legs, immobilizing her.

'I'm sorry about this.' Joanne even sounded sincere. 'But I knew the moment you walked in that you'd guessed, even if you'd only got it half right. And I always knew that if that happened I'd have to kill you. If only you'd stuck to being a gardener, Hari. I always wanted a friend like you. Damn rope. The knots aren't right.' Joanne stood up and eased her back. 'Sorry about the lack of tonic water in your last drink,' she said brightly. 'I thought bitter lemon would best disguise the taste of the poison. You were partly right because I am the arsonist. Not Gareth, he wouldn't have the guts. I also had such fun breaking pots and destroying the plants at Brownlows. Every time I pretended that it was James in person I was attacking.'

Harriet mumbled through her pain, 'Why is Gareth in the car? What's the matter with him?'

'This time he isn't drunk, after all. I've poisoned him. He lost it, you see. He told me … never mind what he told me. But that was that. I knew I'd have to kill him.'

Harriet made a moan of protest.

'I expect you are wondering just what poison I've used? So simple. So apposite, you might say. Do you know – of course you must – that lily of the valley is highly toxic?

'*Convallaria majalis,*' murmured Harriet.

'That's right. Clever you. Then, I seem to remember Felicity telling me that you are a whiz with the Latin names. All you need with lily of the valley, you see, is the water the cut flowers have stood in. It was so considerate of you to have brought me that large bunch last week. I told James how much I appreciated it and that's why he even cut me some more this morning. I saved the water from the last lot, added lemon juice and a little vegetable colouring. When you are dead, all I shall have to do is wash out your bitter lemon bottle and add dregs from mine.'

'Gareth!' Harriet rode the pain from her twisting gut. 'Is he dead?'

'Probably not, but he will be very soon. As soon as it's dark I'm going to drive him to the river. There will be an empty bottle of whisky in the car and enough whisky in his stomach to account for the tragic accident that sent the Land Rover over the bank and into the water. So sad. The question is, shall the two of you have a suicide pact? I'll have to think about that. Once you are dead, too.'

Joanne stooped down to adjust the knots. She was just finishing when the gallery door bell jangled. 'Damn! Now I've broken a nail,' she swore. But before Harriet had the sense to call out, Joanne had thrust a wad of tissues into her mouth. 'Coming,' she called, from the top of the stairs, Harriet surmised, for she was tucked away out of sight. 'Who is it? Why, James. I hadn't expected to see you here this evening. Hang on a moment and I'll come down.'

'I'm looking for Harriet. She isn't answering her phone. Have you seen her?'

'Not for several days.'

Harriet struggled to expel the tissues but they were already sodden from the saliva that she was producing copiously and she could not shift them. But she had to alert James because he would be Joanne's next quarry. She did not know exactly what was happening to her or how much longer she had before she was totally helpless – or dead – but James was her only chance of surviving this. She twisted in the chair but the knots held. She tried rocking on it – it was only a flimsy piece of furniture and the chair crashed to the floor.

'What on earth was that?'

'You don't need to go up, James.' Joanne's voice contained

panic. 'I expect it was the cat from next door. Dratted animal has come in through the window several times. It's been so warm today I left the office window open.'

'That sounded rather more than a cat,' James said determinedly.

Harriet kicked out and the chair bumped again.

'Whatever it is, it is still there. Perhaps you'd better get a rolling pin, or something,' James said, and raced up the stairs.

He took in the scene immediately, assessed what had to be done. The man of action wasted no time in wringing his hands over the woman he loved, on the floor, tied to a chair, her face covered in red blotches, strings of soaking tissue adhering to her chin. His hand went into his pocket for his mobile and he rang for an ambulance.

Joanne had followed him into the bedroom. She saw that Harriet was still alive – at least that her eyes were open, staring at her. Was Joanne attempting to evade the fixed stare that accused her? Did she have any thoughts of escaping through the open window?

'Bitch!' Harriet mumbled through the wad of tissue as Joanne came closer. 'You could have killed Ash.'

Joanne looked at her contemptuously. 'Concern myself over a child?' She sidled towards the window and as she passed, Harriet lashed out with her feet. The knots were insecure. The jerk as the chair hit the floor had loosened them sufficiently for Harriet's feet to be freed.

Joanne saw that Harriet was no longer totally incapacitated. She dodged flailing feet, staggering towards the low, open window. There, she lost her balance … and plunged through it. The thud as her body hit the cobbles was audible to both James and Harriet.

'My God!' He scrambled to the window. Joanne lay on the ground, her neck twisted at a grotesque angle. There was nothing he could do for her and Harriet had need of him. He fought with the knots at the back of the chair and freed her.

She sat up and spat out the last of the tissue. 'Poison. Lily of the valley,' she muttered. Then resolutely she put the fingers of her right hand in her mouth and down her throat and was copiously sick.

The rest was noise and hustle, clanging bells of the ambulance, the wail of a police siren. There was pain and confusion, anguish lest she die, followed by hours of discomfort.

'How is Gareth?' Harriet asked James, when finally her mind cleared.

James shook his head. 'He didn't make it. Joanne'd poisoned him a couple of hours before you arrived. The doctors say that, even if you had realized at the time, they probably wouldn't have been able to do anything for him.'

'I'm sorry, love.'

## EPILOGUE

Finally there was total relief when at last James took Harriet home and she knew herself to be safe.

They were sitting on a hammock in his garden, a riot of colour and perfume. 'When will you marry me and move in with Ash?' James asked Harriet, tenderly smoothing the fringe from her forehead. 'You promised me you would, once we knew who hated us so much.'

'You want to stay in Cennen Bridge, even though Gareth is dead?'

'I am saddened by that. When we were young I suppose we were close. But people change. Gareth certainly changed. What's important is that I am here for Jess and Matt. If you and Ash are beside me, I can cope with the death of my brother. So you see, now I want you here more than ever, not just to keep you safe but because I love you more than words can say. I was never more sure of anything in my life and I want the chance to prove it.'

She wanted it, too. There was no reason for any delay. Joanne, who had hated them both, was dead, had died from the fall. They were both safe. She turned her head and reached up and kissed him. 'You are a dear man and I love you, too. I'll come, just as soon as it can be arranged.'

'It's taken you two long enough, but that is the best news, ever,' declared Ash, who had heard their last exchange. 'What's on the telly?'